I0614153

Unseen

by

Cassie Laelyn

The Fallen Guardians, Book 3

Unseen

Contact Information: info@thewildrosepress.com

Cover Art by *Diana Carlile*

The Wild Rose Press, Inc.
PO Box 708
Adams Basin, NY 14410-0708
Visit us at www.thewildrosepress.com

Publishing History
First Black Rose Edition, 2020
Trade Paperback ISBN 978-1-5092-3331-1
Digital ISBN 978-1-5092-3332-8

The Fallen Guardians, Book 3
Published in the United States of America

The silence was deafening, a screaming buzz in her oversensitive ears. Mom's hand squeezed tighter.

Another loud thump sounded outside, this time on the ground. Her legs shook, refusing to move. Mom crept forward and yanked Hailee to follow.

In the dining room, she exhaled silent relief that she left on the small kitchen light. If not, she would've slammed right into the table.

The knob on the back door jiggled.

Mom spun to her. The look in her wide eyes sent an icy chill all the way down Hailee's spine.

"It's too late," Mom whispered.

Praise for Cassie Laelyn and…

***UNFORSAKEN*, The Fallen Guardians, Book 1:**
Winner of the Best Demons, Devils and Angels
PNR for 2019
The Paranormal Romance Guild
Reviewer's Choice Award

~

Best 2019 Paranormal Romance (finalist)
Australian Romance Readers Award

~

***UNFORGOTTEN*, The Fallen Guardians, Book 2:**
"This a brilliant story of longing, survival, enduring love and redemption."

~Internationally Bestselling Author Annabelle McInnes

"The battle between good and evil kept me glued to the page."

~The Paranormal Romance Guild

"Boys with wings are heavenly!"

~The Reading Gypsy

"What an epic story!!"

~Pretty Book Whore

"It is an emotional, roller-coaster ride."

~The Hot Mess Library

Dedication

For you, for being the burst of sunshine
that lights up my life like a supernova.
The good kind of sunshine,
not the nauseating kind like River.

Acknowledgements

As I sit down to write these acknowledgements, I find myself reflecting over the past 18 months since the Guardians made their way into the world. I'm so incredibly humbled by the support I've received for this series and how readers have fallen in love with these characters as much as I have.

For those who are Team EJ, this book is for you! I hope you enjoy his story, his special brand of crazy, and how he fell harder and deeper than I ever expected. He's officially my favorite Guardian…don't tell the others!

A big shout out to the members of my Facebook Reader Group (Cassie's Log Cabin)—you guys are awesome! Thank you for cheering me on, talking about my books, and pestering me for updates. (Tracy—I'm looking at you!!)

Thank you to my amazing street team (Karina, Danni, Mel, and Emma), every blogger and bookstagrammer who featured the Guardians, and every person who read, reviewed, or promoted my books in some way! Your support means the world to me.

See you all back here again for Book 4!

Cassie x

P.S. Reader support is the lifeblood for any series. If you loved reading *Unseen*, please consider leaving a review, recommending it to your friends, or requesting your local library purchase a copy. Thank you. x

Glossary of Terms

Ariel—Angels of nature who regenerate flora using angelic magic, often in the aftermath of a natural catastrophe such as a wildfire. Ariel have bronze wings.

Azrael—Angels of Death who transport souls from the mortal realm to their final resting place in either the Heavens or Hell. Azrael have silvery-gray wings.

Chosen—A mortal created by Fate; whose destiny restores the balance in Fate's favor.

Dumahel—Half angel, half mortal, Dumahel possess the power to enter and manipulate dreams. They are rare and always born as twins.

Fallen—Once angels of the Heavens, Fallen now reside in the many realms in Hell and give their allegiance to Zath, the current ruler of Hell. Fallen have crimson wings.

Guardians—Fate's warriors, tasked with protecting Chosen mortals, so they can fulfill their fated destiny. Fate exiled the Guardians to the mortal realm over three hundred years ago. They have black wings.

Purah—Crystalline water from the Eternal Fountain, found in the Heavens. Purah is toxic to Fallen.

Raziel—Angels who cast magic, commonly used to disguise the immortal world from mortal eyes.

Tartirim—A realm in the Heavens where Fate imprisons angelic souls that require intense rehabilitation.

Prologue
Blaine

Twenty-five years earlier

Blaine swung his legs over the edge of the concrete building, staring down at the glittery lights of the city. Seven stories up, he had a view of the entire town, plus the dark, jagged mountain range in the far distance. This time of year, the dustings of white powdery snow melted and disappeared around lunch time before returning overnight. The clouds thickened and grew darker, preparing for a fresh batch.

In another week or so, those white caps would become a permanent fixture. Then, this world would welcome its newest set of immortals.

To his right, the oversized heating units hummed in the background. Loud enough they drowned out the cars bustling in the peak evening traffic. Not that this town really had rush hour traffic. More like a few extra cars on the road at the same time. Get-home-and-prepare-dinner traffic.

The mortals lived such a boring existence. Relying on cars for transportation. So many destinations remained off limits because of their inability to fly.

Like the top of the hospital where he sat.

Mortals ventured to the rooftop occasionally, he assumed, to fix the heaters, but he bet none of them sat and admired the view. They all lived down there, on the ground. Little ants building tiny colonies for their almighty queen.

Why was Fate so fascinated with creating such boring creatures?

Brisk night air swirled around the heater duct and he flipped up the collar of his leather jacket. The cold didn't bother him, but wind on his neck annoyed the hell out of him. One of the only positives of Hell was the climate.

He drummed his fingers on the ledge. He'd sat here for a few hours now, ever since the Azrael entered the building with his impregnated mortal. The pair came weekly now, but this visit took longer than the others. In the weeks leading up to the birth, he'd tagged along for the appointments, so he didn't miss anything. More like he sat on the roof and waited, they didn't exactly invite him.

Chilling in Hell wasn't an option because of the time difference. He couldn't miss the birth. When those twins came into the world, he'd take a dot of their blood so he could track them later. They were no use to him until they transitioned into immortality. Until then, he'd let them live boring mortal lives.

A male exited the hospital. Leaning further over the ledge, he zeroed in on the smartly dressed gentleman wearing a dark suit and fancy shoes. Even with a view of his back, he recognized Gabe. Strange. Why was he here? With long measured strides, the Archangel strode down the pavement and disappeared into the hospital parking garage. Gabe didn't visit during any of the other appointments, so why now?

Unless…the twins came early.

Blaine clapped his hands together. Launching to his feet, he unfurled his wings and dashed to the rear of the building before leaping to the ground. The day was finally here.

With a spring in his step, he retracted his wings and entered the hospital, making his way to the maternity ward. But he didn't care for just any infant. He only wanted the special ones.

At the gift shop, he compelled the shop assistant for a bunch of balloons, because apparently that was the custom when welcoming new arrivals. Without knowing the gender of the twins, the shop assistant selected a mixture of colors, adding unnecessary ribbon and string. He didn't care which colors, nor whether the parents liked them, as long as he left the hospital with what he came for.

He stuffed the balloons in the elevator and selected the fourth floor. He'd waited so long for another set of twins. Finally, his plan was in motion.

The elevator doors opened, and he strode out on a mission. Before he reached the reception desk, he spotted the Azrael. The twins' father.

Asher froze, no doubt sensing Blaine's presence.

"Congratulations!" Blaine announced, using a pleasant, excited voice customary for these occasions, so the hospital staff didn't bother him regarding their strict visiting hours. Mortal rules didn't apply to him, and he wasn't in the mood for more compulsion.

Asher turned. His face pale, eyes swollen and red.

Mortal infants were wrinkly and ugly but crying about it wouldn't help.

Blaine shoved the balloons into Asher's hand and slapped him on the shoulder. "Why the sad face, friend?

I mean, sure, they'll be mine, but not for twenty-five years."

Asher didn't answer. Instead, he released the balloons from his hand and walked toward the opposite end of the long hall. Blaine paused, watching the colorful balloons drift to the ceiling, all that unnecessary string dangling in his face. So ungrateful.

At the end of the hall, he followed the Azrael to a waiting area. Strange place to keep infants. Two couches, a coffee table with a few magazines scattered on top, and a vending machine. This late at night, they were the only ones here.

"Where are the twins? I want to see them." Even his patience wore thin eventually.

Asher's shoulders drooped as he stared at the floor. "They didn't make it."

Didn't make it? Procreation between a mortal and an angel came with risks, but no more than between two mortals. Occasionally, Fate recalled the infant soul to the Heavens, but she didn't know of the twins. He cloaked his visits with Asher so Fate wouldn't interfere.

How did both die?

He studied the Azrael. As an angel Asher couldn't lie, but the niggling in his gut told him otherwise. He stepped closer, lowering his voice. "We had a deal, remember? It's not wise to cross me."

The Azrael wiped his snotty nose using the palm of his hand. "I told you, they didn't make it. Do you think I'd be upset if they were alive?"

Asher paced back and forth, shoving a hand through his wavy blond hair.

This was Blaine's big chance. The Azrael owed him. He kept those growing souls hidden so Asher could have the family he craved. Why? He didn't understand the fascination.

He probed Asher's mind, searching for the truth. Some angels perfected withholding the truth and others excelled at blocking their thoughts. When he reached a massive brick wall swirling with darkness he couldn't penetrate, he wasn't surprised. Bloody Azrael and their shadows.

"What about the mother? Your precious soulmate?"

Asher stubbed the toe of his boot into the carpet. "She survived."

"Then create another set of twins."

"There were complications during the birth. She can't have any more children." Asher gazed out the window. "I did this to her."

Fist clenched, Blaine swung and punched the closest object. The glass of the vending machine shattered, exploding brightly colored packets of candy over the floor.

"You better be right." He clutched the front of Asher's shirt and twisted it in his fist. "If I find out you're hiding them, I'll come for you, too. And when they reach immortality, I'll make you watch while I take them both to Hell."

Blaine shoved Asher in the chest so hard the Azrael's back slammed against the wall. Asher was no use to him anymore. He needed Slater to get those infant souls before Fate did.

Storming out of the waiting area, Blaine kicked the coffee table for good measure. Bloody hell. Now he needed to find another Azrael and start all over again.

Chapter One
EJ

Current day

EJ curled his fingers around the smooth, taut leather, brushing the pad of his thumb over every tiny crease and groove, reacquainting himself with the surface. The leather warmed slightly under his fingertip as though coming to life with his touch. Inhaling, the rich smell of aged hide seeped into his nostrils. He'd never tire of how the birch and musk scents stirred together in a wicked combination that sent his heart into a frenzy.

"I've missed you, Stella," he murmured, feeling her underneath his hands after too long an absence.

He tightened his grip, then relaxed back in the seat, eager for this little get together to progress to the next level.

Beside him, Willow snorted, totally ruining the moment.

"EJ, it's a car, not an actual female."

EJ glared at the Ariel sitting in the passenger seat of his Shelby GT500. The same Ariel he might never permit inside his car again. "You're lucky you're Ric's soulmate, Red. I've thrown women out of this baby for way less."

Willow screwed up her face. "I do not need an

image of you in this car with other women."

Tayla stuck her head between the front seats. "Please tell me you don't use the back seat with said women. Eeew, EJ! That's so gross."

Pfft. As if she could judge. "Oh, please, are you telling me you and Raven don't get all freaky outdoors?"

Tayla didn't reply, and she didn't need to, the redness creeping across her cheeks told him the answer.

"Right, has everyone finished dissing my car? Can we leave now?" He raised an eyebrow at Willow, then Tayla.

Willow laughed, her voice full of pure joy. "Sure, EJ. Let's go."

"How did I get stuck on Wingless Warrior duty tonight?" he grumbled to himself, putting the key in the ignition.

Stella roared to life, the engine rumbling through the seat. Accelerating, he skidded out of the garage at the Guardian mansion, into the night.

Once on the highway heading down the mountain to Summit Creek, the girls settled in and chatted away as though he wasn't there. But it didn't bother him. This is what mortal males experienced with a family full of sisters. That's how it felt for him. He'd treated Willow like a sister ever since she and Ric became soulmates more than a thousand years ago. So long ago, he couldn't remember a time when she wasn't around. Well, except for that little spell where she remained in the Heavens while Fate exiled the Guardians. After Willow's detour through Anahel as a half-Fallen, she and Ric were now back together, and everything returned to normal.

Thank Christ. Ric was one moody sonofabitch without Willow.

He steered Stella into a sweeping bend, leaning in his seat as they drove around the corner, knocking it back a gear before kicking her in the guts on the exit.

Tayla was his newest sister. Her inclusion in their thrown-together family happened about two years ago when she found Raven. Though she fit in so effortlessly, it felt like she'd always been there. Her and Raven, well, those two were perfect for each other.

He was happy for his brothers. They deserved soulmates, and he knew soulmates made them better Guardians. He wasn't envious one little bit. That kind of attachment or responsibility wasn't his thing. Stella was the only constant female he ever needed.

The trip into town took about forty-five minutes or so. He made a point of driving slower than usual with the girls in his car. Thinking of the pain Aric and Raven would inflict on him if their soulmates got a scratch while under his care terrified the hell out of him.

Easing off the accelerator, he turned down the narrow alleyway beside SubZero, his frequent hangout. Tires crunched along the gravel drive as he parked in the rear parking lot and killed the engine.

Tayla leaned between the seats again. "Raven just texted me. He and River are calling it a night and heading to the club now."

Willow swung open the door and slid out, leaning back in to lift the lever on the seat, folding it forward. Tayla climbed out.

"Ric won't be far behind, I reckon," he added after locking the car.

Willow peered across the hood at him. "When is

Raine coming?"

He slipped Stella's key in his pocket. "She prefers to fly. She's probably already inside."

"I wish Ellen came, it doesn't seem right celebrating without her," Tayla said, shrugging on her jacket.

"She'll no doubt have a monstrous cake waiting when we get back." He smoothed his palm over the warm metal as he rounded the hood. "Be safe, Stella," he murmured.

Willow chuckled. "EJ, your obsession with this car is rather unhealthy."

"Maybe." He lifted a shoulder. "But she's the only one for me."

He trailed behind the girls as they made their way down the alleyway toward the club's entrance. They chatted about all the potential gifts Raven bought Tayla for their anniversary, which Raven insisted they celebrate each year. The list was goddamn endless, ranging from skimpy lingerie to romantic weekend getaways. The mental image of either of those made him shudder.

Another reason Stella was a better match for him—she appreciated gifts in the form of gas and oil, with a fortnightly detail.

Just before the end of the alley, a wave of nausea washed over him, flipping his stomach upside down and inside out. His arm shot out, bracing against the brick wall to prevent face-planting on the gravel. One second the lights of the bustling street lured him toward the club, the next he squinted against the impossibly bright glare reflecting off the whitest sand he'd ever seen.

Inwardly, he groaned. Fate and her frickin' visions.

He knew the drill by now—stand still, remain upright, and chill out until it ended.

Using his hand, he shaded his eyes from the glaring sun, and he peered around, hoping for some clue as to where he was and what Fate wanted him to know. Not that it ever helped. No, that little twist of hers meant he never prevented the vision from happening in real time. Fate cursed him to always arrive too late, and it became the bane of his almost four hundred years stuck in the mortal realm.

Picturesque coastline trailed off far into the distance. Pristine white sandy beach, a cloudless, crystal blue sky with an ocean to match. And he stood in the middle of it. Lazy waves lapped at his ankles, carrying a warm hint of summer through his jeans. The water so clear, his black designer lace-ups stared back at him.

A shudder worked through him.

This wasn't the first vision he'd experienced of this place. In fact, this was number three. But this time felt different, like the vision warped into reality more than any previous one.

Visions from Fate felt real while he experienced them, but they were more like standing at a distance watching a scene play out. Like watching a movie on the big screen where he could get up and walk away whenever he wanted. This? This was different. The water in his shoes felt real.

Sun beamed down on his back, heating his leather jacket to an uncomfortable temperature. Sweat coasted down his spine. He slipped it off, holding it in his hand, well above the water. The only time he bothered with a jacket and now he needed to frickin' carry it. Another wave washed over his shoes making him sink into the sand.

This wasn't his idea of fun. In fact, this vision sucked balls. He'd take a road trip to the fiery pits of Hell over another visit to this tropical not-so-paradise. But grinning and bearing it was his only option until the vision gave him a clue, or it ended. Then he could carry on with the night. Maybe knock back a few extra vodkas to hold off another assault until he sobered up tomorrow.

Movement to his left caught his attention. Without adjusting his feet in case he sank so far into the sand he couldn't escape, he twisted at the waist. In the far distance, a female exited the tree line, strolling along the sand toward the shore. Her wavy blonde hair lifted in the breeze causing a weird sensation inside his chest.

The female dipped her toe in the water before continuing forward until it reached her knees. What sane person willingly stood in the ocean? Dressed in a singlet top and a casual pair of jean shorts and no shoes, at least her clothing was safe. Unlike his.

In the previous two visions, he was the only one on the beach. He'd stood the entire time on the scorching sand, under the blazing sun, alone. This was the first time he saw someone else.

The woman probably held a clue to whatever Fate wanted him to know. Unless she was…He couldn't even finish that thought. No frickin' way. Fate doomed his existence if she assigned him a Chosen—a mortal created by Fate to fulfill an extraordinary destiny. Since arriving in the mortal realm, the only Chosen assignments Fate dished out ended in his brothers finding their soulmates.

He did not need one of those right now. Or at any time for that matter.

The safer option was to avoid the whole soulmate possibility and remain standing in the warm, irritating saltwater until the vision ended. Which could take forever. Fate neglected to give him a "Receiving Visions from Fate" manual when she cursed his ass.

The sooner he found clues, the sooner he could leave this nightmare destination for good. Approaching the female wouldn't magically turn her into his soulmate. He hoped. Whatever, he needed to take the chance. If it meant ending this failure, so he moved onto the next, then all the better.

Heaving his feet out of the sand one at a time, he trudged along the shore toward the woman. A few yards down the beach, her head swung his way, though she was still too far away for him to make out her features.

She retreated a step, then another, as though she wanted to flee as much as him.

Hang on. She saw him?

"Wait," he shouted, quickening his pace the best he could in waterlogged shoes.

How the hell could she see him? No one ever saw him in the visions. He was a ghost.

The landscape warped, blinking in and out like bad reception. No! He needed answers before the vision ended.

"Wait," he called out again.

The woman spun and bolted to the trees, leaving his pleas unanswered. In an instant, the beach scene collapsed and disappeared.

Blackness. He squeezed his eyes shut, counted to

three, waiting for the nausea to settle before reopening them. Blurry rings of light illuminated the end of the alleyway. Damp air cooled the back of his neck. Where the hell was he?

A firm hand squeezed his shoulder.

"EJ, you okay, man?"

He shook his head, clearing his foggy vision, like he'd just woken with an epic hangover. That was a side effect he never experienced before, yet his blood felt supercharged with energy.

Aric stood before him, brows drawn tight, concern etched over his expression.

"Yep. Just another doozy from Fate." Even though the knot parked in the pit of his stomach said otherwise. He scanned the alley. "Are the girls okay?"

"Yeah, they're inside. I landed in the parking lot just as your vision started, so I told them I'd wait with you."

It scared the shit out of him every time Fate left him defenseless when she sent one of her visions. A Fallen could cut off his head while he was in la-la land. He also hated relying on others to protect him while it happened. "Thanks, Ric."

"Don't mention it. Fate show you anything new?"

Hell yeah, she did. But until he knew what the deal was and the identity of that female, he'd keep those developments to himself. "Confusing as always."

Aric clapped him on the shoulder.

"Let's grab a drink."

After Aric turned and strode out to the street, EJ hot-footed behind him. A drink was exactly what he needed, and maybe a little action on the side.

After no more than three steps, a weird, squishy

sensation inside his shoes made his socks slip down his ankles. He stilled. He wriggled his toes. The waterlogged slushing was a sure sign his feet resembled a wrinkly old man who'd soaked in a tub for oh, about a year or so.

His heart raced. No frickin' way. It couldn't be real.

Fate sent him a vision. If he misted, Aric would've told him. How the hell did he explain the water currently residing in his shoes?

Swallowing the lump lodged in his throat, he peered down, inspecting the smattering of pearly white sand over his black lace-ups. He slipped off one shoe and lifted the sneaker, turning it upside down. Gooey, wet sand slopped onto the gravel.

"Holy shit."

Chapter Two
Hailee

"Excuse me, miss."

Hailee jolted awake at the tap on her shoulder. What? Where was she? A middle-aged man stood beside her seat.

"This is your stop," he said, pointing to the sign outside the window.

Eaglewood Station.

"Shoot." Hailee shot up with her paperback still clutched in her hand. "Thanks." She snatched her backpack off the floor and raced out the train door before it closed. A few times, she'd missed her stop and ended up needing to catch the next train back, adding an extra hour onto her already exhausting ride home.

When the doors hissed closed and the train departed, she waited until her heart rate steadied from waking with such a start. All those late nights caught up with her. She never fell asleep on the train. Usually, she used those precious moments on the ride home for a fictional hero to whisk her away until the cold, hard truth of reality set in once again. On occasion, she closed her eyes, but the nap was more sleeping with one eye open. To fall into such a deep sleep where she dreamed? That was a first.

More evidence she needed to stop doing double shifts at the restaurant.

Shoving the well-read novel inside her backpack, she slung it over a shoulder and ascended the steps connecting the train platform with the street above. Eeriness at this time of the night always caused a shiver down her spine, but no evidence supported the fear. Her house was less than a block from the train station, in a fairly safe suburb. Of course, her mother disagreed. Mom thought the boogeyman hid in every dark corner waiting to strike. Nothing cured that level of paranoia. Nevertheless, Hailee vowed never to let her guard down, regardless of the fatigue seeping into her bones. The reason she kept to the well-lit sidewalk rather than cutting through the park, which knocked off a few minutes. One foot in front of the other.

Today, she pulled a grueling double shift in the kitchen again, working her lunchtime shift and then she filled in for a colleague and worked the closing shift as well. More money, more experience, more bills paid—her mantra for this year.

Not that it changed their circumstances.

Ten minutes later, she trudged up the drive of her shoebox home with one clear destination. Bed. She focused every ounce of energy on making it there rather than falling asleep on the concrete drive.

Sticky, humid air coupled with her exhaustion made her body weak and lethargic, until even her lungs would rather deflate than draw in another breath. Muscles in her lower back burned, a constant reminder of the hours she spent on her feet and the uncomfortable sitting position she fell asleep in on the train.

Dying on the front lawn seemed like a decent idea right now, if it weren't for the overgrown weeds. Maybe the concrete was more comfortable?

Finally, after what seemed like forever, she made it to the front porch. As quietly as she could, she removed her boots, unlocked the door, and slipped inside. She tiptoed around the sofa but drew up short near the coffee table. Light from the outside streetlamp spilled around the edges of the closed curtains, illuminating a few bulky shadows in the center of the room. Any remaining air left her lungs in one punch. Packing boxes.

"Not again," she muttered, hoping her mother had just rearranged the living room rather than packed it for another move.

In the kitchen, a heavy weight sank on her chest. Nope, Mom wasn't redecorating.

After switching on the small nightlight above the stove, she found the same cardboard packing boxes stacked on the counter with the cupboards underneath open and bare. Her backpack slipped off her shoulder and fell on the linoleum with a thud. Like her body wanted to do.

Moving again? Why did her mother insist on fleeing from town to town, forcing them to start again over and over? When would it end?

At the nearest open box, she snagged a cup and forced her feet to the fridge, pouring a glass of OJ. The icy goodness soothed the burn in her throat. She sagged against the closed door. Just once, she longed to stop and smell the roses, or even the weeds in the half dead grass out front. She just wanted to stop and set down roots.

Led by the dim kitchen light, she trudged to the adjoining dining area to inspect the extent of the moving situation. More packing boxes. Not a surprise.

She also wasn't surprised to find her mother asleep in a chair, her head resting on her forearms, on top of the small circular table. A half empty bottle of bourbon within arm's reach. Again, no surprise. Beside the bourbon were Mom's sleeping pills. Magic tablets prescribed to help her drown out the imaginary demons in her nightmares. Nightmares she'd suffered for as long as Hailee could remember.

Instead of dealing with her mother, she screwed the cap back on the bourbon and washed the used glass.

"Happy twenty-fifth birthday, Hails," she grumbled, when the time on the microwave clock ticked over to midnight.

If only she was a normal person. What twenty-five-year-old celebrated their birthday by working two shifts to make ends meet? Plus, she cared for a mother who everyone thought was crazy. And to top it off, she played mom to her twin sister who was the same freaking age.

Speaking of which. Ignoring the all-consuming need to join her mother in slumber-land, Hailee shuffled down the narrow hall of their compact three-bedroom flat, halting at Ebony's bedroom. Her twin sister.

She creaked open the door, but she couldn't see a darn thing in the dark.

"Ebony?" she whispered. "You awake?"

She paused in the doorway for a few minutes waiting for an answer. When none came, she shut the door and headed to her own room. A note was stuck on the door.

Got a gig tonight. Happy b'day. Eb

In Ebony language, gig meant DJ-ing at an illegal

rave party, most likely in the dodgy area of town. For twins, she and Ebony were polar opposites. But battling eyelids as heavy as boulders, Hailee didn't have the mental capacity to worry about another single thing. For the next few hours, she'd give herself permission to stop. To take a breath. Gift herself the present of sleep for her birthday and maybe even dream of the sexy hero she read about on the train.

Referring to Ebony as a handful was an understatement. She constantly did stupid shit, but she always made it home. She planned to give Ebony an earful in the morning. God only knew their actual mother wouldn't say anything about her behavior.

Back at the dining table, she stirred her mom and half dragged, half carried her to bed.

"They're coming…" Mom groggily murmured as Hailee eased her onto the bed.

"Yes, Mom."

By now, she knew arguing or reasoning with her mother was an absolute waste of time. The only thing coming for them was sleep.

After draping a thin sheet over Mom's legs, Hailee bee-lined for the bathroom and showered off the greasy kitchen smells caked into her pores.

She placed her favorite paperback within arm's reach on the floor beside the bed. Reading when she woke was a small pleasure. Constantly moving around the country didn't bode well to a house full of novels, so she only kept her favorites, content with re-reading the same happily ever afters.

Books were the closest she'd ever come to exotic places where valiant heroes swept her off her feet. Those kinds of happy endings didn't happen in the real world. Her father proved knights in shining armor didn't exist.

Chapter Three

EJ leaped to the left just in time to avoid the wave gunning for his shoes. He really should wear flip-flops or something 'cause this shit boarded ridiculous.

While adjusting his beanie, he scanned the landscape, not expecting any changes since the previous vision. Yep, he was right. The same unnaturally white sand curved around a horseshoe bay. More of that crystal-clear blue water washed onto the shore before slowly dragging out again as though it had all the time in the world. The same line of tall, thin palm trees swayed in a gentle breeze.

The blonde was the only thing missing. Damn him for even noticing her absence.

On the dry sand, he slipped off his shoes and socks. If he was stuck here again, then he may as well keep that cringe-worthy wet sand out of his shoes.

Big mistake. Fire burned his soles the second they touched the sand. "Sweet Jesus!"

He leaped from foot to foot to dull the pain. It didn't help. The sand was straight out of Hell's sauna. He bolted into the water and steam practically rose when he submerged his feet.

A wave washed over his ankles. "Frickin' hell, now my jeans are wet."

At least his feet no longer felt like Ellen cooked them on a hotplate.

He scowled up at the cloudless sky, shielding his eyes from the sun. "Fate, cut out the bullshit already and show me what I need to know so we can get this over with."

He scoffed. Not that knowing made it any easier. Fate still made sure he never got there in time. Only once had she shown him mercy—when Aric skipped down to the fiery gates to become a Fallen. That vision of Ric with crimson wings and red fiery eyes came through so clear that, when it finished, EJ threw up his dinner. He hadn't wasted a single second deciphering it, and flew straight to Ric's cabin, hoping for once he made it on time. Thank Fate, he had.

He swept his foot through the water. At least out here he didn't get sand stuck to his clothes. But now that his feet were wet, he couldn't return to the dry stuff otherwise that shit would glue to his wet skin.

Pivoting, he faced the endless ocean. Gabe told the Guardians Fate needed time to recover after Blaine took the last Chosen's soul. Maybe Fate sent him a vision, but the connection wasn't strong enough to show him the entire thing.

He groaned. This vision better not last until Fate regained her powers. He'd seen it for long enough already.

Hands on his hips, he stood there for who knew how long, staring at the pristine water. A pair of shades would be helpful. If this became a regular gig, he needed to prepare himself better. Flip-flops and shades. And maybe he should stop wearing his beanie for a while. Nah, that took it too far.

A rustle in the palm trees made him spin around. The same blonde female from the last vision strolled onto the sand. With a pair of flip-flops dangling in one hand and her eyes watching her every step, the woman wandered toward the water. Toward him. Clearly, she was more prepared for a beach visit.

A few feet away, her gaze lifted. She froze. His stomach did that stupid flip thing again.

Her brows knitted, head tilted slightly. "You're here. That's weird."

She found him being there weird? Nope, not even close. The fact she saw him was the weird part.

Participants in Fate's visions never knew he was there, never saw him. But this woman was different. She spotted him in the last vision, too.

Did he speak? What if speaking screwed up the vision? What if words changed her path in some way?

And what the hell did this vision mean?

A soft grin curved on her face, lighting up her sapphire blue eyes. "Oh, I get it." She chuckled. "I'm dreaming of that scene I just read on the train."

Her gaze roamed over his body and for the first time in his entire existence, he shifted under the weight of a woman's stare.

"Though I don't think the hero would wear something so…grungy in the nineteenth century."

He drew back. What the fuck? She thought he was a hero from a book?

He stepped out of the water but remained on the cool, soggy sand. No need to repeat the feet-burning thing. "Firstly, I don't know what the hell's happening here, but I can assure you I'm not a fictional character. Nor am I a hero. And secondly." He motioned to his jeans which contained more holes than not. "This isn't grungy. It's designer."

"Designer?"

She laughed, a deep, infectious giggle that swirled over his skin like waves.

"For a rave party maybe, but definitely not for the beach."

Who the hell was this woman? More to the point, how did she so effortlessly twist his tongue into tiny knots so he couldn't form proper sentences?

"Maybe you should try rolling up the hems?"

He screwed up his face. "Ah, nope." Rolling his jeans made him look like some country-club mortal.

"Suit yourself."

Out of nowhere, a bright, colorful beach towel appeared in her hand, and she flipped it onto the sand before sitting.

Clues. He needed clues rather than staring at the golden curls tumbling to her shoulders. *Stop that shit right now.*

Clues first, before the vision disappeared again. That way he never needed to return to this hellish sauna. Then Fate would carry out her twisted plan and he could move on to his next failure.

He dashed to the beach towel, internally cursing at the dry scorching sand. He sat down beside her, knees bent so sand didn't stick to his wet jeans. Wriggling his toes deeper into the sand took away the sizzle and prevented him from bolting back into the water like a loser.

He wrapped his arms around his legs. "Who are you?" Clue number one.

She drew back. A slight frown creased her brow. Jesus. Her eyes matched that ocean, endless pools of blue he could stare at forever. Each time they met his,

his stomach somersaulted.

"It's strange dreaming about a guy who doesn't know who I am. Shouldn't dreams of sexy heroes kickstart with the…you know, action? Not with getting-to-know-you small talk."

Fuchsia dusted her cheeks as the words fell from her mouth. He zeroed in on her full lips and the slight part between them.

His brain scrambled and clue discovery flew away with the breeze. "All I hear is you telling me I'm sexy."

****

Dreams weren't places of awkwardness. Nor were they places where Hailee embarrassed herself in front of a gorgeous stranger. There was a first time for everything.

How could she concentrate while staring at his impossibly square jaw line? She bit the inside of her lip. "That's not what I meant."

"Really?" He drew the word out, nice and slow.

"Yeah, so don't get all full of yourself."

A wolfish grin curled his lips. "What's your name?"

"Hailee."

She'd dreamt of book boyfriends before, but nothing like this. This guy didn't seem fictional, and the historical romances she read never contained a bad boy wearing clothes like his. Yet, something was familiar about him, like they'd met before in real life. Maybe he was a waiter at the restaurant, but she took no notice. Only now, her subconscious brought him to life.

No, she would've noticed him. How could she not?

The beanie he wore, with bits of shaggy blond hair sticking out from underneath, gave him an edgy look.

Strong, straight nose, and a natural pout in his bottom lip completed the rock star vibe. Her gaze drifted over his torso. Through his white form-fitting T-shirt, she spotted an intricate masterpiece of artwork, extending all the way to his wrist. She'd give just about anything to rip off that shirt and trace the lines across his chest.

Muscles clenched low in her belly as her gaze lifted back to his. He cocked a brow. Busted! Her cheeks set on fire.

She diverted her attention to the ocean instead, though it didn't dull the tingles dancing along her skin. Shouldn't he at least kiss her? Being this close to him made breathing a little difficult.

She dreamt of this place a few times now. It reminded her of when they lived in Crystal Bay. Of all the towns they lived in that one was her favorite.

But having a companion on the towel with her was totally new.

"What's your name?" she asked, drawing a pattern in the sand with her finger.

"EJ."

"EJ as in…"

When he didn't answer, she paused and glanced at him.

That cocky grin widened. "As in we're not nearly naked enough for you to find out."

Oh, man. Those tingles went into overdrive, centering in one spot. She crossed her legs at the ankles, which only squeezed her thighs together. Gah. She uncrossed them again. "I'll just make up a name then."

"Until we're more naked?"

She shifted on the towel, but it didn't ease the ache. "Until you tell me."

He laughed, a deep and throaty sound that stirred low in her belly. It felt good, relaxed, carefree.

Leaning back, she braced her palms in the sand behind her and lifted her chin toward the sky, soaking up the sunshine. Though inside, her body already flooded with heat.

If he wouldn't tell her what his initials stood for, then she'd guess. E…What guy names started with E? Given his grungy rock star vibe, she bet his name was equally cool and trendy. She didn't keep up with trends, one of her many faults. Ebony did, and she'd probably guess his name straightaway. Half the guys at Ebony's rave parties probably had the same name.

A few names drifted through her mind, though they were all too formal, too biblical or traditional. But she needed to start somewhere. "So, Eamon Jackson, why am I dreaming of you?"

He laughed again, warming her cheeks. Please don't end, please don't wake up. This dream was so much better than reality.

"Nope. Wrong. But points for trying."

"Did I get anything right?"

His ice-blue eyes locked with hers. For a second, she swore her heart stopped beating.

"Mmm. I think you'd get lots of things right."

Next time, she'd sit in the shade. Sitting directly in the sun next to EJ made her all hot and bothered. "Um, your name. Did I get your name right?"

"You guessed the initials correctly."

She shook her head but couldn't wipe the smile off her face. Smiling again made her feel so darn good. "All right funny guy, tell me—"

The silver bracelet on her wrist warmed slightly as

though, for a split second, the sun's rays beamed down in that exact spot. Not hot but enough to draw her attention. She sat upright and shook her wrist to loosen the bracelet.

EJ grabbed her hand. She froze. His touch shot tiny sparks through her entire body. He turned her wrist, inspecting the single dreamcatcher charm dangling from her bracelet.

"Where did you get that?" The playfulness vanished from his tone.

She pulled back, but his grip tightened, enough to make it clear she wasn't moving anywhere. "My mother."

His gaze darted between the charm and her. "She gave this to you?"

"Yeah, when I was a kid. She said it protected me." She jerked her arm again and he let go.

This dream got weirder by the second. Since when did dreamy heroes inspect her jewelry? She'd worn the bracelet for so long she no longer noticed it. Ebony had an identical one, though on nights when it clashed with her outfit, her sister left it at home.

Dreams were an escape from reality, just like her trusty paperbacks. Why did this guy have to ruin it? With yet another move looming over her head, why couldn't her subconscious give her one night off? One dream of a swoony hero who smelled like expensive cologne with a hint of wild and danger. Right now, reality was too darn hard to deal with.

"Protect you from what?"

She fiddled with the charm, now cool, flipping it around with her finger. "I don't know. Mom's imaginary demons? Ever since my dad ran out on her when I was born, she's suffered from nightmares. Pining over a guy for twenty-five years will do that to a person."

His gaped. "You're twenty-five?"

"Today actually. Happy birthday to me." She dug her fingers through the warm, velvety sand, something she never tired of. Though now it just felt gritty. "I'm not sure why age matters in a dream."

He brushed the bracelet with his thumb. "Please tell me you don't have a twin."

Another strange question to ask in a dream. Where the hell was her subconscious going with this?

This time when the bracelet warmed, it glowed iridescent blue.

"What the heck." She fiddled with the clasp, trying to remove it.

"Don't," he growled, stilling her hand.

"This is beyond weird."

"Hailee, listen to me." Urgency in his tone made her heart stop. "Don't ever take this off, do you hear me?"

"Why?"

She wore the bracelet to make Mom happy, not because she believed it actually protected her.

EJ let go of her wrist.

Before she could ask him any further questions, the scene warped. A ripple appeared through the air, flickering between the sunny beach landscape and blackness. Beside her, EJ faded in and out.

He shot to his feet, scanning the beach. "What's happening?"

She knew this part all too well. That was a nice dream while it lasted.

She stood, brushing the sand from the backs of her legs. “Someone’s waking me.”

The last thing she remembered before the dream collapsed was the dark, dangerous fury swirling in EJ’s stormy eyes.

Chapter Four

EJ shot out of bed like the whole damn house was on fire. Landing in a half run, half leap, he tripped over his shoes on the floor, flailing his arms in the air.

"Fuck."

The second he regained balance, wicked pain slammed into the base of his skull. Immortality didn't make him immune to the effects of alcohol. It just made wiping out reality that much harder. The stabbing pain was a small price to pay for a few hours of peace from Fate and his bloody curse.

He froze. Fate. Curse.

He raked a hand through his hair as the foggy events of last night resurfaced. Tayla and Raven's anniversary celebration at the club. Endless supply of drinks thanks to their favorite bartender, so many in fact, EJ couldn't remember how he got home. At some point, likely the early hours of the morning, he collapsed into bed fully clothed. Fate sent another vision, though he couldn't quite remember the details. Either she seriously upped her game, or that wild concoction he drank at the club screwed with his head. But even with the hangover, he couldn't ignore the supercharged sunlight firing through his veins.

Halfway to the shower, a gritty sensation irritated his bare feet. He stilled, peering at the tiny grains of sand scattered on the wooden floor. Was that real?

Maybe his questionable drink choices caused wicked hallucinations and any moment, the tiny grains would sprout wings and fly out the door. He slid his toe through the sand, creating a track. Yep, real. Next, he peered at his jeans, noticing the dark rim around the hems. They were wet.

The ocean. White sand.

Why couldn't Fate go back to sending visions of doom and gloom, filled with toppled buildings, hellfire burning the streets, and screaming, terrified mortals? Those dreams were better than scratchy sand between his toes. How the beach ended up in his bedroom, he'd never know. He never took home a souvenir from Fate's visions. And no one ever saw him.

Hailee.

Her name rolled around in his head. Last night, she spoke to him. Fate toyed with him 'cause a mortal that perfect didn't exist.

Pinching his forehead, he stumbled to the bathroom. The cool tiles under his bare feet simmered some of the heat coursing through his body. He stripped and flicked on the shower—the ultimate hangover cure.

As fog steamed the glass, he slipped off the leather bands from his wrist. One foot inside the shower, he paused. Something important tried to break through the thumping in his head. Something about the vision? Did he find a clue?

He eyed the leather bands on the basin. Something…but he couldn't quite remember. From now on, he'd stick to vodka. Who knew what those other crazy drinks contained?

Shaking off the uneasy feeling, he stepped into the shower and immersed his pounding head under the soothing spray.

Washed, semi-refreshed, except for the ache in his skull, he threw on some clothes—another pair of ripped jeans Dream Girl labeled as “grungy.” He chuckled to himself. Every other woman he encountered thought his clothes were sexy.

A knock pounded on the bedroom door. “EJ, you up, man?”

Aric’s voice hammered through his skull, even from outside in the hall.

“Barely,” he replied, squeezing his forehead. It didn’t help.

“Meeting in five,” Aric called back before heavy footsteps disappeared down the hall.

What part of barely didn’t Ric understand?

Seven minutes later, the thumping in his temples calmed down enough to make his way to the war room. He bee-lined for the mini fridge and swiped a can of soda. The opening hiss made him giddy. Without wasting time, the colder the better, he took a long, drawn out swig. He sighed, more of a deep groan really, like the cold fizziness gave him a frickin’ orgasm.

“Hard night?” Raven interrupted EJ’s little session with the can.

He lowered the soda and found the other Guardians seated at the table staring at him. Raven cocked a brow.

EJ shrugged one shoulder. “What? It’s frickin’ good.”

Aric, seated to Raven’s left, jutted his chin. “You owe me big-time, man.”

“What for this time?”

“For driving your drunken ass home last night. My legs barely fit under the steering wheel.”

"Pfft. You should be thankful I let you drive Stella at all."

Aric snorted.

He grabbed another can from the fridge before taking his usual seat in front of the laptop next to River. Today, the dude wore the world's most fluorescent yellow shirt. "I'd be fine if Sunshine's shirt didn't send laser beams of brightness into the back of my head."

River frowned, peering at his shirt before looking to EJ.

His lips rolled into a straight line. "Adding a little color to your wardrobe won't kill you."

EJ opened the second can of soda. Today was one of those days. "I have plenty of color in my wardrobe. Black and white."

From the far side of the room, Raine huffed. "Can you idiots get on with it? EJ, you look like shit. River, you dress like you're auditioning for the sun. There, done."

His jaw flopped open. Wow. Just wow. That was the longest string of words Raine had spoken since she and River arrived two years ago. Next time, she'd sit down with the rest of them, rather than butting against the side table.

That would really cause a stir.

Raven cleared his throat. "EJ, by the looks of you, the visions are now happening while you sleep?"

"Yep." EJ opened the laptop and pressed the power button.

"Anything new?"

EJ gulped more soda while the laptop booted up. "Last night, the woman appeared again at nightmare beach and spoke to me."

No need to mention the fact that actual sand somehow made its way into his shoes for the second time. Even he didn't understand that. How could a vision become a reality? Or was he careening into crazy land from his years of partying?

"A woman?"

"Yep."

Raven relaxed in his seat, all smug-like. "Is she a Chosen?"

Aric laughed. Like, pissed himself laughing. "Man, by the shit storm you caused Fate, I would've put money on her assigning you a male Chosen that lived with monks, just to piss you off."

If it weren't for the fact his head weighed like a boulder, he'd leap over the table and smack Aric square in the jaw. "It's not a Chosen vision."

River bit the head off a candied snake. "Fate hasn't assigned us a Chosen since Aric's. It's been what? Almost a year?"

"Where are you hiding that candy?" Raven asked, leaning to the side to look for River's stash.

River grabbed a bag of snakes from below the table and plonked them on top. "You want one?"

Raven nodded, hand outstretched.

Aric shook his head. "I'd reconsider that, man, they were sitting on his balls."

Raven's arm retreated. "Second thought, I'll pass."

River shrugged and bit the head off another. Or was it the tail?

The home screen finally loaded on the laptop and he opened the usual programs, before lowering the brightness to a less retina-burning setting. "I wouldn't worry about the Chosen thing. The Fallen won that last round with Leon's soul. Fate's probably still recovering. I'm sure once she's almighty and powerful again, she'll send me the whole vision and I can stop visiting that hellish place."

Raine exhaled a loud, annoyed sigh.

He glared at Raine, shooting imaginary daggers, which didn't seem to faze her in the slightest. Did she take an extra bitchy pill this morning?

The war room door opened, and Willow slipped inside. "Sorry I'm late. Did I miss anything?"

Aric pulled out the chair beside him for her. "It's fine, baby. EJ just caught us up on his latest conquest."

Her chair was so close to Aric's she may as well sit on his lap.

"Oh, that brunette at the club last night?"

What the hell? He was with a brunette?

Any second now, his temples would explode. He needed to get his shit together, drinking to dull Fate's visions didn't work so well anymore. Usually, she only sent him visions during the day, but now she invaded his dreams, too. That took his curse to a whole new level.

EJ jutted out his chin, about to throw back some smartass comment when the band on Aric's wrist froze the words in his throat. As Aric lifted Willow's hand to place a gentle kiss on it, the band glowed a soft orange—the color of Willow's Ariel magic.

He sucked in a sharp breath. The glowing bracelet. The dreamcatcher charm.

He shot up from the table so fast his chair flung back and knocked into the wall. His chest rose and fell with rapid breaths.

Raven glared at EJ. "What the fuck's going on?"

"She's a…she's a frickin' Dumahel."

Chapter Five

Hailee jolted awake with her mother leaning over her, shaking her shoulders. Moonlight seeped through the open curtains casting her room in an eerie glow. "Mom, seriously. What time is it?"

"They're coming. Get up."

Here we go again.

She clasped her mother's wrists, lifting them from her shoulders and sat up. Mom ripped her arms free and spun around. Next, she began tossing Hailee's small collection of belongings into a box by the bedroom door. That box wasn't there when she fell asleep.

"They're nearly here. Your sister's not home."

Hailee rubbed her eyes before reaching for her cell to check the time. Her shoulders slumped. "Mom, it's four in the morning, of course Ebony's not home yet."

Rolling out of bed, she slipped on a pair of shorts and stood before her mother, firmly gripping her shoulders. Mom had countless episodes like this, usually before each of their many moves, but one had never sparked such urgency in her voice. And she'd never experienced an episode so early in the morning.

"Nobody is coming, Mom. Let me help you back to bed."

With an arm draped around her mother's back, she steered her toward the bedroom door. The charm bracelet on her wrist glowed iridescent blue just like in her dream. She paused. It had never glowed the entire time she'd worn it. Why now? Especially after she just dreamed the same thing.

Her mother noticed, too, gasping as she clutched the charm between her fingers. "They're here…"

Hailee's heart leaped into her throat at her words. "Who's here? You're not making any sense."

Mom's gaze locked with hers and for the first time since she could remember, her mother's eyes were clear and focused. They held true fear.

She tugged the bracelet, about to remove it. This whole thing was too weird.

Her mother jerked Hailee's hand away. "Don't take it off."

The guy in her dream said the same thing. What the heck was happening?

Still clutching Hailee's wrist, Mom's gaze slid to the open bedroom door. They both stood there frozen for agonizing minutes. Waiting for what? Waiting for who? Her pulse thundered in her ears. Her hearing hypersensitive in the darkness.

A loud thud on the rooftop made her jump. Her heart raced so fast it could fly out her mouth and land flat on the floor.

Holding her breath, she peered at the ceiling. "What was—"

Mom's hand slammed over her mouth. With her other, Mom held a finger to her lips.

She nodded. She wouldn't make another single sound.

That failed. Heavy footsteps boomed along the rooftop causing a small cry to escape her mouth. Her mother glared at her with another warning.

When had Mom ever been so alert?

Mom yanked Hailee's hand, leading them out the bedroom door in the opposite direction of the footfalls. Unease stirred in the pit of her stomach. Who were they hiding from?

They hunched over, making their bodies smaller, and tip-toed along the hall. When the footsteps stopped at the opposite edge of the roof, they froze.

The silence was deafening, a screaming buzz in her oversensitive ears. Mom's hand squeezed tighter.

Another loud thump sounded outside, this time on the ground. Her legs shook, refusing to move. Mom crept forward and yanked Hailee to follow.

In the dining room, she exhaled silent relief that she left on the small kitchen light. If not, she would've slammed right into the table.

The knob on the back door jiggled.

Mom spun to her. The look in her wide eyes sent an icy chill all the way down Hailee's spine.

"It's too late," Mom whispered.

The lock jiggled again. Without making a sound, Mom shifted a dining chair and motioned for Hailee to crawl under the table.

"I'm not hiding under the table." Shouldn't they call the police? Shouldn't they escape out the front door?

Mom hushed her, pushing her down. "I vowed to keep you hidden."

This was ridiculous. Robbers were at the back door and Mom wanted to hide under the dining room table. More proof she was crazy.

Yet, something urged her to listen. A strange sensation through her middle told her this wasn't a drill.

This wasn't one of Mom's countless episodes. This was a matter of life or death.

On her knees, she crawled under the table and shuffled to one end to make room for her mom. But she didn't follow. Instead, she straightened and slid the chair back under the table.

"Mom," she raised her voice slightly.

Her mother bent down, peering between the chairs. "Don't make a sound. I love you, baby girl. Find your sister," she whispered, before straightening and turning to face the back door.

This wasn't the best hiding spot. Through the chair legs, all she saw were the backs of her mother's legs, her summer cotton nightgown, her baby pink slippers.

The doorknob jiggled again. Deep voices came from the other side of the door.

This was stupid. They should run out the front door while there was still time.

A shadow passed the kitchen window.

Everything happened so fast. The back door flung off the hinges, landing flat on the floor. Hailee slapped her hands over her mouth. Mom stepped forward. Two sets of heavy boots stomped inside.

Nausea and adrenaline swirled together as her fight-or-flight response kicked into overdrive, making her dizzy. She needed to help her mother.

On her hands and knees, she scooted to one side. Before she crawled out, she needed to know how many attackers and where they stood. The element of surprise worked in her favor.

Through the gap between the chairs, she spotted the first attacker. Thick legs clad in a matte leather material with an open dark overcoat. The other one, only a step behind wore dark denim jeans with a few metal chains hanging from the waistband. Both wore black military style boots. By the size of their legs and the heaviness in their step, she guessed they were large men.

Leather pants guy stepped forward, facing Mom at the opposite end of their kitchen.

"Connie, we meet again. How long has it been?"

What the hell? The attackers knew her mother? If that were true, why hide under the table? That lump tightened in her throat. More importantly, why run from people they knew?

"Twenty-five years, but you already know that don't you, Slater?" Her mom may portray confidence by standing up to those two thugs, but Hailee didn't miss the hitch of fear in her voice.

Leather guy, Slater, chuckled. Her bracelet went into full-on light-up-the-universe mode. She tucked her wrist under the front of her shirt, so it didn't reveal her location. It wouldn't matter though, whoever these guys were, she sensed they didn't come for a casual catch-up.

"I guess I did," Slater replied. Humor vanished from of his voice as it lowered. "Tell me where the twins are, Connie, and I'll let you live."

Her mother retreated a step. "I'll never tell you."

Hailee crawled backward, huddling in a ball. Surely, they weren't talking about her and Ebony? What did they want with them?

The jean wearing guy stepped beside Slater. Mom gasped.

"Hello, darling."

Mom retreated another step.

Questions raced through Hailee's mind, but she couldn't focus on them right now. She needed to stop hiding. She needed to help her mother. Protecting her family was her job and she couldn't do that from underneath a stupid table.

She shuffled to the far end, closest to the wall. Gripping the chair legs, she started to push it out from the table but froze. What if they heard? Holding her breath, she peered over her shoulder through the gap. That was the moment she saw their faces. She released the chair as the pit of her stomach plummeted.

Both the attackers had fiery red eyes and…wings? All her life, Mom warned them of creatures with blood-red wings. She and Ebony laughed it off as another one of Mom's delusions.

Their mother wasn't crazy.

A giant hole split open in Hailee's chest. All this time, Mom told the truth and protected them.

Jean guy stepped closer to Mom. "Please, Connie. Tell me where the girls are."

Mom jutted her chin. "I'll never betray them. Unlike you."

His mouth set in a grim line. He raised a palm inches from her face. "You've left me with no other choice."

Dark shadows swirled from his hand, surrounding Mom in a matter of seconds. Hailee covered her mouth, stifling a scream. Her mother convulsed, her body lifted off the ground by the shadows.

The urge to save her screamed over and over in Hailee's head, but her stupid body wouldn't move, frozen with fear.

Shadow Man's eyes blazed while the dark swirls

continued brewing around Mom, swallowing her in the darkness. The second the shadows retreated, Mom collapsed, her head slamming against the floor in a sickening smack.

Bile rose in Hailee's mouth. Silent tears gushed down her cheeks.

Shadow Man turned to Slater. "One is in the warehouse district on the other side of town. The other is still cloaked. Blaine won't be happy."

"Let me deal with Blaine. At least we found one tonight."

Hailee's breath hitched. They were after her and Ebony. How could they not see her?

As though nothing ever happened, the two strolled out the back door.

Fear seized her limbs. She drew her knees into a fetal position and sobbed while her mother lay lifeless on the kitchen floor.

Chapter Six

EJ stood behind the bar in the entertainment room doing what he did best in times of crisis—making cocktails. Fate should've created him as a bartender instead of a Guardian 'cause this was the only thing that truly brought him peace. Well, cocktails and Stella.

Under his palm, he rolled a juicy green lime along the counter before slicing it into quarters. The air in the war room smothered him. Having the others fire questions at him that he didn't know the answers to felt like someone made a voodoo doll version of him and stabbed it with a thousand pins. He couldn't stand it any longer.

All he knew for certain was Hailee was a Dumahel and last night's vision was likely a dream connection. But he didn't rule out Fate's involvement.

Dropping two lime quarters in a short glass, he muddled them together with a sugar cube. Did Hailee know what she was? How rare she was? Did she even know about their world?

He scooped ice into the glass before pouring in the vodka. A few shots more than usual. From inside the mini fridge, he tore off some basil leaves, thanks to Ellen's stash in the greenhouse, and added them to the drink. A quick stir and presto. He took a swig. The sweet and tart combination buzzed down his throat and warmed his chest. Just what he needed.

Raine strolled into the entertainment room, her heels clicking along the wooden floor. He grabbed another lime and got to work making her a gin martini. Straight-up cringe-worthy rocket fuel. Stirred not shaken, unlike that badass secret agent.

Busying himself behind the bar took his mind off the visions, while drinking alcohol kept Fate out of his head. The more he drank, the less frequently the visions came, the less real they felt when they ended. The less his stomach churned when he thought about how he never got there in time.

Cocktails took away everything except the sting of inevitable failure.

Finished with Raine's drink, he dropped a curl of lime rind in the fancy glass then passed it to her. "Are the others still in the war room?"

Raine tipped her chin in thanks before retreating to her usual spot near the pool table. Standard MO. "They're on their way. Raven summoned Gabe."

A second later, the others filed into the room.

River and Willow sat on the couch, Aric on a bar stool. Even Tayla joined their little what-the-hell emergency and sat beside Willow. Raven included her in all the important shit that happened in the household. Except for killing Fallen. Apparently, she opted out of those gory details.

Finding a Dumahel? That was the biggest shit ever.

He made drinks and handed them out one by one, keeping busy until Raven and Gabe strode through the doorway. Cole followed close behind and perched on the stool beside Aric.

"Why are you here?" EJ asked, reaching for a fresh glass.

The Azrael raised his brows. “Nice to see you too, brother.”

EJ sighed and gave Cole a brotherly handshake. “You don’t visit much anymore, Reaper, it’s lonely without you.”

Cole laughed. “That’s a better greeting.”

EJ slid a drink in front of Cole then grabbed his own and rounded the bar.

Gabe slipped off his dark gray suit jacket and folded it over the back of a vacant bar stool. “Tell me what you know, EJ.”

EJ took a long swig, avoiding a mouthful of basil. When the alcohol settled in his belly, he retold the entire dream-vision to Gabe. “Do you know who she is?”

The sooner they got information, the sooner this dream-vision ended. The sooner he failed and moved onto the next one.

Gabe slid one hand in the pocket of his slacks. “Twenty-five years ago, I discovered an Azrael’s mortal soulmate was with child. On the night of their birth, Fate instructed me to compel the Azrael to believe the twins died.”

EJ rolled his eyes. “Plot twist: they didn’t?”

“Correct.”

Raven crossed his arms. “Why would she do that? Why wouldn’t Fate just recall the souls to the Heavens when or before they were born? Given how rare Dumahel are, wouldn’t Fate rather have the powers under her control.”

“When I queried Fate, she insisted the souls remain in the mortal realm. She provided me with bracelets to glamour the infants, which I suspected protected them from the Fallen. Fate wouldn't explain why, and it wasn't my place to question. I'm convinced they play a part in her plan for this realm."

Of course, they did. Just great. Fate set up his latest failure twenty-five years ago. When would this shit end?

Back behind the bar, he refilled his glass and kept the bottle close. He needed to get through today without Fate's torture piled on top.

Aric swiveled on the stool. "Is the Dumahel a Chosen?"

EJ's drink sprayed from his mouth all over the bar. He'd throw back some snarky comment when he stopped choking. Wild-eyed, he stared at Gabe, waiting for his answer. He might have even held his breath.

"The Dumahel are Chosen until they reach immortality."

Air left the room in one whoosh. Something heavy pressed against his chest. A Chosen assignment? No way, not him.

Aric burst out laughing. "Man, that's gonna seriously dampen your social life. You got a two for one Chosen deal. I wonder if one is your soulmate."

EJ feigned a calm and cool demeanor while inside his stomach twisted so tight it may never unravel. "Pfft. Before Fate banished us to this realm, she assigned us hundreds of Chosen. None of those led to soulmates. This assignment is no different. Anyway, Hailee said she just turned twenty-five, so she's no longer mortal therefore no longer a Chosen."

According to that logic, she was also no longer at risk of being his soulmate.

"Whatever you reckon, man."

EJ glanced at Raven. “Wipe that ridiculous smirk off your face, Rave.”

“I’m not saying a damn thing.” The smirk didn’t disappear.

He turned back to Gabe. The reasonable one. “Do you know where Hailee is?”

“No. But now that she’s immortal, Cole can track her soul’s signature.”

“If she removes the cloak,” Cole added.

EJ pinch his forehead. This day got better by the minute. “I told her to never take the bracelet off. How else can we track her?”

“Through the dreams. But remember, her magic pulls you into her dream. It does not work both ways.”

“How do you explain the vision outside the club? I wasn’t asleep.”

Gabe adjusted his fancy cuff links. “In the beginning, her powers will be sporadic. Like bursts of energy, if you will. As she transitions, they will strengthen until she can manipulate dreams at will. Whether the recipient is asleep or awake. I believe outside the nightclub she had a burst of power, which enabled the connection. But until the Dumahel—”

“Hailee. Her name is Hailee.”

Gabe nodded. “Yes. Until Hailee learns to control her powers, a connection when you are asleep is more reliable because your mind is clear.” Gabe paused, considering something. “Clearer than it is while you’re awake.”

He didn’t retort at Gabe’s dig at his drinking habits. If cocktails dulled the visions, no way he’d opt for sobriety. “You’re saying I need to wait until she pulls me into another dream? What if she doesn’t?

What if something happens in the meantime?"

What if I fail?

He didn't even know what continent Hailee lived on. What if they didn't share the same time zone? His sleep patterns were so all over the place he couldn't even call them a pattern.

Gabe pursed his lips. That answered that.

EJ placed the glass on the bar. "Great. Another one of Fate's destined-to-fail missions. Get sucked into a dream by a Dumahel but never find where she is until the Fallen kill her."

Cole drummed his fingers on the bar. "There's a possibility she doesn't even know what she is. If she's recently turned twenty-five, her immortality wouldn't have shown until now."

The Reaper had a point. "She didn't act like she knew how the bracelet worked. She said her mom gave it to her as protection, but she didn't seem to believe it. Gabe, what happened to the Azrael?"

"Believing his twins died caused him to Fall."

Raven raked a hand through his hair. "Well, that screws that idea. EJ, why don't you try to get some sleep, in case she contacts you again. We'll stay here and research possible locations based on the imagery you described."

"Are you frickin' kidding, Rave? You're putting me on bed duty?"

Aric snorted. "Hang on, Romeo. I thought you had all your best times in bed."

He refrained from giving Aric the finger. "For your information, the best sex happens in the absence of a bed."

Chapter Seven

Hailee waited until her bracelet dulled, returning to its usual platinum color before she crept from her hiding spot. How did they not find her? If the…creatures were after her and Ebony, how didn't they see her?

She glanced again at the bracelet. Maybe it only glowed when…

Everything pieced together. The bracelet warned her when the creatures were near. EJ, the guy in her dream, and Mom told her not to remove it. The bracelet didn't just protect her, it apparently hid her. That theory made sense but also raised more questions. Who was EJ? How was he in her dream? Was he after her, too?

She crawled to Mom's body, choking back the sobs. "I'm sorry, Mom. I'm sorry I didn't listen."

Faint gray lines spread in a web-like pattern under the surface of her mother's skin, a similar color to the shadows that swirled from the killer's hands. As though he'd poisoned her.

She brushed a hand over her mom's pale, lifeless eyes, closing the lids. "I'll find Ebony, I promise."

Bending down, she rested her cheek against Mom's. Her eyes blurred with more tears, but she didn't have time to grieve. Not yet. Ebony was in danger and she needed to find her before the creatures.

She straightened, pushing aside the storm of

emotions whirling inside her with the force of a hurricane. Half crouching, half running, she bolted to Ebony's room. She prayed to whatever god would listen that Ebony left a clue to her whereabouts.

On top of the dresser, amongst a few black pieces of costume jewelry, was Ebony's bracelet—the same bracelet as hers. Her heart sank.

Hailee had never attended a rave party, they weren't her thing. For her, free time consisted of a train ride to and from work each day and regular dates with a book boyfriend.

Scanning Ebony's room, she searched for clues. Nothing. She couldn't let that stop her. She'd search the whole town one warehouse at a time if that's what it took.

Wait. That was her clue. The killer said Ebony was in the warehouse district. She didn't want to know how he used those sickening shadows to elicit that information. At this point, it was her only lead.

Snatching Ebony's bracelet, she sprang into action. First, she draped a thin sheet over her mother, careful not to touch the body and set off the crazy hysteria bubbling under her skin. She'd sort out what to do with the body after she found Ebony. They didn't have any family, nor were they overly friendly with the neighbors. How would she explain it to the police?

Another task to sort out later.

She bolted out of the house and into the car. Dawn trickled along the quiet streets as she sped toward the other side of town, continuously calling Ebony's cell, but it diverted to voicemail every time. If Ebony were in the DJ booth, she doubted she'd answer.

Why didn't she know Ebony's schedule?

Fresh tears blurred her vision and she blinked a few times to clear them. She didn't know Ebony's location because she thought her mother was crazy and keeping tabs on Ebony wasn't necessary. Lately, mothering Ebony became more like a burden. Something she never voiced aloud.

Her stomach twisted tight. What if she didn't find Ebony? What happened if those killers…?

If she finished that sentence, she'd curl in a ball and cry for the rest of eternity.

A car horn sounded. She swerved to avoid the oncoming collision.

"Shit!" She wiped her eyes with the back of her hand. "Focus, Hailee, focus."

Twenty minutes later, she veered into the warehouse district and slowed the car to a crawl, peering left and right at the oversized metal sheds flanking the streets. Some had signs indicating the businesses, others didn't. Convinced the rave party wasn't in a paint shop or mechanic's, she continued further along the dark, deserted street.

Toward the end, where the buildings spaced out, her bracelet glowed. Not as vibrant as before, but enough to notice the change.

The creatures were near.

She pulled the car to the curb and hopped out to survey the nearby warehouses. One across the street drew her attention, no business sign and graffiti tags sprayed on the outside walls. She darted to the oversized roller door and angled her ear, listening for the sounds of partygoers or music. Nothing. Inching open the door, she slipped inside.

Her eyes adjusted to the change in light. She

staggered back, hand covering her mouth.

Right building. Only, she was too late.

Tall stands with giant speakers lay on the floor, the speakers smashed and broken. Strobe lights hung from long cords over exposed beams in the roof, the multicolor bulbs still flashing as though the rave continued in silence. Red plastic cups and printed leaflets littered the concrete floor. Smashed cell phones scattered the floor with tiny puffs of smoke curling from the handsets as though they'd caught fire.

What made her stomach churn lay in between the mayhem. Bodies. Dead bodies. Too many to count. The vacant look in the closest guy's eyes…

Bending over, she vomited, adding the contents of her stomach to the already filthy floor.

Once she pulled herself together, she examined the guy beside her foot. No blood or obvious wounds, but the faint gray lines under his skin were identical to Mom's.

Those creatures killed all these people.

Forcing down the bile rising in her throat, she focused on the DJ booth rather than the horrific scene. With each step closer, the knot in her stomach tightened. She hugged her middle to ease some of the nausea.

Was Ebony dead on the other side of the booth? With shaky legs, she stepped onto the raised platform.

Please be okay...please be okay...

She sucked in a sharp breath. Ebony wasn't there. Relief rushed through her so fast it made her dizzy. She gripped the booth to remain upright, her fingers brushing a cell phone. Ebony's phone. Oh, God. There went the slim chance Ebony was somewhere else.

There went the hope Ebony escaped before those creatures found her.

Call the police. The rational part of her brain screamed, but what would she say? Hey, two guys with crimson wings and red eyes broke into my house. One killed my mother using shadows from his hand and then they came here and did this…

That wouldn't go well. All scenarios ended with her locked in a white padded cell, wearing a matching jumpsuit. No, she had to figure out this herself, including why they wanted her and Ebony.

Mom protected them their entire lives, and Hailee wouldn't let all that running be for nothing. First, she needed to find her sister.

Back in the car, she sped home and dashed inside before the neighbors saw. In the kitchen, she skidded to a halt. Someone took Mom's body and folded the sheet over the dining chair.

Were they still near? Were they watching from afar? Who the hell were they? She needed to leave before they realized she was home.

She raced to the bedroom and stuffed essentials into a backpack: wallets, clothes, money. She wouldn't come back here, ever. In Ebony's room, her hand stilled on a photo of the three of them by the beach before their last move. Before now, she never noticed the spooked look in her mom's eyes. Even in a picture, Mom's gaze was wide and wary of danger. Why didn't her bracelet glow back then?

Mom taught them to trust no one. Now she knew why. Her dad had abandoned them, they spent their whole lives running from creatures, and now said creatures killed her.

Trust led to death. The only person she could trust right now was Ebony.

She shoved the photo in the backpack and grabbed supplies from the kitchen.

Once back in the car, she wrapped her arms around her middle and silently said farewell to her mom.

Each time they'd moved, Mom insisted on going east. Without knowing why, she put her trust in Mom, and pulled out of the drive. She prayed Ebony escaped those killers and headed in the same direction.

Chapter Eight

Ear-splitting beats thumped from the tiny Bluetooth buds in EJ's ears while his feet slammed the treadmill with the same intensity. Hard. Fast. He hoped all the running sent his body into a complete state of exhaustion.

He sucked at sleep. For a good hour after Raven sent him to his room like a mortal toddler, he sulked on top of the covers. The problem was with so many shots of vodka in his system, coupled with his usual I-survive-on-no-sleep routine, his mind didn't know whether to pass out or bounce around dancing. So, he kept busy all day, then hit the gym.

These days his alcohol tolerance and the number of shots required to rid himself of Fate's visions climbed higher and higher. Soon, he'd need another remedy or else he'd have to man up and take that shit. Not likely. Being responsible wasn't his thing. He left that to the other Guardians, the ones who didn't continually pay for an epic screw up in the Heavens.

When Fate exiled the others, she didn't curse them like she had him.

He sure as hell didn't need the reminder Blaine Fell. He missed the memo while in the Heavens and now he paid the price for the rest of eternity.

Fate's visions started the second he landed in the mortal realm post banishment. All doom and gloom, images of this world engulfed in flames. Buildings toppled, choking smoke and ash filling the air, mortals screaming on the streets. Those pathetic Fallen hovered in the dark, sunless sky like frickin' kings.

Then, as a bonus, Fate sent that same vision on repeat every single day. He didn't need the reminder of what happened if the Fallen won and Zath defeated Fate. Hell, he even inked the damn image across his body, so he didn't forget.

He increased the speed on the treadmill and turned up the incline for the hell of it. Sweat coasted down his bare spine, soaking into the band of his sweatpants. Any moment now, his lungs would call it quits, and he'd pass out on the machine.

Two hundred years after their banishment, Fate sent him his first non-doom and gloom vision—an image of the ornamental cherry planted in the front of the Guardian mansion.

That was the day his trek of failures began.

Would Fate stop the visions if they ever returned to the Heavens? Doubt it.

She acted all forgiving to Raven and Aric by pairing them with soulmates. But Fate would never forgive him for as long as he drew breath. Not after what he did to her.

The treadmill halted with a jerk, flinging him forward. In the nick of time, he leaped into the air and spun his body over the side, so he didn't smack his head on the console.

"Frickin' hell."

Regaining his balance, he ripped out the ear buds and faced the soon-to-be-dead man.

Cole stood by the machine with one arm rested on

the control panel, twirling the red emergency stop tag in his hand. “You weren’t listening, so I resorted to drastic measures.”

EJ waved an ear bud at the lunatic. “ ’Cause I didn’t hear you. Next time, slap my arm or something.”

He grabbed the bottle of water from the holder and chugged the remainder, giving his pulse a moment to calm down. “Since when do you visit so much anyway?”

Cole pushed off the machine. “I thought you said you missed me?” At his cocked brow, Cole continued. “Thought you’d want to know what I discovered about the Dumahel.”

A mouthful of water caught in his throat. Of course, he wanted to know. The more information he gathered, the quicker he figured out what Fate planned for him. The quicker he failed.

He never failed an immortal before, except Blaine, so that was a new layer to Fate’s curse. “Hit me.”

Cole threw him a gym towel. “I escorted a mortal soul to the Heavens last night.”

EJ wiped the sweat off his chest and the back of his neck. “Hate to say it, Reaper, but isn’t that your thing? Escorting souls?”

“This soul was a middle-aged female who had her entire memory wiped.” Cole paused and inhaled a deep breath. “By a Fallen Azrael.”

All the dots lined up.

Cole continued, “I took care of the body. Then not long after, a Fallen harvested a group of teenage souls from inside a warehouse. Slater’s signature all over them. The other Azrael was there, too.”

“Who is it?”

Cole's lips thinned into a grim line. "I don't know yet. But that's not all."

"C'mon Reap, spit it out. The suspense is killing me." That lump grew, constricting his airway.

"I picked up a Dumahel trace at the second location, but I couldn't track it any further. They must have access to Raziel magic and used it to cloak their movements."

"Frickin' hell. What did you do with the bodies?"

"I couldn't mist them, there were too many. The authorities will think it was a drunken teenage party gone wrong. A batch of bad drugs, a cult, whatever. It happens all the time. But it's obvious the two incidents are related."

"Where's the warehouse?"

"On the west coast. I gave Raven all the details, but I thought you'd want to know."

He sure as hell did. If he got there fast, he could beat Fate at her own game. "Appreciate it."

Cole gave him a brotherly handshake then headed out of the gym.

Given Fate removed their ability to mist, flying or driving were his only options. Flying was quicker, he'd arrive in hours, but daylight restricted his movements. Driving took days, but he could leave now and only stop for gas.

Sleep duty was the third and quickest option by far. If he spoke to Hailee, he could warn her and tell her to remain hidden until he got there.

After throwing the empty bottle in the trash, he left the gym and headed to his room. If his encounters with Hailee were actual dreams and not visions, then he could use them to stay one step ahead of Fate. That way, when Fate threw a twist, he'd be ready. Because one thing was for sure, if Fate marked Hailee as his mission, he damn well wouldn't fail. Not this time.

After showering off the stench of his workout, he slipped on a pair of jeans but kept his shoes off, so that sand stayed on the beach where it belonged. He also traded his beanie for a baseball cap. See, he could adapt. He just drew the line at rolling up his jeans.

Climbing onto the bed, he lay on top of the covers and thought of Hailee, hoping like hell he found her before the Fallen.

Chapter Nine

Hailee dug her fingers in the sand, closing her eyes as the warmth seeped into her bones. She closed her fist around a handful then released. The action eased the tension in her shoulders and washed away her worries like the gentle waves rolling in and out. The sun, high in the sky, beamed down on her skin, cleansing her mind.

This dream became a ritual she relied on over the past few months. No matter how stressed or anxious she was when she fell asleep, this dream guaranteed she woke refreshed and energized. Her body knew when she needed it, and over the past couple of weeks, it reoccurred more frequently.

She only truly felt at peace in the dreams. Somewhere her real-life responsibilities didn't weigh on her. Dreams were the only time she allowed herself to imagine a better future, one where she and Ebony stopped running. A future where a knight in shining armor, just like the heroes in her novels, adored her more than life. Where a love so strong conquered her fears.

But knights and heroes didn't exist. Her father proved that. Mom trusted him, loved him, and he abandoned her. He abandoned all of them.

She thought of last night's dream, and the guy who sat next to her. A thrill blazed through her center when she remembered the intricate lines tattooed over his defined arms, and the cocky smirk on his lips when she called him sexy.

The air near the shoreline rippled, waving back and forth as though she sat inside a giant squishy bubble and someone poked it from the outside. She narrowed her eyes, focusing on the spot. Someone gradually appeared. First a pair of bare feet, followed by black grungy jeans, then a strong muscular back covered in ink.

A smile lifted her cheeks when she recognized the tattoos.

EJ's form flickered in and out before solidifying, and man, she didn't shy away from ogling his tanned skin and the firm, broad shoulders covered in black swirls. She could stare at that all day. This time he wore a baseball cap, giving him a surfer meets rock star vibe that totally suited him.

Tattooed guys were never her thing, and none of her book boyfriends had tattoos. But most of them came from a different century. Clearly, she needed to switch sub-genres. She had missed out all this time.

"Finally," EJ muttered to himself, loud enough to hear. A wave rolled over his ankles, and he leaped backward but too late. "Frickin' hell."

At her giggle, he pivoted.

"That's what happens when you don't roll up your jeans…" A few names filtered through her mind until she settled on her next guess. "Emerson Jeffreys."

His lips curled with a grin full of mischief and confidence. "Nope. Still wrong."

She laughed and shrugged. "I'll just keep guessing. Unless you want to tell me?" she teased.

"I like you guessing. Plus, we're still not naked enough."

Her heart beat faster with each step he took toward her. He was glorious. Exactly how she imagined those fictional heroes. Perfectly defined arms strong enough to swoop her to the bedroom, out of this world sexy, and he even scored a panty-melting smile. She needed to figure out which book he came from so she could read it again and again.

Hopefully, this dream skipped to the part with the action. She could do with one of those dreams. Action, or any kind of relationship also didn't exist for her in the real world. That led to a commitment she couldn't give. Constantly moving didn't bode well for relationships, especially if she left out of the blue.

When she found "the one" and finally put down roots somewhere, with the whole white picket fence and wide front porch, it would be with someone who also put family first. Which couldn't happen until she and Ebony were safe. Until they landed on their feet.

"May I?" EJ motioned to the vacant space beside her on the towel.

"Sure."

He sat on the towel and bent his knees, curling his arms around them. "I may not have rolled up my jeans, but I came prepared." He wiggled his toes in the sand. "No shoes."

She snorted. "You're still not exactly dressed to ride your noble steed into the sunset."

His gaze slid her way and the pain behind his glassy blue eyes made her breath catch.

"I told you, sweetness. I'm not a hero."

She took a second to steady her pulse. "You forget,

this is my dream. I say you are."

He peered at the ocean. "Then I hope you're ready for disappointment."

How did she reply? This wasn't a sex dream. This was karma for continually reading the same romance story. Her subconscious telling her she needed to branch out and stop wishing for something she couldn't have.

This version of EJ was a bit too broody for her. She wanted the playful side to return. The side that came with a cocky grin and gleam in his unearthly blue eyes.

While he stared at the ocean, she took advantage of his diverted attention to admire his glorious tattoos. On the arm closest to her, an intricate colorless battle scene began at his shoulder blade and extended all the way to his wrist. Angels with swords fighting each other in clouds near his shoulder while black flames swirled up his forearm. In the center near his elbow, lay a massacre. Bodies piled on top of each other with an angel kneeling beside them, arm raised, head lowered. The scene tickled a memory but before she dug further, EJ spoke.

"She was your mom, yeah?" Roughness deepened his voice.

She drew back, unaware how close she'd leaned while admiring his tattoos. "Huh?"

He lowered his head. "The woman who died. She was your mom."

Her gaze returned to the battle scene on his arm. A chill raced over her skin. Mom. Winged creatures killed her mother.

She scrambled up off the towel. "They killed Mom. I have to find Ebony." Her chest squeezed tight.

EJ stood and inched closer. "Ebony? Is she your twin?"

"How do you know?"

"Let's just say it's my job to find out."

"Your job?" Her gaze darted left and right. "What do you mean? What's happening?" She retreated a step, her breaths coming faster. "This isn't real, it's a dream. Who are you?"

"Breathe. It's okay, you're safe. I won't hurt you."

Hurt her? Her eyes widened as realization shook her. "You're one of them." The winged creatures found her and now controlled her dreams.

Clouds rolled over the sun, thick and ominous, scaring away the warmth. A thunderous storm brewed on the horizon.

EJ peered at the storm then back at her. "I'm not the bad guy."

She steadied her feet, preparing to run. "Which one are you? The bad guy or the hero? Is EJ even your real name?"

"I'm neither. And of course, that's my real name. Why would I make up shit like that?"

He inched closer and this time she didn't retreat. She sensed he wasn't the bad guy. But that didn't explain how he knew about Mom without her telling him.

"I have to wake up and find Ebony."

"Wait." He caught her wrist. "I can help you find her."

Her gaze lowered to his hand. When the monsters attacked Mom, her bracelet illuminated blue. Now, it didn't. Could she trust the bracelet to guide her? Did Mom give her the bracelet so she could determine the difference between the good and bad guys?

If the bracelet didn't glow in EJ's presence, could she trust him? She'd never fully given her trust to anyone other than Ebony. For years, while Mom declined further into her self-medicated spiral, she couldn't risk it.

Her gaze lifted to EJ's and his eyes drew her in, sent a wave of calm and reassurance through her body right to the heart of her soul. She wanted to trust someone, ached to. Someone who could help shoulder her burden and weather the storm.

A silent sob rose in her chest. Who were those monsters and how could she find Ebony? At this point, this fantasy guy appearing in her dream was her only confidant.

"They killed Mom."

EJ's grip on her wrist loosened enough to slide down and hold her hand. "I know, sweetness."

"How?" Her chest squeezed air from her lungs. "How do you know? What if they captured Ebony? What if they kill her, too?"

Using his thumb, he brushed light circles over the back of her hand.

"They need her alive. But Hails, listen to me, they'll come for you, too. I have no doubt about it."

He gave her hand a gentle squeeze.

"I need you to tell me everything you know."

She could wake up, recommence her search for Ebony, but so far, she'd gotten nowhere. She couldn't even remember where she fell asleep. "I'm going crazy just like Mom. How did I even dream of you again?"

Still holding her hand, EJ led her back to the towel where they both sat side by side. His thumb resumed the light circles, calming her.

"Tell me what happened."

Where did she even start? A world she didn't know existed flipped her own upside down and tore it apart.

Staring at the raging white-capped waves, she relayed the events to EJ. She started with the appearance of the two monsters who murdered her mother right up until the horrific scene at the rave party.

Thunder cracked over the horizon. Loud booms of angry lashings increased in intensity the longer they sat on the beach doing nothing. The heady scent of stormy rain stirred through the air. Even though EJ remained silent, his thumb never ceased the gentle, calming circles over the back of her hand. The action grounded her somehow, kept her in the moment, so she didn't explode like the brewing storm.

A thunderous crack of lightning made her jolt, and she shuffled a little closer to EJ. "I've had this dream so many times before and there's never been a storm."

He moved their joined hands to rest on his knee. "Make it go away."

"Huh?"

With his free hand, EJ motioned to the ocean. "You're in control. It's your dream, so change it. While you're at it, how about you create someplace cooler with a helluva lot less sand? Instead, throw in a decent amount of snow and some cloud cover."

What the heck did he mean? EJ was as crazy as her. She couldn't make the storm go away and whisk them both to another location. She was dreaming for goodness' sake. Her subconscious conjured this location when she fell asleep.

More pressing questions needed answering right

now, rather than figuring out EJ's riddles for making thunderstorms vanish.

She twisted to face him but kept her hand in his. "There are so many things I don't understand. Like, how are you here? Who are you? How do I dream of you?"

His intense gaze searched her eyes for a moment before he spoke. "You don't know what you are, do you?"

Yep, crazy. Trust her to dream of a lunatic. "You're so weird."

"Me?" His head tilted to one side, studying her. "I've been called creative things in my lifetime: sexy, skillful, charming, God, but never weird."

She snorted a laugh. "God? Could you be any more cocky?"

"Is that a challenge?"

A giggle rose while warmth swelled in her chest. "Who are you?"

"EJ."

"Duh, we've established that. But who are you really? I must've seen you somewhere to keep dreaming of you like this. Because you sure as heck don't match the heroes on my current reading pile."

Using his free hand, he brushed his fingers over her knee sending sparks dancing along her flesh.

"I told you, sweetness. I'm not a book dude."

"But you're in my dream."

"Exactly."

He leaned closer, making her pulse spike.

The smell of his wild cologne heightened her senses. Tiny pulses fluttered through her middle.

"You pulled me into your dream."

"Annnnd?" she whispered.

"This is real. Me touching you is real."

She tracked the slow and delicate brush of his index finger as it circled her knee. If only this was real. If only he was real. He was too perfect for her harsh reality. All her years of avoiding relationships, thanks to the stellar example her parents set, made her dream of a swoony guy.

This wasn't real, it was a fantasy. If she didn't end the dream now, she'd pine over an imaginary hero during her waking hours and end up like Mom.

She dragged her gaze from their hands to his eyes. "You make me feel safe, content, protected, but this isn't real. You're a figment of my imagination, a result of devouring too many romance novels while longing for a happily ever after of my own." She slipped her hand from his and stood, brushing the sand off the back of her shorts. "A happy ending isn't in my future and I accepted that a long time ago. Now my mother is dead, my twin is missing, and monsters I had no idea even existed are hunting me."

EJ rose, stepping into her personal space. Her gaze fell on his smooth, angular jaw and golden tanned skin along his collarbone.

He curled a finger under her chin, lifting her eyes to his. "Tell me where you are. I need to save you before I'm too late."

Oh, she wished he'd save her. She'd give anything right now to have him swoop her up in his strong, tattooed arms and whisk her away to his castle by the sea. They'd live blissfully happy forever.

But this wasn't reality.

She stepped out of his reach. "You're not the hero

in this story."

Three bangs in quick succession boomed around her. Her gaze darted left and right, then up at the ominous clouds. Nothing.

EJ's eyes widened. He reached for her. "Wait, don't wake up—"

The air rippled, the beach scene collapsed, and EJ disappeared all in a matter of seconds.

Blackness.

She woke with a start, jolting upright, banging her knee on the steering wheel.

A bone chilling shiver raced along her spine, causing the hairs on her neck to stiffen. Holding her breath, she turned to the driver's window where a shadowy figure peered back from the other side.

Chapter Ten

EJ shot out of bed. Jesus, he was well and truly sick of jolting out of bed as though his ass was on fire. The sooner this dream mission from Fate ended, the sooner he could return to stumbling out of bed with an epic hangover but vision free. Or even better, not falling into bed in the first place.

He hadn't gone to the club or followed his usual routine for three days. During that time, instead of those pesky the-world-is-ending visions, a breathtakingly beautiful woman invaded his dreams.

Hailee.

Shit. Why couldn't he wake instantly remembering the dream? Why did his brain take precious minutes to catch up? He didn't have time to spare. If he wanted to find her before this whole damn mission blew up in his face, then he needed every second.

Not bothering with a shirt, he raced out of his bedroom and down the hall in search of Raven.

Hailee had no idea about the immortal world. Which made this screwed up situation that much more complicated. *Nice one, Fate.*

Oh, yeah, he guaranteed Fate's hands were all over this little twist. Even with her powers in recovery mode, Fate was the master at manipulation and covert torture. She'd excel as a spy. Some days, he'd rather she tie him to a chair and rip off his fingernails instead of sending riddles that took him too long to decipher. If she tore off his fingernails, at least when the ninth one came off, he'd see the light at the end.

With this vision shit? He had no clue when Fate would end it. Maybe she never would.

He bolted down the stairs, two at a time, swinging left at the bottom. The only thing Hailee knew was that monsters killed her mom and they hunted her and Ebony. She got that right. Labeling those dark angels as monsters was the best description he ever heard.

If keeping Hailee safe was his mission, he couldn't do that in a dream. But he missed the opportunity to tell her that before the damn thing collapsed.

You're not the hero in this story...

Her words stung, but they shouldn't. He wasn't a hero. Once maybe, before Fate cursed his ass but no longer. His entire existence in this realm consisted of nothing but failure after failure. A hero never failed.

He needed to find her outside the dream, get her to trust him, that way they could find her twin. Then, and only then, would this nightmare end. He couldn't add another failure to his overflowing list right now, his docket was already full.

Though, after he saved Aric, maybe, just maybe, he was on a winning streak. Fingers crossed.

Ellen's homemade chicken pie lured him down the hall to the dining room. He burst through the double doors and skidded to a halt. The whole household sat at the table, forks paused at their mouths, eyes gaping, staring at him while he made an ass of himself.

He didn't bother explaining the reason for his interruption, nor did he greet each of them individually. They were used to him running late. Instead, he waved a hand in the air while he headed to Raven at the head of the table.

Tayla sat on his lap. God, Raven was so lovestruck he pitied the poor Guardian brought to his knees by a Chosen.

Thank Fate Hailee had already turned twenty-five. An immortal wasn't technically a Chosen, therefore, she couldn't end up as his soulmate. Except Willow and Aric were soulmates…he hoped that was a one-off on Fate's behalf. She rarely created immortal pairings. In fact, besides Aric and Willow, he only knew of one other.

Anyway, Stella was a jealous kinda gal, he wouldn't want to upset her by gaining a soulmate.

"Rave, you got a minute?"

On the other side of the dining room, Ellen trailed through the kitchen door with a tray of steamed greens. Darting past Raven, he reached to take the tray from Ellen's hands and place it on the table.

She snatched it away from him with a scowl on her face. "EJ, I hope you don't plan on sitting at the table without a shirt."

Some dumbass snorted from behind him. Probably Ric.

"I wouldn't dream of it."

"I bet dreaming is what ripped off his shirt in the first place."

Nope. That punk was River.

Dinner tray forgotten, EJ spun and faced the Guardian. "Unlike you, Sunshine, I don't need a dream for women to rip off my shirt."

River narrowed his eyes. Ric burst out laughing and slapped a palm on the table.

Ignoring River, EJ pulled out the chair to Raven's right and sat.

Tayla stood. "I'm getting out of here before this turns into a food fight."

Raven drew her down for a love-scene kiss. Any minute, tiny heart confetti would fall from the ceiling and a pair of doves would flutter out the window.

"See you in a bit." Raven grabbed his drink and turned to EJ. "Cole filled me in earlier today. Did the Dumahel contact you again?"

"Hailee. Her frickin' name is Hailee."

Raven's brows twitched, but he didn't respond.

"And to answer your question, yep, she did." Forearm on the table, he leaned closer and lowered his voice. Not that it would make a difference, if the others wanted to listen, they would. And could. "She didn't know she's half immortal. She's freaking out about not being able to find her twin and I sensed she's on the run."

Raven took a long sip of his bourbon. "Does she know about the Fallen?"

"Kinda. She saw them kill her mom, but I don't think she knows exactly what they are. She gave an accurate description of Slater and another Fallen, who I don't know. I haven't had time to think of all the angels who Fell while we were in the Heavens. And we have no idea how many Fell since Fate exiled us here. Cole might know more."

Raven's shoulders tensed. "Where is Hailee now?"

"She didn't tell me."

Muscles in Raven's jaw popped with the glass at his lips. "We have to find her. We can't let the Fallen siphon her powers."

With Hailee cloaked, finding her wouldn't be easy. EJ drummed his fingers on the table to lighten the heavy churning in his gut. "Listen, Rave, maybe I'm not the best Guardian for this job. I mean, with my track record. This vision, dream, mission, whatever it is, seems important. What about if I communicate with her in the dreams and you send someone else to find her? Someone who will get there in time."

Raven stared into the glass as though the golden liquid held all the answers. After a long moment, he placed the tumbler on the table but kept it in his palm. "EJ, this mission is made for you. With your charm, you could convince a female to follow you to the end of the universe. All you need to do is get her to trust you."

Sure, he had a way with the ladies. His charm worked in his favor when he needed to relieve tension or escape reality. But using it to convince Hailee to trust him made a weird sensation stir in his blood.

Yet, an even weirder sensation burned deeper when he thought of sending another Guardian in his place.

Nice twist, Fate. Maybe Raven was right. Fate created this mission for him. This was his chance to win two in a row. Save this world one immortal at a time.

If he could earn Fate's forgiveness, maybe then he could forgive himself.

He straightened in the chair. "Righty-o. You want me to head out tonight?"

Everyone ceased eating to tune into their conversation.

Raven's gaze roamed over the faces of those sitting at the table before landing back on EJ. "I'll come with you. We don't know how many Fallen are after Hailee, and if it involves a Raziel, we won't even see them coming."

Raine's chair scraped back from the table as she stood. She slid on black fingerless leather gloves. Why the hell did she wear gloves? As immortals, the cold didn't bother them. She probably had some freakish fetish.

Her violet eyes swung his way. "I'll go. If the Dumahel is scared, she'll react better to another female showing up at her door."

If he weren't so stunned, he'd burst out laughing and fall off his chair. Including Raine in the same bucket as other females just seemed…odd. "In that case, I'd better take Red with me."

Quicker than he tracked, Raine threw a throwing star. His chair shuddered as it lodged in the side of the backrest, wobbling from impact.

He leaped to his feet. "Frickin' hell, Rae." The star missed his arm by less than an inch.

Raven smirked. "Raine's a perfect choice. She'll protect you."

EJ glared at Raven, mouthing, "What the fuck?"

Raven shrugged one shoulder and lifted his bourbon to his lips.

With an exaggerated huff, he turned to Raine. "Fine. Let's go. And just so you know, I don't need protection."

"Sure, you don't." She pushed her chair in under the table and gathered her empty plate and cutlery. "I need to change my shoes." She waved a hand at his bare torso. "You should put on a shirt. Not everyone wants to see that."

"For your information, Rae, there's a line a mile long waiting for a glimpse of this." He motioned to his perfectly defined six-pack.

Raine ignored the comment and carried her plate to the kitchen.

After Raven filled him in on where Cole found Hailee's mother, EJ ducked to his room and grabbed a shirt so Raine wouldn't bitch the entire way. Loaded with weapons, he made his way out the front door. With only six hours left of darkness, he itched to leave straight away.

Raine stood under the porch light with her black wings unfurled, still wearing a pair of kick-ass heels.

He jogged down the steps to her. "I thought you were changing into, I dunno, sneakers?"

She screwed up her face like he'd suggested she wear a pair of bright orange flip-flops.

"No. I swapped for a black pair. They're less obvious in the sky."

Oh, sweet Jesus. Why did he always draw the short straw?

Chapter Eleven

It took a goddamn agonizing number of hours to fly to Hailee's home. By the time he and Raine touched down in the bare backyard, his wing muscles burned like a bitch. In hindsight, they should've stopped somewhere along the way, at the halfway point. But he'd pushed on and Raine didn't complain. Stopping meant they lost the cover of darkness and without a car, they'd need to wait another twelve hours until they flew again.

Waiting that long wasn't an option.

An urge, a bone deep pull to find Hailee, hummed inside his veins. It kept his wings moving, refusing to let him rest until he found her. Since arriving in the mortal realm, Fate hadn't assigned him a Chosen, but he still remembered the connection. This was different. The pull he experienced now was way more intense. Clearly, because of the dreams.

New to immortality, Hailee's powers were stronger, heightening their connection in the dreams. That was the only logical explanation and the only one he entertained. Admitting she was his soulmate? Nope. She wanted a hero. She wouldn't get that from him.

"I'll scope the perimeter," Raine said, heading around the side of the home while her wings retracted inside her back.

He stood in the yard a bit longer, taking in the

residence—single story, red-brick, standard-looking, nothing out of the ordinary. Three windows faced the rear of the property and one door. He narrowed his eyes. Correction, one hole in the wall in the shape of a door.

Doing a three-sixty, he scanned the backyard. The darkness didn't hinder his vision. Sure, he saw better during the day, but with sharp immortal eyes, he saw damn good at night, too. It would suck if he didn't, given nighttime was the only time he could fly.

The yard wasn't anything special either. Some grass here and there, plenty of dirt, a couple of mature trees, a six-foot wooden fence that had seen better days.

A train clunked over tracks in the distance. Besides that, the neighborhood was quiet. An average suburb in a standard city.

Not somewhere he expected the daughters of an Azrael to live.

Removing the Glock from the back of his jeans, he held it in front while he strode to the house. He entered through the hole in the wall and glared at the door on the floor. A weird bubble fired his blood. Those shitty Fallen knocked down the damn door. It must've terrified Hailee. No wonder she wouldn't tell him her location. Her only experience with immortals were two dumbass Fallen crashing into her house and murdering her mom.

Gaining her trust might be harder than he thought.

Stepping over the door, he roamed the compact kitchen, then the dining room. He sensed there weren't any Fallen inside the house, no mortals either, so he and Raine could take their time.

Clicking heels identified Raine before she appeared

in the doorway and he lowered the gun.

"All clear out front."

"Yeah, same out back. Though someone kicked in the damn door. Probably Slater."

Raine twirled a throwing star around her index finger. "I'm surprised they didn't do more damage."

Next time he saw that loser, he'd smack him upside the head using one of Raine's heels. "Hailee's not here, but I wanna see if she left any clues as to her whereabouts."

Raine nodded and proceeded down the hall. He followed but diverted into a bedroom at the far end, lured there by the sunshine and salty breeze lingering in the air. Just a hint, but he caught it.

The pull inside his soul deepened as he searched her room. For what? He didn't know.

The bedroom was just as basic as the rest of the house. A single chest of drawers, a handful of clothes in the wardrobe. The only items that gave away someone lived here were the three novels on the floor beside an unmade bed.

He grabbed the top book and rolled his eyes at the cover: a dark-haired dude dressed in clothes Gabe wore more than a century ago, cradling a woman in his arms. If this was Hailee's version of a hero, then he was well and truly off the hook.

He dropped the book on the bed. Judging from the half-packed box by the door and the matching ones throughout the house, Hailee and her family were about to move.

Did her mother know about the immortal world? Did she know how rare her daughters were and that the Fallen hunted them? If so, why the hell didn't she warn them before they turned twenty-five? The magical age when a Dumahel entered immortality.

Dawn trickled through the open curtains. He twisted, following a thin beam of light that shone across the floor, up onto Hailee's bed before landing on a handmade dreamcatcher hung on the wall.

He brushed his fingers over the soft teal feathers dangling from the bottom. Raziel feathers. All the signs were there. How could Hailee not know what she was?

After unhooking the dreamcatcher, he hung it from his finger. Magic buzzed through his skin as it spun in slow circles catching the morning light. If a Raziel spelled the dreamcatcher, as he suspected, it prevented the Fallen from entering Hailee's dreams. His chest tightened at the thought of her sleeping without it. Unprotected, she could pull a Fallen into her dream without even knowing.

The urgency to find her jumped a notch.

"Look what I found," Raine said, startling the hell out of him. He'd never know how she was so stealthy with those eye-gauging heels.

He spun and found her standing in the doorway waving something in her hand. "Show me."

Chapter Twelve

A shadowy figure loomed outside the car window. Hailee screamed and scrambled for her seatbelt. The quickest escape was to drive away. Without seeing the eyes, she didn't know if the figure was one of those creatures or not.

A fist banged on the glass. Hang on. Her hand stilled, key in the ignition. Would a murderous creature really knock on the window?

With her heart lodged in her throat, she eyed the bracelet on her wrist. It wasn't glowing. Did that mean the person outside the car wasn't one of them?

She braved a second look out the window. Once her eyes adjusted, her brain registered things she missed moments ago. Headlights came from behind her car, shining on the figure. A police officer uniform. A badge held up to the window.

Relief burst inside her. The police? She'd plenty of practice handling their inquiries. So many in fact, some might say she was an expert.

Unless he knew about what happened to Mom and all those murdered innocent teens. No amount of experience could explain that.

The officer pointed downward, motioning for her to lower the glass.

After turning on the ignition, she pressed the button and lowered the window just enough to speak through.

"Can I help you, Officer?" She steadied her voice as best as she could with her pulse racing.

The police officer glanced through the small opening. "Are you lost?"

Yep, totally lost, both in life and direction. Not that she said that aloud. Instead, she shook her head. "No, why?"

The officer narrowed his eyes. "It's not safe traveling this road at night, let alone by yourself. Where are you headed?"

No idea. But she sensed the police officer wouldn't like that answer. "To my sister." That wasn't exactly a lie.

The officer didn't respond right away, instead he paused as though waiting for her to continue. He probably wanted her to add where her sister lived. Instead, she remained silent. She'd never had a problem with silence and the urge to fill it with senseless rambling. Plus, remaining silent was better than lying. Lies always caught up with people in the end.

Finally, he nodded. "You can't sleep here in the car." He pointed up the road. "The next town is about an hour down the road. Do yourself a favor and book a motel for the rest of the night."

She exhaled a ragged breath. He didn't quiz her about her mom or the other murders. Thank goodness, because running from those creatures was enough without adding a police chase into the mix. "I'll head there now."

When she put the car in gear, the officer stepped back from the window. "Drive safe."

"I will, thank you," she replied before closing the window.

She sat there for a few moments, willing her heart rate to lower to something that resembled her new normal. That steady drum prepared to run at a second's notice but calm enough to concentrate on the task at hand.

After giving the officer a wave goodbye, she pulled out onto the road and headed to the next town. In the rearview mirror, the police officer did a U-turn and drove in the opposite direction down the highway.

She really should've thought this through. Sleeping on the side of the road in her car was one of the stupidest decisions she'd made. She was the logical one, not the risk-taker like Ebony.

What if it wasn't a cop that tapped on her window? What if those creatures found her? If they took her too, or worse, killed her, then she'd never find Ebony.

Just another day in the life of Hailee Mitchell. Ebony did something stupid, got herself into trouble, and Hailee stepped in and bailed her out. Literally. Illegal rave parties were Ebony's specialty. A few times, the police caught Ebony and Hailee stepped in as her legal guardian. Of course, she'd used the "Ebony's just acting out because our mother is ill" excuse which gained Ebony nothing more than warnings and threats that next time the police wouldn't be so lenient. Though they always were. Her sister had charm specifically tailored for compelling law enforcement.

She was so fed up with having to drag Ebony out of trouble.

Tears filled her eyes. That was a horrible thing to think. This wasn't Ebony's fault. Ebony didn't know about the creatures. She was in the dark like her. Neither of them knew—

The road distorted before her eyes, flickered in and out. One second, she saw the dark, single lane highway, next an image of a formal living room. She slammed her foot on the brake. Tires skidded, the car swerved off the road. She flung her arms up to protect her head, bracing for impact. Just before she slammed into a tree, the car slid to a halt.

The landscaped distorted again. She no longer sat inside the car. Now, she stood beside a lit hearth in an unfamiliar living room.

What the heck? She spun in a tight circle.

Her breath hitched as Ebony strolled into the room. "Hey, sis."

She ran to her, wrapping her arms around her, hugging her tight. "You had me so worried." Drawing back, she squeezed Ebony's shoulders. "What happened? Are you okay? Where are you? What the heck happened, Eb?" Hysteria overtook her voice and she sucked in a gulp of air to level it.

Stepping back, she scanned Ebony for injuries, touched her face, turned her this way and that. Ebony wore her usual DJ clothes—black singlet top, tight-fitting jeans, tucked into knee-high boots with heavier than usual eyeliner. Dyed pink and electric blue streaks weaved through her blonde hair.

No ripped clothes, no smudged makeup, no blood. No dark, swirly lines on Ebony's skin.

"I'm fine." Ebony frowned. "What's got you so worked up?"

"Really? Besides the fact our mother is dead, you're missing, and I'm running from some terrifying creatures. Wait a second." The last thing she remembered was driving along the highway after the cop woke her. She surveyed the living room again. "How did I get here?"

Nothing made sense. Like she was in some strange reality, where she caught glimpses of her current life and a parallel alternate. If she'd left work a few minutes earlier the other night. If Mom woke her an hour earlier. If they fled the house in time.

"Mom's dead?" Ebony choked on the words.

She didn't answer. "How is that even possible? What's going on?"

Ebony glanced over her shoulder toward a doorway. "They told me no one would get hurt."

The hairs on the back of Hailee's neck stood at attention. "What did you say? Who's they?"

As she whispered the words, her bracelet exploded with iridescent blue. A warning. It didn't react to Ebony. Someone else was nearby, hiding.

Hailee retreated a step as the fireplace roared to life, emphasizing the evil and foreboding doom.

Ebony's brows furrowed. "Hailee, listen to me."

"Someone killed Mom. I saw it." Her chest heaved in and out. What the heck was happening? Who else was here?

"Tell me where you are."

"Why are you so calm?" Hailee's gaze darted between the doorway and her sister. "How am I here? Where is this?" Her voice rose. "Why won't you answer me?"

Ebony stepped closer and touched her arm. "Just tell me where you are."

Her stomach plummeted. This wasn't like Ebony. Her sister constantly made dumb decisions, but she never avoided questions like this. Usually, Ebony's honesty and nonexistent filter got her into trouble.

The bracelet glowed brighter. “Why do I get the feeling I can’t trust you?” she murmured.

Ebony’s lips formed a grim line. Behind her, a shadow appeared in the doorway. Gradually, the dark swirls retreated, revealing his features. She staggered back. It was him, the creature who killed Mom. Before she warned Ebony, he raised his arm. Black shadows swirled from his palm toward her sister. Hailee screamed, lunging for Ebony—

In an instant, the living room vanished. She opened her eyes in the car, the headlights shining on a tree inches away from the hood.

“No!” she screamed, ripping off her seatbelt.

She bolted from the car and scanned up and down the roadside. Nothing. No fireplace, no leather couches, no evil murderer. No Ebony.

Her pulsed raced, and she inhaled deep breaths to calm it. Did she fall asleep at the wheel again? Dreaming of Ebony made sense, considering all that had happened. She was more exhausted than she thought. Driving in this state was too dangerous. She was useless to Ebony if she crashed and killed herself.

Once back in the driver’s seat, she cradled her head in her hands and thought for a moment. The dreams seemed so real. Was it possible she connected with Ebony just like she did with EJ? EJ said he was real. Could it be true? The bracelet didn’t glow in his presence. Did that mean she could trust him?

All she knew was she needed answers and to find Ebony, she needed help. If the dreams were real, then that confirmed her greatest fear. She was out of time. The creatures kidnapped her sister, and she needed EJ’s help to save her.

Chapter Thirteen

EJ sidestepped seconds before a wave engulfed his lace-ups. Thank Fate. He didn't bring spares and explaining why his shoes were full of wet sand made for an awkward conversation with Raine.

By now, he expected the beach dream, prepared to leap out of the wave's war path as soon as he closed his eyes. He readied himself for the uncomfortable, gritty sensation of all that sand in his shoes and the salt plastered to his skin.

Though lately, the sticky, salty air wasn't so bad. It reminded him of Hailee.

Waves crashed into the shore, the white caps breaching the surface far into the distance. Thunder boomed and dark, ominous clouds pelted the ocean with rain, but the storm hovered out at sea.

Turning, he spotted Hailee huddled under the protection of a swaying palm tree, knees bent, staring at the sand by her side. Her golden hair flicked over her face, and she gathered it, holding it back with one hand while drawing patterns in the sand with the other.

His heart squeezed. He needed her to trust him, yet he was about to blow apart her whole damn world. But to beat Fate at her own torturous game, he needed to suck it up and get this over with.

Her head rose and her gaze drifted to him. His heart did that stupid flip thing again, but he tried to ignore it. Now wasn't the time for distractions. If he didn't keep his head in the game, he'd miss a critical clue and all Hell would break loose. Literally.

A smile curled her lips, though it didn't reach her eyes. Even from the shoreline, she remained guarded, wary of him.

He strolled up the beach to her. "Hey."

"Hey…Eric Jeffery."

He couldn't stop his grin. "Sweetness, you're not even close."

She laughed and the sound warmed his chest.

"Just tell me already!"

No one outside the Heavens knew his real name, and he wasn't about to ruin his awesomeness by telling a mortal. Half mortal. Plus, he kinda liked hearing her guesses. With so many combinations, it would take her years to figure out the real one.

"Nah, this is way more fun." He gestured to the towel. "May I?"

When she nodded, he eased down beside her, careful to not get a shoe full of dry sand. That shit was stealthier than Raine.

Hailee eyed his footwear. "You forgot to take off your shoes."

"I gotta keep them on this time. Would probably hurt like hell if I chased a Fallen bare foot."

A tiny frown creased her brow. "A Fallen?"

He peered at the ocean while he figured out how to tell her. In such a small amount of time, he needed to reveal who and what she was, who he was, and also convince her to trust him, so he didn't screw this up and add her to his endless list of failures. Plus, he also needed to warn her of the dangers. Honesty always scored mega brownie points with women. But sometimes the truth hurt more than a tequila hangover.

"You're getting better at this. I only just closed my eyes."

"Better at what? You say weird things in my dreams."

He pivoted to face her, and his gaze locked with hers. For a second, the wind ceased blowing and the waves stilled. Sunlight burst through the clouds, encasing her in a yellow halo of light. But as soon as she noticed, the light vanished, and the clouds converged together again.

He swallowed, moistening his dry throat. "Hailee, I need to tell you some things…"

She startled. "Wait! I need to tell you something first."

He tensed. Even in a dream, he responded to the quiver in her voice and readied for battle. "What? What's wrong?"

It took a second too long for her to answer. "I…something's happened…I need your help." She paused and inhaled a deep breath, seeming to calm herself. "How do I know this is real? How do I know you're real? You say you are, but how do I know for sure?"

That was the easy part. He touched her hand, brushing his thumb along the back. "Does this feel real?"

"Yes."

He trailed a path up her arm, circling her bare shoulder. "And this?"

She nodded.

Continuing, he tucked a strand of hair behind her

ear, while trying to ignore the buzzing in his blood. "This too?"

"Yes," she whispered.

His thumb followed the same path back down her arm to take her hand and place it on his chest. "Now, touch me."

The words sounded so frickin' hot, but she missed the innuendo. Or ignored it. He should do the same.

Instead, her hand slipped free from his and traced along his stubbly jaw. Sweet baby Jesus. Her touch was full-on electric. It made every cell in his body buzz with energy like the biggest high he ever experienced without popping a single damn pill.

Her chest rose and fell. If he weren't so mesmerized, he'd move and adjust the hard-on lengthening in his jeans. The last thing he needed was her mistaking him for a fictional hero he could never compete with.

He coaxed her hand away from his jaw and held it in his. Now, he could at least concentrate. "I'm going to tell you a few things. Just hear me out, yeah?"

She nodded.

"As you've seen, there's a whole other world out there hidden from mortals. Good and bad." Using his free hand, he twisted her bracelet until the dreamcatcher charm dangled underneath her wrist. "Angels, Fallen, and rare Dumahel." He paused. "Like you."

Her gaze found his. "Like me?"

"Yeah. That's how we're here right now."

"I figure angels are good and Fallen are bad? What exactly is a Duma…?"

He traced light circles on the back of her hand. "A Dumahel. Half angel and half mortal. The abilities of an immortal while mortal enough to age. Until you're twenty-five."

"And you think I'm one of those?"

"Not think, know." He meshed his fingers between hers. "And for the past few weeks you've pulled me into your dreams."

Her eyes sparkled. "To be honest, there are worse things than dreaming of a gorgeous guy at the beach."

He bit his tongue hard, so the conversation didn't divert to the fact she just labeled him gorgeous. That topic was so much more fun but wouldn't help him find her. "You're not dreaming of me, sweetness. I'm actually here, in your dream."

"I don't understand."

"Dumahel are born with the ability to dreamwalk."

"How can I pull you into a dream if I don't know you?"

Good question and one he couldn't answer. He'd ask when he next checked in with Raven. "Fate plays a mysterious game and we rarely know the rules."

Hailee sat in silence for the longest moment, staring at their joined hands. He didn't pull back. The connection showed her the dream was real, that he was real. To win this battle, he needed to prove he wasn't the bad guy. He just wasn't the hero either.

Finally, her gaze lifted to his, searching his eyes. "Can I trust you?"

Releasing her hand, he reached under his T-shirt and pulled out the secret weapon he stashed there before falling asleep. Her dreamcatcher.

Chapter Fourteen

Fallen? Angels? Dumahel, or whatever. It all sounded so far-fetched, yet, she believed it. How could she not? She saw it with her own eyes. Creatures with crimson wings and glowing red eyes.

EJ dangled her dreamcatcher from his finger. The one that hung above her bed since she was an infant. How did he get it? And how was it here now in her dream?

He offered it to her. "This only works if you hang it where you sleep."

She took it and lay it flat in her palm, tracing her fingertip along the intricate weaving in the center. "I don't understand any of this."

"It prevents the bad guys from entering your dreams."

She chuckled at his choice of words. "No, I mean the whole situation. I have so many questions."

His hand returned to her knee and the touch seemed so familiar, so comforting. Affection was a luxury over the past few years, something she never sought, but EJ touching her felt…right.

"Hit me with your questions." He tilted his head, pausing for a moment while his thumb drew lazy circles on her knee. "First, I'll get the small-talk questions out of the way. Beach or forest? Easy, forest. I like the serenity and stillness even when I think I don't need it.

Plus, as you know, sand and I aren't BFFs. Steak or salad? Steak. Salad is only good for cocktails and even then, I limit it to basil and lime." His cocky smirk lifted at the corner of his mouth. "Boxers or briefs?"

Heat flashed through her entire body. She guessed he chose those questions to make light of their situation, not for her to mentally paint a vivid picture of underwear, or lack of, beneath his ripped jeans.

Probably best if they remained on less intimate topics. In the beginning, she'd wanted all sexy action, but now she knew he was real, she should focus on getting answers. "You mentioned angels and Fallen. What are you?"

"You don't want to know my underwear choice?"

"I, ah…" Where the heck had all the air gone? She cleared her throat. "Maybe it's best if we start at the beginning before divulging personal details."

"Fair enough." He peered in the thunderstorm's direction, far out in the ocean. "I'm an angel, a…protector of sorts."

She mentally cheered. "I knew it. You are a hero."

"No, sweetness. I'm not."

Her heart ached a little at his mellow tone and the way his shoulders slumped, erasing his earlier playfulness. EJ may not believe he's a hero, but in her dreams, he saved her in more ways than he knew. They were her only escape. A few hours of freedom. Even in a dream, he whisked her away, lightened her spirit, and reinvigorated the joy in her life. Before reality came crashing back when she woke.

But now she knew they weren't just dreams. Trouble and danger still waited for her when she woke. That required her attention. She needed to save Ebony, and she needed his help.

"The creatures who killed my mom…"

His features hardened through the rigid set of his jaw. "Fallen."

Even if she hadn't seen it with her own eyes, his scathing tone left no doubt in her mind the Fallen were the bad guys.

"They kidnapped my sister."

He tipped his head back to glance at the sky before pivoting to face her. "I figured they did. How do you know?"

"I had a dream of her. Well, maybe I pulled her into mine? Wait. Can Ebony dreamwalk, too?"

"Maybe, and yes. She's a Dumahel, too. They're always born as twins. It doesn't matter who initiated the connection. Did she tell you where she is? Where the Fallen are holding her?"

"No. She kept asking where I am."

He adjusted his beanie. "Don't tell her, yeah? Not until we know it's safe." At her nod, he continued, "Tell me about the dream. Where was it set? Did anything stand out?"

She relayed the dream with Ebony, right down to the creepy Fallen with shadow hands.

EJ waited a few minutes before responding. "Our best chance of finding your sister, without tipping off the assholes who took her, is through your dreamwalking. You need to learn to control it. Manipulate it. How about you experiment a little while we have time?"

"What do you mean experiment? Experiment with what?"

He shrugged a shoulder. "Anything. I'm game."

Oh, she sensed that wasn't a lie. She bet his game was in a whole other league than hers. Majors verses little league.

"Change something. Except, if we stay on this beach, please don't make it rain. Wet sand sticking to my jeans would seriously sucks balls."

He said strange things. "I can't control the weather any more than I can control my sister."

A memory scratched the back of her brain, but she couldn't focus enough to bring it to life. Dreams were thoughts and images rolling around in her mind while she slept, made up of past experiences and actions. Hopes and fears. If that were true, she couldn't control them.

Could she?

"Try."

He reached out and tucked a loose strand of hair behind her ear, his touch so tender it stole her breath.

Heart racing, she focused on the white caps crashing against the shoreline. How did she change anything? Think of it? Imagine it? How?

Narrowing her eyes, she stared at the ocean and envisioned the waves calming. They didn't.

"Nothing's changing. You've lost your mind."

"Probably, it wouldn't surprise me." He peered left and right, then back to her. "Start with something small, like changing the color of your shirt."

She glanced down at her gray shirt. This was insane. Was she even trying this? But with everything she experienced over the past few days, she couldn't deny the fact things existed beyond her understanding.

She held the hem of her shirt between her fingers. How did she change the color? Just imaging the cotton was green instead of gray? The second the thought formed, her shirt changed from soft gray to lime green. Instantly, like she'd snapped her fingers.

She turned the hem this way and that, inspecting the fabric. "Did I just…"

"Yep." Playfulness returned to his tone. "Change something else."

The grin on EJ's face made a bubble of excitement dance in her chest. What else could she change? The wind picked up again, flinging her hair in front of her face. A hair tie would come in handy.

Opening her palm, she imagined a small brown tie, and not a second later, it appeared. She pulled her hair into a ponytail. "Thank goodness, it was driving me insane."

"I kinda liked it down," EJ murmured.

When she turned and found his gaze locked on her, heat flashed along her skin. His ice-blue eyes darkened.

Having him there gave her an escape, an outlet. Someone to share a blissful moment with to recharge before reality returned. But it wouldn't last. It couldn't. At some point, she needed to wake and find Ebony.

"This is all a bit of fun, but how will changing my shirt color protect me from the Fallen who killed my mother. How will it help me find Ebony?

"It won't protect you from the Fallen. That's my job. But I can't do that in your dream."

He took her hand, giving it a gentle squeeze, making her heart flutter like crazy.

"Together we'll find your sister. You have my word. First, let me find you."

This time, she did.

Chapter Fifteen

"Are you sure this is the place?" Raine landed beside him in the corner of a parking lot and retracted her wings.

He eyed the two-story motel that had seen better days. More accurately, how did it remain upright?

"Yep." He pointed to the top floor. "Her room should be at the top of those stairs."

Raine strode forward, death-defying heels crunching along the gravel. "This place is a dive, even for a mortal."

"Half mortal," he corrected.

They ascended the external stairs and proceeded left until they reached a weathered door with number eleven, curtains closed on the only window. Good, Hailee listened to his instructions.

He scanned the balcony, up and down, checking out how many rooms were on either side. He inspected the concrete, the rust stains on the railing, watermarks on the curtains.

"You gonna knock anytime soon?" Raine grumbled from behind him.

Yeah, he'd knock. In a minute. When his pulse calmed the hell down.

Impatient, Raine shoved past him and banged twice on the door. Loud enough to wake the whole damn motel. He glared at her, about to snap, but didn't get the chance. The door unlocked and opened as far as a security chain permitted.

Hailee's gorgeous blue eyes peered through the gap. Up went his pulse again. Seeing her in person took his goddamn breath away.

"EJ?"

"Yeah." He cleared his throat. "It's me."

Her gaze darted past his shoulder.

"That's just Raine, she won't hurt you. She may look all badass, but she's really not."

Raine huffed. "You didn't say that when I kicked your ass the other day."

Over his shoulder, he screwed up his face at Raine. "I have no recollection of that happening. Ever." He turned back to Hailee, so Raine didn't lower his manhood any further. "May I come in?"

Hailee's lips formed a hard line. After a quick glance at her bracelet, she nodded and closed the door. A second later, the door reopened chain free.

As agreed, Raine remained outside. They didn't know who watched Hailee. A Fallen could ambush them at any moment and fighting immortals in a motel room wasn't the smartest plan. They wouldn't be there long anyway. His mission was to get Hailee to the Guardian mansion stat. Plus, he had no idea when or if—likely when—Fate would throw another twist. This could be a trick. Fate's mission for him could implode without notice, her standard MO.

A quick scope inside revealed a dismal room. Small bed, TV, tiny bath toward the rear, and carpet he wouldn't walk on barefoot. A backpack slumped beside the door.

"I can't believe you're actually…real."

He spun. Hailee hesitated just inside the room with a wide-eyed, freaked-out expression on her face.

A much as he ached to ease her into this world of horrors, time wasn't on their side. He'd save those conversations for others more skilled than him when they got back to the Guardian mansion. "I know it's loads to process, but we gotta get moving."

She nodded.

He motioned to the backpack. "Is this everything you have?"

She nodded again. Damn, she must've left in a hurry. He should've grabbed that handful of books at her house before he and Raine flew here. He'd call in a favor later to fix that lapse of judgement.

He picked up the backpack and slung it over his shoulder, before reopening the door. "Let's go, yeah?"

Raine stood at the metal railing, scanning the parking lot. He waited a second, and when Hailee didn't follow, he closed the door again.

She just stood there, frozen to the spot.

He softened his voice. "Sweetness, are you okay? We really need to go."

She stared at the door. "No, I'm not okay. I don't understand what's happening. You're real, my dreams are real. The same Fallen that killed Mom also abducted Ebony. It's too much."

He cupped her face, rubbing his thumbs along her jaw. They didn't have the luxury of time. Once they were at the Guardian mansion, she could freak out all she wanted but not now. Not until she was safe.

"Look at me." When she did, he continued, "You're safe with us. Raine really is badass, just don't tell her I said that. We can't stay here in plain sight, we have to go."

In the last dream, he told her about the Guardian mansion and that once there, Raven would coordinate a search for her sister. Dumping all that information on her plate at once was a shitty move. But knowing the Fallen hunted her made his stomach twist into a dangerous knot. Bad enough they killed her mother and kidnapped her sister. They wouldn't get their hands on Hailee, too. Not on his watch.

He tuned into her heartbeat, thumping as fast as his.

"I know you barely know me, and this must be super overwhelming, but I'm not a bad guy. I'll protect you. All you have to do is trust me."

When her gaze slid to his, a bizarre feeling shifted deep in his chest. Tightened. Twisted around his…Nope. Not going there.

He dropped his hands and stepped back. Fate could suck it. He wasn't falling for that soulmate trick.

Hailee's chest lifted with a deep inhale. "Okay."

This time he waited until she opened the door and exited the room before he followed. They shared some sort of epic connection outside her dreams, and until he confirmed it wouldn't bite him in the ass, he'd lay off touching her. There was no need to strengthen it.

Keeping Hailee between him and Raine, they darted across the parking lot toward where he landed earlier. Halfway there, Hailee stopped beside a car.

"What are you doing?"

"This is my car."

His gaze darted between the old silver hatchback and Hailee. "Are more of your belongings in the car?"

"No, it's all in my backpack. Why?"

"We don't need a car. We're flying, remember?"

She withdrew keys from her jeans pocket. "And how do you suppose we get to the airport? Walk?"

He lowered his voice. "When I said we're flying, I meant I'm flying you. Using my wings."

Behind him Raine snorted. He shot her a glare, and a mental, "Shut the hell up."

Raine turned away with a dumbass smirk on her face while twirling a throwing star between her fingers. Probably best Hailee didn't see that.

Hailee held up a palm. "Hold on. Exactly how will you fly me? In your arms?"

That sparked his interest.

Put your dick away and let's get the hell out of here. Raine, always killing the moment.

"I'll carry you, yes. It's faster if we fly. And it's fun, especially at night."

She crossed her arms. "For you maybe. That's a deal breaker. Besides, what will I do with my car? And what happens when the sun rises? I don't imagine angels fly around in broad daylight, do they?"

He shook his head, unsure he liked where this conversation headed.

"With my car, we won't need to stop, we can drive in shifts." She gestured to the rust bucket as old as this realm. "Besides, you can't expect me to just leave it here."

Why not? Though she probably wouldn't appreciate that answer.

He thought for a moment. If the roles reversed, he wouldn't ever leave Stella deserted in a parking lot. As much as he refused to admit it, Hailee also had a point. With a car, daylight wouldn't slow them down.

He sighed and turned to Raine.

"No way. I'm not driving in that," Raine warned.

Too bad. If traveling in that bomb meant Hailee going with him, then he'd suck it up. It wasn't cheating on Stella if he did it in the line of duty. He'd apologize to his car as soon as they got back, she'd understand.

"I'm driving," he announced, holding his hand out for the key.

"I didn't sign up for a road trip," Raine replied in full-on hard-core bitch mode.

"Suck it up, Rae."

Hailee dropped the key in his palm, and they piled in the car. After refusing to sit in the back and more bitching, which he ignored, Raine sat in the passenger seat—a better spot for keeping watch, apparently. He guessed she was apprehensive of cars after the accident she had with Tayla a couple of years back. No one could blame her. Hailee didn't mind and sat in the middle of the rear seats with her backpack hugged on her lap.

To his surprise, the engine started immediately, and he drove out of the parking lot.

****

They needed tunes. Something to fill the silence. Road trips should be fun singalongs, not so quiet he fell asleep at the wheel and never woke. He fiddled with the stereo dial until something other than golden oldies played through the speakers. Modern music was more his thing. Beats that kept him in party mode because life without a party was a downright drag. After an advertisement for some windshield repair business, a top forty song started. He settled into the seat, tapping his free foot in time with the beat.

Hailee fell asleep about an hour into their little road trip. Arms wrapped protectively around her backpack, she laid her head on top. Through the rearview mirror, he checked on her now and again. Not frequently. Just every minute or so. Thank Fate she didn't pull him into a dream while he drove. Crashing her car would be a dick move and hard to avoid while in a trance.

For a four-cylinder rust bucket, it did all right. Nothing compared to Stella. This car lacked a hint of musk and aged leather trim and the rumble of a decent engine. But the four wheels were enough to drive them to the mansion, and that was all they needed. At the speed this baby went, they'd arrive in about a year.

A half decent song came on and he turned up the music.

Raine hushed him and turned it back down. "She's asleep, dumbass."

Car trip from freaking Hell. Now he couldn't even hear the damn music.

"It's okay. I'm awake." Hailee yawned, stretching her arms above her head.

He forced his eyes from the rearview mirror to the line in the center of the road. "See? She's awake." He screwed up his face at Raine. "Can I have the music on now?"

As usual, Raine didn't bite, just gave him her lethal glare.

"Where are we?" Hailee asked, leaning forward between the seats.

"Middle of nowhere, almost at somewhere." He had no goddamn clue. But a sign twenty minutes ago said they were fifty miles from the next town. "We'll stop for gas and food up ahead."

Hailee nodded. “Can I ask something?”

He met her gaze in the mirror. “You finally want to know the answer to that last question?”

Pink dusted her cheeks. “Ah, no.” She fiddled with the bracelet on her wrist. “How can you both see me, when those two Fallen couldn’t?”

“I dunno.” He’d asked Raven the same question when he checked in earlier. They didn’t know. “Each cloaking spell is unique to the Raziel who creates it. Given Fate created your bracelet, it’s highly likely we’ll never know the full extent of its powers. The bracelet could cloak you from danger, or immortals who want to harm you.” Though that didn’t explain why Cole couldn’t see her either. “Maybe I see you because you told me your location and wanted me to find you.”

Raven suggested EJ saw through the cloak because of his soulmate connection with Hailee. He dismissed that theory real fast. That didn’t explain how Raine saw her. But he struggled to come up with another plausible explanation.

Chapter Sixteen

Could the seat be more uncomfortable? Hailee stared at the sun setting over the vast desert landscape. Dirt, scattered trees, pink and purple strewn across a cloudless sky. Her bum was numb. Oh, just great. Now she needed to pee.

In the front passenger seat, Raine remained an elegant stationary statue. Only her head moved, alternating between the front and side windows. She suspected the calmness was a guise. Raine pinched a silver star between her fingers, her hand rested on top of her thigh. Each time they got back in the car, Raine planted a handgun in the center cupholder. She pitied any Fallen who dared attack.

EJ acted more low-key but seemed equally as lethal. From her seat, her gaze roamed over his gorgeous body. He was even better looking in person, hotter than any book boyfriend, but not her usual type. Though what was her type? All the guys she fell for in the past were figments of an author's imagination, not real flesh and bone.

Outside the dreams, EJ still wore a charcoal beanie. At their last stop for gas, he took off his leather jacket, and she shamelessly used it as a lap blanket. His wild and earthy scent drifted through the back of the car causing a simmering burn low in her belly.

His short sleeve T-shirt gave her a perfect view of

the tattoos covering his arm. Thick, dark swirls gave an ominous vibe as though they represented a world full of death. Now the etchings of fighting angels made sense. Were they Fallen? Through the white shirt, more lines and pictures extended up his shoulder blades. Did they also go down his back?

Warmth tingled across her nape and her gaze slid to the rearview mirror. She didn't need to see behind his reflective aviators to know he stared back at her. She sensed it, the spark in her blood, the slight flutter in her chest. How her heart beat faster.

In person, his eyes were a haunting blue, light and clear—duller than in her dreams but no less mesmerizing. Last time, Dream EJ's eyes swirled with dark clouds. Did they do that in reality? She had so much to learn.

Veins popped in his forearm as his hand curled tight on the steering wheel. She sensed the moment his gaze returned to the road, the same moment the tingle on her neck vanished.

EJ cleared his throat. "We'll stop for the night up ahead. You must be exhausted."

Quite the opposite. She hadn't sat still for this long in years.

"Don't stop for me, I'm okay. The quicker we get there, the sooner we can find Ebony. Though I could use a restroom break."

The corner of his lips twitched, and that tingle at her neck returned. "I think Raine's getting a little cabin fever. She doesn't do people."

Quicker than she could track, Raine jabbed her elbow into EJ's upper arm.

He yelped. The car swerved onto the other side of

the road before righting again. "What the hell, Rae?"

Raine glared at EJ.

Instead of looking her way, he simply turned the music back up and tapped his thumbs on the steering wheel in time with the beat. Raine resumed her graceful statue pose as though nothing happened.

Hailee sank back into the seat. She returned to drooling over EJ's tattoos, occasionally alternating between his strong, angular jaw dusted in a dark blond five o'clock shadow. If only she could see his chest.

As the sky transformed into night, they arrived at the next town and EJ pulled up in front of a motel. Much classier than the last place she stayed. While she and Raine waited in the car, he chatted with the older lady at reception before returning and parking in front of their room.

The second he unlocked the door, she bolted inside and took care of business. Relief never felt so sweet. She exited the bathroom and found her backpack on the bed with Raine standing by the closed door, arms crossed over her chest like a bodyguard.

"Where's EJ?"

More to the point, why did it bother her that he wasn't there?

"Gone for food."

With everything going on, the last thing she wanted to do was eat. "I think I'll take a shower, I'm really not hungry anyway."

That was better than watching the clock tick while Raine guarded the door against murderous Fallen who could bust in at any moment.

From her backpack, she grabbed toiletries and a clean set of clothes and returned to the bathroom. The hot water didn't remove her worries or answer any questions. It never did. But just like the dreams, the shower served as a brief escape from reality. For a few precious minutes, she pretended the horrors on the other side of the shower curtain didn't exist. She imagined Mom and Ebony sitting in the motel room rather than strangers she only just met. Her mind pretended EJ was there to sweep her off her feet and carry her into the sunset, rather than protecting her from dangerous creatures.

Of course, none of that was true. Those creatures existed, EJ wasn't her knight in rock star jeans, and Mom and Ebony weren't in the motel room. Once again, reality proved so much crueler.

A door closed outside the bathroom, followed by EJ's voice. Finishing up in the shower, she dried and dressed then returned to the room. EJ sat at a round table, ankle crossed on his knee, an open bottle of vodka within reach. Raine perched on the bed eating noodles from a takeout box.

EJ motioned to the stack of various containers on the table. "I didn't know what you liked, so I grabbed one of everything."

"Thanks." The thought of eating made her stomach churn. But how could she decline when he'd obviously gone to so much trouble? "Are you eating?"

He lifted the vodka and took a long swig from the neck. "Yep. Potatoes." He tipped the bottle to the food. "Eat."

She shifted the weight between her feet. "I think…I'm too worried to eat. Sorry."

EJ gave a half-hearted shrug and swigged the vodka again. "It's fine." A hint of disappointment seeped into his tone.

She sank down on the corner of the bed. Could she feel any worse?

Raine dumped an empty container on the table and grabbed a full one. "I'll take the first shift," she announced, slipping out the door, closing it behind her.

EJ capped the vodka and stood. Instead of leaving the room, he grabbed a spare pillow from the closet, threw a blanket on the floor under the window and lay down on the makeshift bed.

Her heart fluttered. "Hang on. We're all staying in the same room?"

He folded his arms behind his head in a casual, super sexy pose. If only he knew how much the thought of him sleeping in the same room affected her.

"Why wouldn't we?"

For starters, she thought Raine would share a room with her. Not the three of them. Holy crap. Having EJ in her dreams was one thing, but him sleeping in the same room just a few feet away? Every nerve in her body became hyper-sensitive with the idea.

How did he appear so relaxed?

She eyed the double bed, meant for two people. Her mouth went dry. Politeness nearly made her offer to share the bed with him, but she'd get no sleep. Not from anything they'd do, especially while Raine was just outside, plus the fact they only just met. Their proximity, him lying beside her under the covers, would keep her awake all night. Him in the same room still might have the same effect.

EJ closed his eyes, unaffected by her internal freak out. "Night, sweetness."

After a few shallow breaths, she crawled up the

bed and slipped under the covers before switching off the lights. Once her eyes adjusted to the darkness, she lay there for what seemed like hours, staring at the flecks of peeling plaster on the ceiling, illuminated by the glow from the streetlamp peeking around the blinds.

Was EJ asleep? Was he waiting for her to pull him into a dream? Did he want her to? The flutter in her belly wouldn't go away and kept sleep at bay for far longer than she expected.

****

Glaring sunlight behind her closed lids and heat tingling her shoulders were the first clues she'd finally fallen asleep. Salt and sea lingered in the balmy air, warm sand spread between her toes, and with each second, her breathing relaxed as the dream took shape.

The waves were once again calm and tranquil, rolling in slowly and dragging out even slower. With everything that happened in the past twenty-four hours, she thought sleep would never come, especially with EJ in the same room. Thankfully, it did.

She fell asleep in sweatpants, socks, and a sleep shirt, yet on the beach she wore the same denim shorts and singlet top she always did in the dreams, with her usual flip-flops. Maybe EJ was right. Maybe she controlled the dream more than she thought.

Near the shore, the air blurred and rippled. She still didn't understand how all this worked but knowing EJ entered her dream every night caused a thrill inside her chest like nothing she'd ever experienced. Did he expect it, too? Was he excited, even though he told her several times how much he hated sand? *He hated sand...*

The air shifted at the shore. In a few seconds, EJ

would appear. She concentrated on the spot where the air rippled, focusing on the tiny grains of sand while she imagined a wide, long stretch of lush green grass. Her breath caught as the grass appeared like a deep green carpet unrolling along the sand, stopping when it reached her. Next, she concentrated at the spot where the grass met the ocean, waiting for the exact right moment. EJ's form solidified, and he leaped backward. But there was no need. The second he appeared, she froze the wave and stopped it from wetting his shoes and jeans.

Mental air punch.

EJ peered at the grass beneath his shoes then twisted to face her. When his gaze met hers, that thrill intensified, stalling her breath.

The corner of his mouth lifted in a lazy grin as he swaggered along the lush grass carpet toward her. No other word described his walk more accurately. Full of confidence and sex appeal, like the grass beneath his feet should worship his every step.

"Nice move with the grass. You're nailing this."

"Thanks." She couldn't hide her own grin and sense of achievement.

EJ shoved his hands in his pockets and surveyed the beach. "I wasn't sure if you'd want company tonight."

Of course, she wanted company, especially his. This became the time of day she looked forward to the most, but it felt a little weird admitting that to him. After all, they'd only just met. Instead, she changed the topic.

Kicking off her flip-flops, she sat cross-legged on the grass facing the ocean. "Do you actually rest while you're in a dream with me? Is it like normal dreaming? Or is it more like being awake but not awake at the same time?"

He sat beside her, legs stretched out in front and crossed at the ankles. "I think so. I dunno. I've never really been much of a sleeper to compare the difference. But I feel more energized after a dream with you."

So did she. The dreams gave her more energy like she fell into a deep sleep that restored every cell in her body.

He leaned back, bracing on his hands. "No guess today?"

A chuckle bubbled in her chest. She forgot all about guessing his name. "I need a list or something, so I know which names I've tried and which ones I haven't."

She angled her body to study his eyes. Really look at them. What kind of name went with his vibe? Cool, grungy rock star. Though he looked late twenties, she sensed he was older. Much older. A decade or two, or more?

She bit the inside of her lip. How old were immortals?

EJ was an angel. Possibly a really old one. If that were the case, he'd have a strong, traditional name he'd somehow made trendy in this era.

Eric short for Ericson? No. Maybe Edward? "Eddie…no, Ed. Yes. Ed, um, Jenson?"

The smirk on his face lit her insides on fire. Totally worth the guess.

"Nope. Still wrong."

She laughed, really laughed, for the first time in ages. It felt darn good. With all the worries waiting for her beyond the dream, this was a perfect little slice of paradise. Bliss.

"As soon as I wake, I'm researching every name starting with E." She paused, lifting her brows. "Unless you want to give me a hint?"

He held her gaze for a few heartbeats. "All right. Come here." He crooked his finger, encouraging her closer.

She shuffled to his side little by little until their legs touched, sending bursts of heat through her middle. Her heart sped, thumping so loud it drowned out the gentle swish of the waves. His finger hooked underneath her chin, lifting her gaze to his. The endless pools of his blue eyes spelled her.

Still, he leaned in further until only a sliver of space remained between their mouths. Her chest squeezed.

"What are you doing?" she whispered.

"Giving you a hint." Roughness tinted his voice now, deeper with a layer of rawness and pure, wild male.

The back of his fingers trailed along her jaw and she swore she stopped breathing. He was going to kiss her. She'd wanted this since the moment he first appeared in her dreams. Her lips burned to taste his and trace a path over the tattoos hidden beneath his shirt. But the responsible part of her butted in, screaming that she shouldn't want this. Ebony needed her. The last thing she should do was engage in a steamy, fantasy dream.

Instead of pulling back though, her gaze slid to his full lips.

Chapter Seventeen

Sweet Jesus. He wanted to kiss Hailee so goddamn bad. Her breath tickled his lips driving him crazy.

But he held back. Why the hesitation? He'd never put the brakes on kissing a woman before, especially one he wanted. Why now?

Kissing was his favorite part. Okay, maybe not his favorite, but in the top three. Definitely the top five. The intoxicating taste of desire on a woman's lips, the flavor of her lip balm, the anticipation in her soft, sweet moans. The needy ache his tongue created when it swept over hers.

Kissing shut off his mind, so he forgot all about the shit visions from Fate and the torturous eternity she crafted for him.

This was different. Hovering at Hailee's lips, something felt different. Like this kiss meant more than all the others he ever had. As though an invisible line ran between them and kissing Hailee meant not just crossing but catapulting over it with no hope of return.

Certain boundaries and lines he never crossed, but this moment didn't fall into any of those categories. Hailee never mentioned a boyfriend other than the fictional dudes she drooled over. She wasn't drunk or high. And going by the slight part in her lips and the heat in her intense blue eyes, she wanted this as much as he did.

What the hell made him hesitate? Escorting Hailee to the Guardian mansion was his mission, and Raven encouraged him to use his charm to gain Hailee's trust. Kissing was one of his most trusted moves. He never had any complaints. Quite the opposite. His reputation with women surpassed any other guy, mortal or otherwise. Yet touching Hailee didn't feel forced. He didn't turn on his charm to win her trust. In fact, it seemed natural, comfortable, as though his hands were made to caress only her. It felt right, and that alone scared the bejesus out of him. Because if this felt like the right path, then there was a three hundred percent chance Fate's hands were knuckle deep in this pie.

Hailee's eyes fluttered shut as she held still, waiting for him to close the distance. He couldn't do it. The tightness at the back of his throat made it hard to swallow, and the realization Fate was involved muddled his brain.

This wasn't the right time or place. Hailee trusted him to find her sister. Kissing her only complicated things, and he was shit at dealing with complications. He needed to deliver her safely to the Guardian mansion.

It took every ounce of willpower to redirect his movements, bypass her mouth to whisper against her ear. "My name isn't a girl's name."

Jesus. Was that even his voice?

She inhaled a sharp breath, and the sound sent a thrill through his body, snapping a sliver of his self-control. He couldn't stop himself. Angling his head, he brushed his lips against her jaw. By accident, he didn't mean it. His mouth had a mind of its own and wanted to taste her even though his brain decided against it.

Control wasn't his thing either. But right now, he needed it. Needed every ounce of that control to pull himself out of this mess.

Fate set him on a path, and instead of a standard Chosen assignment, he found a beautiful woman who yearned for a hero. That reminder diverted necessary blood to his brain. Instead of delivering a sweet kiss, he dropped his hand and peeled himself away from her. If Hailee expected a hero, he'd only disappoint her.

He couldn't look at her, not yet. Not until his pulse calmed down. If he looked at her now and still saw desire in her pretty blue eyes, he'd lose every thread of that control.

Sex on the beach was a spectacular cocktail choice, though the real thing never made it on his list of fun things to do. Not with gritty sand that could wriggle its way into the smallest crevices. The thought alone made him shudder. But he already demonstrated his ability to compromise and adapt to any situation, and Hailee took care of the sand issue. So maybe…

Nope. Still not going there.

He cleared his throat and stared at the horizon.

Awkward silence passed between them and he wished for something funny to say or a smartass remark about their almost kiss. He didn't though. For the first time in his entire existence, a girl had stolen his words.

"Do you think I'm immortal? As in, I'll live forever and never die?"

The question threw him. Exactly what he needed. A diversion from thinking about her warm breath on his lips and her rapid pulse beating beneath his fingers.

He twisted to face her. "How much did your mom tell you?"

"Nothing." She twisted her finger around a blade of grass.

"That sucks. Growing up, never knowing what you are or that another world exists and you're a part of it, must've been tough."

Her gaze lifted to his. "I guess I never knew the difference. A few things make sense now that I know."

He moved to link his finger around hers but forced his hand back by his side. Touching her led to wanting to kiss her, which before long would lead to actual kissing, and then he'd be right back to the sex-on-the-beach predicament. For now, touching and kissing were off limits.

"Yeah, you're immortal. From an infant, you grew and changed like a mortal, but once you turned twenty-five and your powers fully developed, you stopped aging. I bet you never got sick or broke a bone, you just didn't know why."

Hailee's gaze grew distant for a moment before landing on him. "I fell from a tree once. I snuck up there to read and slipped on the branch, landing on my arm. It hurt so bad, I could've sworn I dislocated my shoulder or maybe even broke my collarbone. A neighbor rushed me to the hospital, but by the time the doctor examined me, I felt fine. Mom wasn't surprised. I guess she knew all along, just never said anything to us."

Her lips thinned as she fiddled with the grass. "That was before Mom's nightmares began."

"Nightmares?"

"She had dreams of creatures with blood-red wings hunting us, said she sensed them coming. Which is why we moved so much. But she never told Ebony and me those creatures were actually real."

A strange tug pulled in his chest when her eyes washed with unshed tears.

"I wish she had." She plucked a blade of grass and twisted it around her finger. "Maybe I could've helped her. If I knew the danger was real, instead of brushing it off as Mom going crazy, I would've listened when she warned us. If we left the house before the Fallen found us, Mom would still be…"

Alive. A single word that held so much emotion.

He could shoulder some blame, too. He experienced the beach dream for months before he saw Hailee, and each time he shrugged it off as another confusing vision from Fate. He dreaded finding clues because that meant his next failure was one step closer. Instead, he stood on that burning sand and cringed every second until the vision ended. He should've tried harder.

Breaking the rule he made a second ago, he curled a finger around hers. "Don't blame yourself. The weight of a burden like that will crush you. More so for an immortal."

She slipped her hand in his, causing his stomach to flip again. What the hell was up with that? Every time he touched her, his insides somersaulted and swung around like an acrobat.

"So…my dad is an angel like you?"

"An Azrael. Angels with the wicked power to escort souls to their final resting place. Their shadows are a cool party trick."

"I don't understand why my dad wouldn't want us. Mom said he abandoned us when we were born, that he wasn't cut out for fatherhood. Why would he bother having kids if he never wanted them?"

"Relationships between immortals and mortals are rare. Plus, only an Azrael and a mortal can create Dumahel twins, so they're even rarer. Maybe that scared him?"

"What's so special about being a Dumahel? Why are the Fallen hunting Ebony and me?" She shuffled closer, lifting their joined hands onto her thigh.

Touching her face and hands was one thing. Touching her thigh? That made his pulse rocket into the atmosphere with no hope of return. Salt air, the sunlight catching in her golden hair, and the closeness of their bodies all messed with his head. He couldn't catch his goddamn breath.

"Dreamwalking is an epic power. Especially when you can pull anyone into your dreams. Mortal and immortal."

Before he knew it, Hailee moved so close her side fit snugly against his and she rested her head on his shoulder. His heart rate kicked up another gear and now a whole team of acrobats on a shit load of caffeine flipped inside his stomach.

"Do you know my dad?"

He swallowed, trying to clear that damn lump in his throat. "Nope. But Gabe did, he's an Archangel, like a big boss in the Heavens. He'll be at the Guardian mansion waiting for you."

She lifted her head to meet his gaze. "Did? Did my dad die? You just said immortals live forever."

Shit. Delivering bad news was another talent he lacked. He should summon Gabe once they woke. That Archangel excelled at delivering shit news and making it sound like the recipient had won the lottery.

"Every immortal can die, some are just harder to kill than others. For angels, it's possible for our bodies to die under the right circumstances but if that happens, our souls return to the Heavens."

"What happened to my dad?"

"You should talk to Gabe about it when we get to the mansion."

Her eyes softened. "Tell me what happened. Please."

He couldn't deny her, not when her eyes pleaded with him for answers. "Your dad…he thought you and your sister died at birth. He must've thought Fate recalled your souls to the Heavens to keep you both safe. But that knowledge, the guilt that he failed you, the pain, darkened his soul." He paused, searching for the right words but none came. He just needed to come right out and say it. "He became…a Fallen."

Her breath hitched. "A Fallen like…"

Like the creatures that killed her mother.

He nodded. "Gabe hasn't heard from your father since he Fell. We don't know where he is."

That wouldn't soften the blow, but it was all the information he had.

Her lip quivered, but as she turned away, he cupped her jaw, stopping her. Her chest rose and fell in quick succession. Perfectly timed with his. Their gazes locked as unsaid words floated between them. Nothing he said aloud took away her pain, but seeing her hurt made his chest ache so goddamn bad his lungs struggled to inhale.

The air shifted between them as her breath quickened. He needed to get into the shade, the heat or something made him lightheaded.

Her eyes dipped to his lips again. “Why won’t you kiss me?”

Lost in the moment, he leaned closer, one hand cupping her jaw, the other still entwined with hers. Every point connected with her skin tingled, stirring through his blood.

“Do you want me to kiss you?”

“Yes,” she whispered.

Control slipped away real goddamn fast. “Sweetness, when I kiss you, I want it to be real. I want it to be so perfect it’ll make your toes curl and erase any memory of guys who came before me.”

She sucked in a sharp breath. That forbidden line between them blurred by the second until he only saw a squiggly faded pencil mark. “When I kiss you, it’ll be because you want to kiss me in reality. Not just in your dream.”

“I already do.”

Sweet baby Jesus. His palm curved around her face, brushing the pad of his thumb along her full bottom lip. A lip he’d give anything to taste. To bite. “Wake up then. Wake up and let me kiss you.”

Chapter Eighteen

Hailee's eyes shot open to darkness. Her breath caught in her throat, heart pounding against her ribcage. She lay there frozen, hyperaware of everything in the room. The distant hum of the mini fridge, the fluorescent red alarm clock on the nightstand, the buzzing in her ears. Dust particles fluttered in the stale air of the motel room, caught in the pale light sneaking around the closed curtains. Still, she didn't dare move.

Was EJ awake? Ever so slowly, she turned her head in his direction and found him still lying on the makeshift bed on the floor.

Even though it was a dream, her lips burned where his thumb traced. A hot coil tightened deep in her belly, warmth pooling between her legs. She danced around her attraction to him, fumbled with a little flirting, and was happy to skip to the action while in a dream state. Dreams gave her false confidence, something she lacked in the real world. Especially when it came to drop-dead gorgeous guys who were way out of her league. Then she discovered EJ existed outside her dreams. He wasn't a book boyfriend she fantasized about. He was here, in the same motel room, lying on the floor a few feet away, wanting to kiss her.

She wanted to kiss him too, so badly it made her dizzy. His warm breath still lingered on her mouth. Her skin tingled every place he'd touched. Dream or not, kissing him would be heaven. She knew that without a doubt. He'd make her toes curl just like he said. Kissing him would be better than any pleasure she ever experienced. All she needed to do was open her eyes and let him.

One kiss. One amazing kiss she could dream about for the rest of eternity. This was her chance to experience real life at its best.

EJ cleared his throat and her breath hitched. He was awake. Was he waiting for her? Should she sit up?

She rolled onto her side at the same time he did. Just as his eyes opened, she slammed hers shut. What the heck was she doing? She didn't need this complication. Nor was she ready for any kind of relationship, let alone with a guy she just met. She needed to find Ebony, not humiliate herself. EJ was so out of her league his ball game was on a different planet.

EJ shifted. Nervous energy made her peek. He peeled himself up from the floor. Her heart leaped into her throat. She couldn't do this. She squeezed her eyes shut, which only sent her other senses into overdrive. Her pulse drummed in her ears. EJ's wild and earthy scent stirred through her blood, tingling low in her belly. She sensed his presence draw closer, warmth bloomed along the back of her neck. Just as she did back in the car, she felt his gaze on her.

Beads of sweat broke out on her palms. The room was too hot. She needed to kick off the blankets, but nerves seized her body.

More than anything she wanted to open her eyes. She wanted him to kiss her, to take away her worries and whisk her off into the sunset. But she…couldn't.

A heartbeat later, the warmth on her neck vanished. The motel door opened, and night air rushed into the room, cooling her burning cheeks.

"Tag, you're it," EJ said, his voice thicker and deeper than earlier in the dream.

"You look like shit. Did you even sleep?" Raine replied.

"I can't tell the difference anymore. Get some rest, Rae. We'll leave as soon as Hailee's awake."

They may as well leave now because that dream wired her body so much she'd never fall back asleep.

****

As soon as the sun rose, EJ announced they were leaving, and she barely showered before he grabbed her backpack and started the car. Once she settled in the backseat again, he passed her a muffin, takeout coffee and told her they'd arrive at the mansion at nightfall. He made it super clear they weren't stopping for anything but gas.

EJ made no mention of their almost kiss and asked no questions, as though he wanted to forget the whole thing ever happened. She didn't discuss it either, especially with Raine in the car. He was probably just as embarrassed as her. Relieved even. Tomorrow, they'd laugh about the whole thing and focus on finding Ebony.

Until then, the vibe in the car was the most strained, painful, uncomfortable silence she ever experienced. Nothing could top it.

EJ fiddled with the music, switching songs so frequently they never listened to a whole tune from start to finish. In the passenger seat, Raine tapped a dagger on her thigh to her own beat, never in time with the music.

Being stuck in the backseat was the worst. Most of the time, she pretended to sleep, avoiding any conversation.

The whole road trip was downright awkward.

After twelve torturous hours, the car slowed before turning off the highway and onto a dirt drive flanked with towering trees. Rounding a bend, they exited the forest. The car's headlights landed on a ginormous house, no, mansion. Lights were on inside, but with the curtains drawn she couldn't see through the tall windows.

She didn't need to. Even at night, she recognized the house from a picture her mother kept in her drawer. All along, Mom knew not just about the immortal world, but also this place.

EJ pulled up in front but remained in his seat with the engine still running. "Rae, you take Hailee inside."

Raine's head swung in EJ's direction and she stared at him like they engaged in a conversation in their minds. Hailee didn't wait. She didn't need handholding. After grabbing her jacket and backpack, she slid out of the car. Raine joined her and slammed the door a second before the car drove away.

"Follow me," Raine grumbled, not bothering to wait as she strode toward the front door.

She trailed behind Raine, her stomach fluttering more with each step. Just inside, a stunning woman with deep auburn hair greeted her.

"You must be Hailee. I'm Tayla."

Raine stepped to the side. "Safely delivered. I'll speak to Raven once I've changed. I've been wearing the same clothes three days straight."

Tayla laughed. "Where's EJ?"

"Bailed," Raine said over her shoulder, already halfway up the stairs.

Bailed? Did she upset him? Was she such a burden he couldn't wait to drop her off and be rid of her?

Tayla led her up the stairs, chatting away, but she barely listened. They walked down a hall to an entertainment room. Inside, two guys stood by a bar, deep in conversation. One of them, the taller guy with dark hair, dressed in a black button-up and jeans, approached her.

"This is Raven," Tayla said, leading Hailee to the leather couch. She sat beside her.

Raven sat on the opposite couch, drink in hand. "I appreciate you coming. I know this must be a lot to take in."

"I know this place."

Raven tilted his head. "How so?"

She scanned the room. Although it had all the modern fixtures, including a bar, pool table, and the biggest TV she ever saw, the antique chandelier hanging in the center gave away its age.

"My mom had a picture of this house. She took it everywhere with her. I think she knew to come here. I think she searched for this place with every move."

Raven peered past her in the direction of the other guy sitting on the bar stool.

Tayla leaned closer and whispered, "That's Aric."

These guys weren't great at introductions.

Raven turned his attention back to her. "Someone must've told your mom it was safe here."

She fiddled with the bracelet on her wrist. "Maybe. Mom always said it was her dream house, that one day we'd stop running and live in a place like this."

Hailee treated it like a pipe dream. They could never afford a house like this. She worked double shifts at the restaurant just to pay the power bill and rent on their tiny shoebox. The money Ebony made put food on the table and paid for Mom's medical bills. She couldn't afford the flat screen hanging on the wall behind Raven, let alone the entire house.

But Mom knew this place existed. Did her father tell her before he ran out on them? "Why would someone give Mom a picture and not the address?"

Raven sipped his drink before answering. "Your mother was safer without that knowledge."

Warmth spread along her nape a second before EJ waltzed through the door. She tried not to look but couldn't fight the pull, like some magnet drew her eyes to him.

When he caught her gaze, her chest tightened, breath halted in her throat. He'd changed into a non-crinkled version of the same clothes. He didn't speak, just held her gaze for a heartbeat then continued toward the bar.

She looked back at Raven. Maintaining eye contact with EJ meant swiveling in a one-eighty, which only made her staring more obvious.

Raven fired more questions about Ebony and Mom, and she answered best as she could. Where they'd lived, what she knew about her father, what she knew about herself. She couldn't concentrate on any of it. The hushed conversation occurring behind her between EJ and Aric stole all her focus. If only she heard the words.

EJ appeared beside the couch, startling her like he

caught her listening to his conversation.

"Drink?" He offered her a tall cocktail glass filled with orange liquid and garnishes along the rim.

"Oh, ah, no thanks. I don't drink alcohol."

His brows creased.

Raven snorted.

Tayla tsked him. "That's not nice, Raven. Hailee doesn't have to drink alcohol."

The smirk softened on Raven's lips. "Honey, I wasn't making fun of Hailee. Only EJ."

She glanced up at EJ, feeling the need to explain. "I just…I dunno. I don't sleep well. Alcohol gives me weird dreams and—"

"You don't need to explain. It's fine." EJ abandoned the glass on the coffee table and addressed Raven. "I've done my part. If you don't need anything else, Rave, I'm gonna head into town."

Raven frowned. "Sure you don't wanna stay here?"

"I've got somewhere to be."

Tayla stood. "I should show Hailee around the mansion anyway. You can quiz her again once she's settled in and freshened up." Tayla turned to Hailee. "Let's go find you a room."

Chapter Nineteen

Friday night dance party at Subzero. Exactly the distraction EJ needed. Tonight, he didn't even bother with the VIP area. Instead, he mingled with the ordinary mortals at the crowded bar.

"Another," he shouted above the music to Jimmy, the club's owner, and the only guy he considered an equally skilled bartender.

Jimmy flipped a fresh shot glass in front of him and poured the vodka.

EJ shot it back in one go, wishing like hell shot glasses came in larger sizes.

He tipped his chin to Jimmy who refilled the glass.

What he needed was something to take his mind off the almost kiss with Hailee and the fact he'd woken with the hard-on of the century. Palming his cell, he flipped through the contacts searching for someone to take the edge off. Emma? Nah, she preferred hookups at her place, and he wasn't in the mood to leave the club. He scrolled further down. Kristy? No, she was a little wild for his mood tonight and the last thing he wanted was foreplay for hours. Any other night, he'd jump at the opportunity, but not tonight. So wound up from the drive across the country, he needed something fast and now. Nat? Nope, he wanted a blonde not a brunette.

His thumb paused over Zoe. Perfect. Zoe was

always up for a no-questions-asked hook up in the private rooms at the club. He shot her a quick text and waited for her reply. Maybe she was out of town, maybe she was unavailable.

Maybe he should take his drunk, tired ass home.

River leaned his elbow on the bar, having just arrived at the club. "I'll have a beer," he shouted to Jimmy.

EJ peered inside the shot glass. Empty. Again. "Who the hell doesn't drink alcohol? And since when does someone not like my frickin' cocktails?"

River swigged his beer. "Huh?"

"Screw it. Never mind," he grumbled, knowing River heard regardless of the thumping music. He checked his phone for a text and came up empty. "Go home, Sunshine. I don't need a babysitter."

"I'm not here for you." River nodded in the DJ's direction. "Tonight's the night. She's gonna play my request, I can feel it."

Jesus. If the DJ played a sappy eighties love song, he'd snatch that bottle of vodka right out of Jimmy's hands and down the whole damn thing.

Instead of checking his phone again, he glared at River's outfit. Tonight, the Guardian outdid himself in the wardrobe department, wearing a ridiculous shirt covered in tropical leaves. "When the club advertised party night, it's the music, Sunshine. Not a dress code."

River frowned and pointed at the dance floor. "Nah, bro. Tonight is a beach party theme. You're the odd one out."

Yeah, he'd realized that the second he stepped foot in the club. Another reason he needed the whole bottle of vodka.

The dance floor resembled a makeshift tropical island. Beach balls bounced off hands. Mortals danced, dressed in clothes identical to River's wardrobe. Inflatable palm trees lined the outer edges with a truckload of sand dumped in the center. He couldn't escape that shit. The scene resembled a blinding vomit of sunshine.

Of all the nights he needed a distraction, they'd turned the club into a frickin' beach.

His phone vibrated in his ass pocket and he snatched it out to read the text.

Zoe: *I'm at the club.*

A weird feeling stirred in his gut. He needed more vodka. He waved the shot glass at Jimmy who refilled it for the umpteenth time before he replied to Zoe.

EJ: *Meet me at the bar.*

After shoving his phone in his pocket, he shot back the drink and slammed the glass on the bar. As the music switched to some song about the temperature of the room being hot, he turned to face the dance floor and scanned the sea of mortals for Zoe.

A mortal distraction was a perfect idea. Sex worked way better than vodka.

He spotted Zoe weaving through the middle of the beach party, heading toward him. Her straight, bleached blonde hair glowed under the strobe lights. He adjusted his beanie, not sure why. Zoe would rip it off anyway. She curved around a group of females dancing near the steps of the dance floor—

Nausea slammed into him. His stomach flipped upside down and he gripped the edge of the bar to remain upright. No frickin' way…

One second, he stood in the club, the next a vision

transported his mind to Hell. Not exactly Hell, but a scene mimicking what happened to this earth if the Guardians failed their mission. Fate and her shitty timing.

From his vantage point on the rooftop of a seven-story building, he stared down at a fiery apocalypse. The city looked like a dragon torched the whole damn thing. Acid and sulfur burned in the air, layered with death. So much death. Thick, black smoke blanketed the sky in darkness. Heat billowed from fires burning on the streets, explosions booming in the background—cars, windows shattering, buildings toppling to the ground.

But the screams were the worst. They got him every time. Piercing cries of pain from hundreds of mortals fleeing onto the streets. There wasn't any point. They wouldn't survive, regardless of their location.

All he could do was wait. Since the first time Fate sent him this vision, he'd searched for clues, hidden meanings or familiar faces. Nothing helped. There were no hints. Fate didn't send him scenes of pristine sandy beaches with calm, tranquil waters. She repeatedly sent him this shit, a never-ending sea of blood and fire. A storm of Fallen unleashing Hell on Earth.

Until now, Fate hadn't sent him an apocalyptic vision since he met Hailee. Guess Fate's powers were back online.

A sedan exploded directly outside the building he stood on, making him cringe. What came next was worse than the screams.

He counted the seconds. Three…two…one…a Fallen swooped down from the sky, soaring low over the road, its target in sight. He couldn't watch. Not again. Turning his back on the scene, he gagged as a woman's curdling scream ripped through his ears.

Jesus. He couldn't do this anymore. This curse frickin' sucked.

Closing his eyes, he imagined sitting on the beach with Hailee. Sand was a helluva lot better than this shitty place. He knew the drill by now. Fate's vision would end soon, but that didn't mean he needed to watch. Or listen. Once the vision was over, he'd return to his night at the club. He inhaled a deep breath and thought of Hailee's smile, her bright eyes as she peered at the ocean, her hand laced with his. His heart rate steadied. Calming sounds of waves washed out the screams.

His stomach lurched again. Darkness swirled before his eyes. Crisp, salty air replaced the sulfuric stench.

Snapping open his eyes, he gawked at the beach. What the hell? He didn't have time for this, he was in the middle of the club.

In reality, Fate's visions were a speck of time, but he'd no clue how much time passed in Hailee's dreams. Right now, his body stood at the bar and, from what the others told him, his eyes looked freaky as hell.

Someone would discover what he was. Zoe would've reached him by now.

He spun, found Hailee sitting on a patch of grass, and marched toward her. "I can't do this right now," he snapped with more attitude than he intended.

Hailee winced. "Sorry." She stood and brushed the back of her shorts. "I wanted to thank you for finding me. And apologize for the…you know. The last dream."

"It's fine." His shoulders sagged. She didn't need to apologize. He was the loser who made it all weird. "I'm just at the club."

"Oh, I'm sorry." She stepped back, putting distance between them. "You're busy… with someone else."

It wasn't a question, nor an accusation, but his damn stomach churned anyway. He ripped off his beanie and raked his fingers through his hair. "You pulled me into a dream while I'm in public, that's all. We can talk later."

"Sure. I'm sorry to bother you." She turned, about to walk away.

He reached for her. "No, you didn't bother—"

Before he finished the sentence, the scene warped and twisted. Blackness. Blinding lights pierced the back of his skull as he came back online in the club.

"Babe, are you okay?" Zoe touched his arm.

He flinched. No, he wasn't okay. What the hell was he thinking? He didn't want this.

Zoe inched closer until he felt her breath on his neck. "Want to hit the back room?"

His stomach lurched for a completely different reason. This was all kinds of wrong. He needed to get the hell out of there before he did something more stupid than sending a hook up text.

Grabbing the nearest drink, he shot it back, unsure whose it was. "Nah, I just remembered I gotta be somewhere."

He didn't wait for a reply. Turning his back on Zoe, he slapped River on the shoulder and hightailed it out of the club.

Realization smacked him in the face in the form of freezing night air. Distracting himself with random blondes at the club wouldn't work. That weird feeling humming beneath the surface of his skin told him the only one who could cure the damn itch was back at the mansion.

Chapter Twenty

Hailee opened her eyes to an oversized bed, chest of drawers, and a window seat. Regardless of the luxurious furniture, she didn't feel at ease. Now that she controlled the dreams more easily, she'd connected with EJ after slipping into a trance while still awake.

She wiped away the wetness underneath her eyes. EJ at a club with someone else shouldn't sting. They weren't in a relationship. The last time she pulled him into her dream, she chose not to kiss him. He had every right to see other people, every right to kiss others.

The thought made her breath jam in her throat. His body language and the tone of his voice made it clear he didn't appreciate the interruption. So, she ended the dream. No need for further awkwardness between them.

She glanced at her backpack on the floor beside the bed, and her heart ached for the belongings she left behind. Especially the novels. She yearned for a happily ever after right now to fill the gaping hole in her heart.

In need of a distraction, she pulled on a sweatshirt, left the bedroom, and wandered downstairs. This late at night, she assumed everyone was already asleep. Her body clock was out of whack thanks to her many double shifts.

Desperate for a bit of normality, she gravitated to the kitchen, but pulled up short as she walked through the door. Ellen, an older lady who Tayla introduced her to earlier, stood by another door, about to switch off the lights.

"Oh, sorry."

Ellen smiled. "Don't be. Is there something you need?"

"No." She peered around the kitchen. "I just, I don't know, felt like being in the kitchen."

Ellen moved behind the counter and gestured to a breakfast stool for Hailee to sit. "Do you cook?"

Hailee settled onto the seat. "Yeah. I work in a restaurant. Well, I used to. I guess I don't have a job any longer." She shook her head, dismissing the subject. "Anyway, desserts are my passion, but I cook whenever I can. Do you cook for their entire household?"

Ellen nodded. "The Guardians are always offering to help me prepare meals, but I find it quite therapeutic."

"Me too."

"When I'm in the kitchen, the worries of this world fade away. I can imagine the mortals safe, the Fallen defeated, and the Guardians happy."

If only.

Ellen rounded the counter to stand before her. She had the loveliest eyes, warming and welcoming, as Hailee imagined a grandmother's would be. Though she suspected Ellen wasn't that old. Or was she older? Was she immortal like the others?

"Would you like to cook something?"

"Oh, no, it's okay."

Ellen placed a hand over hers on the counter. "My kitchen is your kitchen, my dear. You may cook in here whenever you like."

Her throat closed, preventing words. Ellen patted her hand, then with a smile, walked out the kitchen leaving Hailee alone.

She sat there for a moment in silence. Cooking always eased some of her tension, and like Ellen, maybe it would help her forget all the craziness of the real world, if only for an hour.

Mind made up, she wandered about the kitchen, familiarizing herself with the space. Then she gathered ingredients and set about making her favorite vanilla bean cupcakes with cream cheese frosting.

Within no time, the sweet aroma of freshly baked cakes filled the kitchen, soothing the tightness in her chest. She removed the last batch from the oven, placed them onto wire racks to cool, and collapsed on the breakfast stool.

Exactly what she needed. A distraction.

She reached over the counter and grabbed a cupcake. Using a butter knife, she scooped a generous amount of frosting, slathered it on top, and took a bite.

Icy shivers skated down her spine, and she spun on the stool, searching for the source. Blackness dotted her vision. The knife fell from her hand and clunked on the tiled floor.

“Damn it.”

She pushed out from under the counter. The legs on the stool wobbled. She flailed her arms, reaching for the counter, but too late. The stool tumbled backward. Sharp pain exploded in the back of her skull when her head hit the floor. At the same time, the kitchen morphed into an extravagant living room.

She waited for the scene to solidify before sitting upright, pressing her hand on the wetness at the back of her head. "Argh."

"What happened to you?" Ebony stood before her.

Blood stained Hailee's palm. "I fell off a darn stool. Jeez, Eb. First you pull me into a dream while I'm driving and now you do it while I'm using a knife. This really isn't safe."

Ebony raised a brow. "What are you doing with a knife?"

"Icing cupcakes."

That sounded so stupid. How could she ice cupcakes with Ebony still missing? What kind of sister was she? A crappy one.

Ebony helped her off the ground. "At the restaurant?"

She almost corrected her, but the words caught in her throat. EJ warned her to not reveal her location. If Ebony was with the Fallen, they were all in danger. If she told Ebony, the Fallen could attack everyone in the household. She didn't need a history lesson in all things immortal to know that wouldn't end well.

She wiped the blood on her sweatpants. "Where are you, Eb? I'm worried."

Her sister stoked the fire. "I'm fine. Actually, I'm better than fine. I'm here with Dad."

She snagged Ebony's arm. "What did you say?"

"I said I'm here with Dad." Ebony shrugged her arm free. "He's helping me build my powers. Learn how to control the dreams better."

Her heart thumped faster and faster, making her lightheaded. "That's impossible. Our father is missing."

"He's not missing, he just hasn't been on Earth. The mortal realm as he calls it."

How was that possible? EJ said her father became a

Fallen and no one had seen him since.

"If you're not in the mortal realm, where are you?"

"A place Dad calls Aralim. But keep that between us, I'm not supposed to tell you."

Bile rose in her throat. Where the heck was Aralim?

She lowered her voice. "Listen to me, Ebony. You're in danger. EJ said our father became a Fallen, which means—"

"Who's EJ?"

"It doesn't matter. What matters is that whoever this guy is, he can't be our dad."

"He sure knows a lot about Mom and us, including where we lived, where we were born. He even told me about what the bracelets do. Did you know they cloak us?" Ebony laughed. "Our whole lives, Mom made us wear them so Dad couldn't find us. She made us believe he abandoned her. What a load of shit."

Air rushed from her lungs. "No, it's a lie. He thought we were dead."

"Yeah." Ebony shrugged one shoulder. "He told me about that, too. Then when he found out we were alive, Mom started running."

Holy crap. Could it be true? Was their father alive and looking for them the entire time?

But if he was a Fallen, then shouldn't he be…bad?

She took Ebony's hand and squeezed. "Tell me where you are so I can come to you. So I can see for myself."

"You need to take the bracelet off."

Warning bells rang loud and clear. Not real ones, but a prickly sensation she experienced just prior to Ebony pulling her into the dream. So much conflicting advice. Take the bracelet off, keep it on. Who did she trust? Her twin sister or an angel who took her to his home to meet others of his kind. Other freaking angels.

EJ also helped build her powers and vowed to find Ebony. That counted for something. But Ebony…she was family.

"How do I know this is all true? The Fallen might have you under some sort of spell, a trap to get me to come to you."

"You want proof? How about meeting Dad for yourself?"

Her heart stopped. Of course, she wanted to meet their father. She lived her whole life thinking he abandoned them, she'd hundreds of questions only he could answer.

The scene warped, flickering in and out of focus.

Ebony tugged hard on her arm. "Hailee, focus on the dream. Someone's waking you."

She couldn't. What if it were important? *This is important!* "Tell me where you are, Eb, so I can find you. So I can meet Dad." She rushed the words out before the dream collapsed.

The scene faded. Ebony's form blinked out then back in. Hailee concentrated, curled her toes in the rug, anchoring herself in the dream. But she wasn't in control. This was Ebony's dream.

Ebony grinned. "No need, he's right here."

In the lit hearth, the fire roared, throwing waves of heat against her side. A tall, solid figure cast in swirling shadows stalked through the doorway. Light from the flames shone over his features, highlighting his wavy blond hair.

Hailee slapped a palm over her mouth.

Even with the glowing red eyes, the resemblance was uncanny. Why didn't she notice last time she saw him? When the shadows from his hand killed her mother.

"Ebony…" She staggered back, losing her anchor on the dream. "He…"

Ebony extended an arm toward the Fallen. "Meet Dad."

Chapter Twenty-One

EJ patted Hailee's cheek. "Hails, wake up."

He returned from the club through the back door and found her on the floor. A small pool of blood behind her head. A stool knocked over beside her.

He mentally shouted for Aric. EJ hadn't learned first aid. Why bother when he was immortal? But Aric picked up a thing or two over their centuries in the mortal realm. If they needed one, Aric was their designated patcher-upper.

Only Fate knew how long Hailee lay there on the floor while he screwed around at the club. She could've fallen ages ago.

He leaned over, patting her cheek a little harder. "Wake up, sweetness."

Aric burst through the door, a medic kit in his hand. He dropped it on the counter then crouched beside Hailee to inspect her head. "She's not human anymore, man. I'm sure she's—"

Hailee shot upright with a gasp. She clenched the front of EJ's shirt, holding on for dear life. "Why did you wake me?"

Aric straightened. "Case closed. She's fine."

Her pounding heart through their shared connection told EJ otherwise.

He cupped her cheek. "You hit your head."

Her gaze darted to the fallen stool, up at Aric, then

back at him. "She's with him. Ebony. She's with our Dad. I saw him."

His heart sank. A fucking Fallen pulled her into a dream and he wasn't there to protect her.

"What the fuck?" Aric muttered.

EJ took a few deep, long breaths before he spoke. "Sweetness, I need you to calm down a notch. Take a deep breath." When she did, he continued. "I want you to tell me everything. But first, let Aric make sure your head's all right, yeah?"

Her wild and frantic eyes settled on him. Her breathing steadied. Finally, she nodded.

Aric opened the kit, grabbed a bottle of something, and squirted it on a gauze. Hailee didn't even wince when he dabbed the wound.

"She's already healed, man. No need to panic."

Relief never felt so goddamn good.

Aric stood and threw the gauze in the trash before he packed up the medic kit.

"Take Hailee upstairs while I get Raven. If she feels up to it, maybe she can finish icing those cupcakes first? They smell fucking amazing."

"Are you kidding me? She's got a head injury."

Aric rolled his eyes at him. Frickin' rolled his eyes before turning to leave.

Wait! He mentally shouted to his brother.

Aric paused at the doorway and glanced back at him. *What?*

There's a stack of books beside Hailee's bed, back at her old place. Can you pretty please ask Red to mist there and grab them?

Aric smirked. *Man, you're in so deep you can't even see the surface.*

Whatever the hell that meant.

Aric nodded and left the kitchen without waiting for a reply.

He curled an arm around Hailee, helping her stand. "Are you okay? Dizzy? Headache?"

Once on her feet, she stepped back, putting space between them. "I'm fine. There's no need to worry or pretend to care."

Ouch. That stung. "I'm not pretending."

"I'm just saying, there's no need to change your ways on account of me being here. It was wrong of me to expect…it doesn't matter."

Now, he was no expert on moods, but even he knew she was pissed at him. He hadn't changed his ways. In fact, since meeting her, he felt more himself each day. She just needed to realize he wasn't a hero. He couldn't live up to those expectations four hundred years ago. Why would now be any different?

Even though he didn't reply, she must've sensed his reluctance to talk because she turned, hands splayed on the counter. "I should clean up this mess."

"We'll worry about that later. Right now, we need to tell Rave about your dream."

He reached for her hand, but she pulled back. *Shit.* He'd done it now. Pissed her off so much she couldn't even look him in the eye.

"I don't need help. I said I'm fine."

Maybe he was the one who needed help, not her. After a moment, he nodded and led her upstairs to the entertainment room where Gabe and the other Guardians were waiting.

Hailee sat beside Raine on the couch opposite Gabe. Hang on. He did a double take. Yep. Raine sat on the couch like a normal person. Were they in an alternate universe?

He glanced at Gabe, Raven, then Aric…They all seemed normal. Well, normal wasn't a word he'd used to describe them, but they didn't look like aliens.

Then why the hell was Raine acting so weird?

To be safe, he veered around the couch and stood behind Hailee. In case she experienced side-affects from hitting her head or on the chance the world fell off its axis because of Raine's little sit-on-the-sofa stunt. Either way, he was ready.

Raven stood at one end of the sofa with his hands shoved in his pockets. "Hailee, this is Gabe. He's the Archangel who knew your father before you were born."

"I wish we were meeting under more pleasant circumstances."

EJ peered at the bar where Aric sat, drink in hand. Vodka called him, but his feet wouldn't move. Maybe his body also suspected the female sitting beside Hailee might turn into a mutant zombie at any second.

When Hailee spoke, a hint of bitterness tainted her tone. "EJ said you made my father believe we were dead."

Uh-oh. He'd done it again. He braced for a scolding from Gabe.

"I did. A Fallen marked your mother, and we needed to protect you both."

False alarm. Before he relaxed, a weird sensation buzzed in his blood. He ripped off his beanie and raked his fingers through his hair.

"Why would he kill my mother?"

What the hell? The whole room froze. Aric nearly

pulled a Hailee and fell off his stool.

Raven cocked his head. "Did you just say your father killed your mother?"

"Yes."

Raven glared at EJ. "Did you know this?"

He shook his head.

Raven narrowed his stare before addressing Hailee. "How do you know your father killed your mother if you've never met him?"

"He was in my dream with Ebony. He's helping her develop her powers, helping her manipulate dreams." She stood, hands clenched by her side. "He murdered my mother and now he has Ebony."

"He won't hurt your sister," Gabe interjected.

"How do you know that?"

Gabe's expression softened and settled into his standard it's-more-complicated-than-you-think face. "He loved all three of you."

"He killed my mom," Hailee snapped.

EJ rounded the couch and took her hand. This time she let him. Her gaze locked with his and his heart did that flip thing again. The same thing it did every single time she looked at him. "Hails, we'll find Ebony. Let's just hear Gabe out."

Her chest rose in a deep breath. "Sorry," she muttered before sitting back down.

With her hand in his, he perched on the armrest.

Mutant Raine twirled a throwing star around her index finger. "How do we track him? The father."

Gabe leaned forward, elbows on his knees. "Hailee, do you remember anything else from the dream? Anything that could give us a hint to his whereabouts?"

Hailee lowered her head in her free hand. The pull to comfort her was more than his need for the bar. Which said something. But before he got the chance, she straightened.

"Ebony said they were in a place starting with A. Ara…Ara-something."

"Aralim?" Gabe prompted.

"Yeah, that's it."

"Fuck."

Raven muttered it, but they all frickin' thought it.

Gabe pivoted to face Raven and given the twitches in Raven's face, a little conversation for two happened in their minds.

Not on his watch. If the conversation involved Hailee, then she deserved to be a part of it. "Rave, Hailee has a right to know."

Raven pursed his lips. "You're right." Raven addressed Hailee. "Aralim is a realm of Hell. If you think of the gates of Hell as a foyer in a hotel, then Aralim is the rooftop bar."

Little creases appeared in her brow. "How is Ebony there?"

Gabe turned to Hailee. "Because you are both half Azrael, you and your sister can pass through gateways between the realms without affecting your soul. Provided you don't linger too long."

Hailee sank further into the couch as though absorbing the information.

EJ crossed his ankle at his knee. "That's cool and all, but why did a Fallen mark them? And who the hell was it?"

Gabe leaned forward. "Dumahel are unique because of their ability to dreamwalk."

"We know that part, Gabe," he snapped, impatient with the drip-by-drip information.

"Shut the hell up and let Gabe finish," Raven barked.

Gabe should hurry up and get to the point. He waved his hand for Gabe to continue.

"Dumahel are twins where one is light and the other is dark. The reason they are targeted is their ability to pull immortals into their dreams. The twin with light flowing through their soul can pull any angel into their dream. The twin with darkness can do the same for the Fallen."

Raine jammed the throwing star into the coffee table. It wobbled from impact. Immortal or not, Ellen was going to kill her. "What's this got to do with Hailee? Clearly, she's the light twin if she pulled this loser into her dream."

She hitched her thumb at him.

"Why does the deadbeat dad need her?"

Pressure built in his chest so tight he couldn't even throw a smartass remark back at Raine. He jiggled his foot, waiting for Gabe's answer.

"Any angel. Hailee can pull any angel into her dream. Including those in the Heavens. And I know of at least one Fallen who would do anything for that ability."

The penny dropped and tumbled along the floor.

"Blaine," Raven growled.

Shit reached defcon five. Code frickin' red.

Hailee sucked in a sharp breath. "The two Fallen said that name when they killed my mom. They said Blaine wouldn't be happy that they didn't find Ebony and me."

"Goddamn it." Raven growled. "Why would Fate leave their souls in the mortal realm if she knew Blaine wanted them?"

Gabe stood and slid on his suit jacket in preparation for his imaginary boardroom meeting. "I think it's time that I have a word with our queen." While adjusting the checkered fabric in his breast pocket, he spoke in his mind to everyone but Hailee. *It is imperative that Blaine does not find Hailee.*

He already knew that, but he answered anyway. *Roger that.*

"I will return with answers," Gabe said before his corporeal form wavered and misted away.

"Holy crap!" Hailee jolted forward in her seat. "He just...disappeared."

"Misted," EJ said.

She angled her body to face him. "Where did he go? Can you do that? Can I do that?"

"To the Heavens, not anymore, and I have no frickin' clue."

Raven cleared his throat, drawing their attention. "Hailee, don't leave this house until we know it's safe. Okay?"

Hailee nodded, but through their connection he felt her pulse spike.

"EJ, follow me."

He placed Hailee's hand back in her lap before standing. "I'll be back in a second."

Slipping his beanie back on, he caught up with Raven out in the hall. "What's up?"

Raven didn't waste time with small talk, it wasn't his thing. Just like technology. Or decent music. "For once, Fate clued us in early on her plan. This is Hailee's path, my man."

He'd roll his eyes if Raven wouldn't punch him for it. "She's not a Chosen, Rave. She's immortal. Fate doesn't pave paths for immortals, and she's never assigned us to protect an immortal before."

"Times have changed. Hailee might not officially be a Chosen anymore, but she became your assignment the moment you strolled into her dream."

"I safely delivered her to the mansion, didn't I?"

"It doesn't end there. Protecting her is your assignment until further notice. Understand?"

He huffed, voicing his dissatisfaction loud and clear. Protecting Hailee meant spending more time with her, and right now that wasn't wise. But he never questioned Raven's leadership, and he wasn't about to start now. "Yep."

"Do whatever it takes to keep her safe." Raven lowered his voice and added a damn lot of authority to it. "Don't screw this up."

Chapter Twenty-Two

"I'm not staying in your room." Hailee hesitated in the doorway of EJ's room.

EJ ignored her protests, waltzed in, and dropped her backpack onto a chair. "You'll love it." He pointed out different things in this room that weren't in the one she previously chose. "Look, there's a monstrous flat screen for watching baseball, movies or…I dunno, what do you watch?"

She shrugged. TV never interested her, and she didn't care to watch the movie adaptions of books because they were never as good. Why didn't movie producers include all the pivotal points and perfect lines from the book? Who cared if the movie went for six hours? She'd watch it. It'd be worth the numb butt.

"This room faces the back of the mansion, so it has a view of the estate and the Snowy Mountains. The room you chose faces the driveway."

She raised her brows. He grasped at straws now, but he kept going.

"My room also has an adjoining bath, so you won't have to share with the next person who moves in."

She sighed. "I'm not moving in. Just because I can somehow pull any angel into my dream, doesn't mean I'm staying in this house forever."

He lifted a shoulder. "Sure. But why not have all the luxuries while you're here?"

Fair point. She took a tentative step forward and peered through the open doorway to the bath. Positioned under a window, the deep tub was so darn inviting. She hadn't lived in a house with a tub for years. Oh, the serenity of reading in one.

Her gaze drifted back to the oversize bed with black plush bedding and matching padded headboard. A cozy spot to read, but still… "Where will you sleep?"

EJ eyed the bed, then a random spot on the carpet. "I'll take the floor."

Because that turned out well last time. Not. "This is ridiculous. You said so yourself, I'm safe while I'm in the house. It shouldn't matter which bedroom I sleep in."

As though she hadn't spoken, he slipped off his shoes, climbed onto the bed, and removed the black and white painting hanging above the headboard. In its place, he hung her dreamcatcher.

"I'd feel more at ease with you in the same room."

But she wouldn't. Having him in the same room just seemed weird given their brief history. She barely knew him. And the last time they shared a room she nearly kissed him.

A soft knock rapped on the door and she turned to find a stunning woman with bright copper hair standing in the doorway holding a stack of books. Hailee's books. The ones she left behind when she fled.

EJ leaped off the bed to greet the woman by the door. "You're awesome, Red. Thanks for getting those." He accepted the books.

"It's the least I can do." She peered around EJ. "Hi, Hailee, I'm Willow. Are you staying in EJ's room?"

Her cheeks heated. Did everyone know? "He

seems to think so. I'm still not sure."

A warm smile brightened her hazel eyes. "Our Guardians are protective like that."

"Oh, he's not my—"

"I'm about to win our little debate anyway," EJ interrupted, cradling the books in front of him.

Willow chuckled. "I'll leave you to it. Hailee, if you need anything, let me know. I'm just down the hall."

Hailee nodded, unable to speak. How could Willow think she and EJ were a couple?

"Thanks again, Red."

After Willow disappeared down the hall, EJ closed the door and handed her the books. A soft sigh escaped as her fingers connected with the covers. Almost like she'd come home. The gesture was enough to win her over. Her argument and restraint crashed and burned.

"How did Willow…?"

"I asked her to mist there and grab them. I saw them when I was at your place, but Raine and I left in a hurry to get to the motel before daylight." He inched closer until he was well and truly inside her personal space. "Are you happy?"

Mouth dry, she nodded. "I'm just not sure it's a good idea," she murmured, not sure whether she referred to accepting the books or staying in his room.

She hugged the paperbacks close to her chest like a security blanket, fighting back a fit of tears.

"I do," he whispered. "Stay. At least until we find your sister."

He reached out and brushed a thumb along her jaw, making her skin tingle. This was such a bad idea. But the bath…the comfy bed…having his scent in the room when she fell asleep.

She couldn't say no, the word wouldn't even form on her tongue. "Okay. Until we find Ebony."

He grinned like she just signed over her heart. Which, in that moment, maybe she did.

"It's settled then. Right." He retreated a few steps. "Well, I gotta go…ah, do…things." He slipped his shoes back on. "Make yourself at home."

****

As tempting as the deep tub was, she couldn't bring herself to use it. What if EJ came back to his room? What if he walked into the bathroom while she soaked in the bath? Naked. The thought horrified her as much as it created other sensations she refused to acknowledge.

Instead, she settled under the covers and grabbed a well-worn paperback from the top of the stack on the nightstand. As she opened the cover, a crinkled photo fluttered onto her lap. The photo of the Guardian mansion, the same one Mom always carried with her. Tears burned her eyes as she brought it to her chest. EJ couldn't possibly know how much this meant to her. She left her house in such a hurry, she hadn't thought to take keepsakes or personal belongings. She only grabbed necessities.

She should thank him. He did all this for her.

After tucking the photo back between the pages, she placed the book on the nightstand and slipped out of bed. Halfway along the hall, music from the entertainment room drew her attention, and she diverted in that direction.

She inched the door open and found EJ with his back to her, leaning over a pool table. No one else was in the room. He clearly didn't want or need company. Maybe she should wait until he came back to his bedroom.

As she eased the door closed, he spoke. "Hey."

She paused a moment before poking her head through the doorway. "Sorry, I didn't mean to interrupt. I just…"

"S'all good. Ric just left in a fit of loser tears. He gets so sad when I kick his ass. I thought he'd be used to it by now." He held the pool cue upright on the floor. "Do you play?"

"No." She stepped into the room. "I never had much of a social life. That's always been Ebony's thing, not mine."

He tipped his head for her to come closer. "Have a game with me. I'll teach you."

Flutters erupted low in her belly. His grin cheeky and mysterious, and totally sexy. He wore a pair of ripped jeans and a T-shirt, sadly covering a bulk of the glorious ink over his chest.

At the pool table, she scanned the set up. "All I know is I have to get all the balls into the holes."

"Pockets. Yeah." He rounded the table, collecting balls from the pockets, and placed them in a triangle at the far end. "But you have to stick with your group. Big or small." He held up two different colored balls, pointing out the difference. "No aiming for my balls."

She nearly choked on air.

He held up a black ball. "Leave the black one 'till last. Knock it in early and you lose," he said, adding it with the others. "Ric always forgets that."

EJ removed the triangle and hung it on a rack. "I'll break."

Oh, God. The way he stretched his body over that table made her stomach flip. Muscles flexed in his bicep as he drew back the cue, making the inked angel wings flutter and take flight. Tingles crept down her middle, inching between her legs. Bad enough his words made her melt in a puddle, but to be that damn good looking, too. There was no hope for her.

The white ball clanked into the others at the opposite end of the table, scattering the balls in all different directions. Two fell into pockets.

EJ flicked her a glance. "I'm big."

She gulped. "I'm not responding to that."

With a chuckle, he moved to the other side and took another shot, stretching over the table. The ball rolled across the felt at a sluggish pace halting directly in the center.

He passed her the cue. "Your go."

"Why do I get the feeling you missed the pocket on purpose?"

"I have no idea what you're talking about."

Cue in hand, she mimicked the way he'd held it, but it just felt awkward. Did it rest on top of her finger or between them? Where did her other hand go? At this point, she'd look like an idiot either way, so it didn't matter.

She eased the cue back then nudged it forward. It completely missed the white ball, instead hit another color, and sent the ball careening across the table like a drunk driver. "It's not as easy as it looks."

"Here."

In a heartbeat, he stood behind her with his front pressed against her back. She inhaled a quick breath which was a huge mistake. His wild and dangerous cologne drifted through her nose making her toes curl. Those tingles returned with a vengeance.

"Move your hand back a little," he whispered, his warm breath tickling the side of her neck.

He placed his right hand over hers and slid it up the cue. His left hand grazed down her arm until his fingers curled between hers. With slight pressure, he stretched them both forward over the table. Holy Mother of God. Her mind blanked. Absolutely blank.

"Place the cue between these fingers."

The what? At this point, she forgot all about the game and couldn't focus on anything except EJ's groin pressed firmly against her butt. And she couldn't miss the hardness behind his zipper.

Her breath quickened.

In a casual manner, he placed his chin on her shoulder. Though, to her, nothing about the encounter seemed casual.

"Ready?"

"Mm-hm." Words no longer existed.

With his hands controlling hers, he glided the cue backward then jolted it forward. The white ball tapped its target, knocked into a small-circled ball, and popped it into the pocket.

"It went in!" she cheered, her voice a little breathy.

EJ cleared his throat, released her from his hold, and stepped back. Cue in hand, she spun to face him.

His smile portrayed something between pride and downright agony, an interesting mix. "Your turn again."

Chapter Twenty-Three

Despite his raging hard-on, he continued helping Hailee with each shot until she got the swing of it. Touching her became a drug. A sweet, euphoric drug that gave him the highest, most exhilarating thrill he'd ever experienced. Denying the pull to her became an impossible task.

If he thought his itch needed scratching before, it was nothing compared to now.

Across the table, Hailee knocked another ball, just missing the pocket. Her gaze lifted to his. "I missed."

"You're still kicking my ass."

Her answering grin set his blood on fire. This game needed to end, so he could put distance between them. Except, that couldn't happen now because he moved her into his bedroom. *Dumbass.*

Thanks to his mad teaching skills, Hailee only needed to sink the eight ball. Her next shot would end the game.

Accepting the cue from her, he lined up his target. Nine in middle pocket. He knocked the ball, aiming to the left so it missed the target, ricocheted off the side then hit the black, stopping it right in front of the back-corner pocket. For her.

"I missed again." He handed back the cue over the table.

He didn't know what was worse. Standing on the

opposite side of the table, hiding his erection while he watched her bend in the most erotic way known to man. Or while she did it with his front pressed against her back.

"I just have the black one left, right? The one that's now positioned directly in front of the pocket?"

"Would you look at that? How convenient."

Her laugh ended in a yawn. She should be asleep, not playing a game of pool with an insomniac like him.

Hailee lined up her shot, and he forced his gaze to the white ball, so he didn't increase blood flow to his groin when she bent over the table. The cue knocked the ball but with a little too much force, popping both the black and white into the pocket. Shit. He forgot to mention that rule.

"I won!"

Not technically, but he kept that to himself. She'd had enough buzzkills to last a lifetime.

"Look at you, winning your first game."

"Maybe next time you could not let me win?"

She was on to him, but he feigned ignorance. "I dunno what you mean. Sometimes I'm just not as awesome as everyone thinks. Rare. But it happens." *Not.*

While she laughed, he slipped the cue from her hand and placed it in the rack.

"We're not playing again?"

"Sweetness, you're so tired I don't know how you're still standing."

Resting her hands on the edge of the table, she stared at a spot in the felt. "I…can't sleep."

Oh, he knew that feeling. "Complaining about your bed already?"

"It's not that." Her gaze lifted to his. "It's just…with everything that's happened…"

He moved into her space and smoothed his hands over her shoulders, pivoting her to face him. "I know. But you gotta rest. You'll be no help rescuing your sister if you fall asleep in the hallway."

Moments passed where he thought he'd have to break out the big guns and throw her over his shoulder to carry her to bed. No such luck.

She sighed a long, ragged breath. "You're right."

Sliding an arm around her waist, he led her to his room. Their room.

The way she leaned into his embrace made it hard to concentrate on putting one foot in front of the other. After he delivered her to bed, he'd hit the vodka. At this point though, he wasn't sure whether he wanted alcohol to prevent sleep or make it come quicker.

Inside his room, at the edge of the bed, heat flashed through his body at the precise moment she took off her sweater and tossed it at the end of the covers. His pulse spiked, sending a weird sensation through his blood. Not the usual heat of sexual awakening, more a spark that lit inside his chest.

Diverting his gaze, he concentrated on the dreamcatcher. She was a rare Dumahel, hunted by Blaine and his pack of dimwits. Raven tasked him with her protection and that didn't include watching her undress like a creeper.

With a flick of the lamp, the room fell into darkness and he stood there in silence while his eyes adjusted. "Right. See you in the morning then. I mean, it's already morning, so see you in a few hours. Once you're rested and all that."

Jesus. He couldn't even form a proper sentence.

"Will you stay with me until I fall asleep?"

Sweet baby Jesus. This was a bad, bad idea. The mother of all bad ideas. Like if there was a gigantic, flaming meteorite filled with bad ideas shooting toward Earth…this was it.

He should leave. If only his feet and brain were on the same wavelength.

Instead, he nodded. Frickin' nodded. To himself, apparently, because she wouldn't see it in the dark. Unless her eyesight was as good as his. Which it would be once she completed her transition to immortality.

He inhaled a deep breath. How long had he stood there rambling to himself like a loser? He needed to get his shit together.

When the bed dipped as he crawled on, she scooted over to her side. Her side? Now he divided up the mattress space? What the hell was wrong with him?

On top of the covers, he propped his head up with his hand and lay on his side facing her. Hailee shuffled under the duvet, angling her body to him, tucking her hands between her cheek and pillow. He didn't dare move. Not one little bit.

Her eyes drifted closed. Silence filled the room for so long he was positive she'd fallen asleep. Her heart rate steadied along with the slow inhale and exhale of her breath. Adrenaline from earlier seeped from his body leaving a strange and foreign sense of calm.

"Sorry for disturbing you at the club," she whispered.

Negative. Not asleep.

"I'm sorry for being an ass and snapping at you. That wasn't cool." His hand twitched but instead of inching toward her, he clasped the bedding. "I had a shit night."

At least words formed properly in his brain this time.

More silence and quiet breathing followed, and his shoulders sank further into the bed. This wasn't so bad. Not if it helped her sleep. It made him kind of sleepy, too.

"Were you with someone?"

She whispered the words so softly he wondered if she spoke in her sleep. He hoped so. Because what the hell did he say? No, he wasn't with someone at the club. But he'd considered it until he'd realized his error and abandoned the idea.

Her eyes fluttered opened. "Sorry. You don't need to answer that."

Shit, she mistook his silence for an answer.

"I don't think I want to know the answer anyway."

He repeated her words in his head. "Why don't you wanna know the answer?"

A lump tightening in his throat. His pulse kicked up a notch. *Bad, bad idea...*

"It's none of my business."

This time when his hand reached for her, he didn't stop it. He swept a loose strand of hair from her face. "Don't you like the idea of me being with someone else?"

Her body remained completely still, and he swore he stopped breathing for a second.

"Not really," she murmured.

"Not really or not at all?"

"Not at all."

The weird tug shifted in his chest, beside his

thumping heart, and this time he couldn't ignore it. "What about the idea of me kissing someone else?"

"No," she whispered.

That meteorite shot toward Earth with so much speed he couldn't stop the inevitable destruction. If Fate paved destinies for broken immortals like him, then she had a wicked sense of humor to pair him with Hailee.

"Good."

She shifted closer on her pillow. "Why is that good?"

He trailed his fingers along her cheekbone, curving under her chin. "Because it seems I don't like that idea either." Her breath hitched when his fingers dipped down the side of her neck along her racing pulse. "What about the idea of me kissing you?"

The last thing Hailee needed was him dragging her into his world of devastation and endless failure. But a selfish part of him wanted her in this moment, wanted to taste her lips. He wanted to kiss the breath from her lungs.

"I like that idea."

Without thinking, he inched closer until he lay flush against her front. Through their connection, he sensed her pulse quickened. "Then why are you so nervous?"

She took a second to answer. "I've never…"

"You've never been kissed?"

"Well, I kissed Tim Duncan back in eighth grade when we were playing Truth or Dare in his parents' attic. But I was so nervous I puked."

He snorted. "Should I move back in case that happens again?"

As she chuckled, her heart rate steadied. "I think

you're safe. Plus, if I puke on you, you'll never tell me your real name."

"Exactly." Brushing the back of his fingers along her jaw, he inched his mouth closer. "So, you've never had a real kiss?"

"After that disaster, I decided reality was too raw and turned to romance books instead. In books, kisses are perfect. Slow, sweet, tender moments that bleed into your soul."

"That's one helluva standard for me to compete with."

A slow smile lifted on her mouth. "I get the feeling you're up for the challenge."

"Losing has never been my thing."

While rubbing his thumb over her cheek, he kissed her. Slow and sweet at first, little brushes of his lips against hers, easing her into it. She caught on quickly, kissing him back, until soft and tender was no longer enough. He slipped his tongue along her lip and she opened for him, deepening their kiss. Air squeezed from his lungs. All control and sensible thoughts collided with that meteorite in one fiery explosion.

Rising on his forearm, he moved his body half over hers, pressing her into the mattress. By now, he didn't give a shit if she felt his hardness. His hand curved around her neck to tangle in her hair.

While kissing resided in his list of top five favorite things to experience with a female, nothing compared to kissing Hailee. The way her lips moved against his, the achy need in her breath as it exhaled into his mouth, like his lips waited his entire existence to connect with hers. She'd officially ruined kissing anyone else forever. He could never come back from this.

If Fate recalled his ass to the Heavens tonight and threw him into Tartirim for his epic screw ups, he'd live for the rest of eternity a happy Guardian.

Hailee's hand glided down his chest and curved around his waist, slipping under the back of his shirt. His brain turned to mush. Fate should siphon this euphoric feeling from his veins and bottle it. It would probably cure Fallen.

Twisting his fingers through her hair, he deepened their kiss, craving more of the salty warm sunshine on her lips. He could do this all night. But this was her first kiss. Her first real-life experience with a guy and he wouldn't ruin it by rushing.

When they were both a panting, tangled mess, he slowed down. He should stop this altogether. Everything he touched eventually turned to shit. He didn't want that for her. She'd had enough damage and disappointment to last an eternity.

Easing back, he paused with his mouth hovering at hers, while their heavy breaths collided between them. His lips sizzled with the most delicious after-kiss-burn he'd ever experienced.

"So, we're clear." His voice sounded a thousand times rougher than a few minutes ago. "I'm not cool with someone else kissing you either."

"But we can kiss each other?"

"Yep." He couldn't say no even if he wanted. "How was it?"

"Well…" Her nails circled his side. "As far as first kisses go, that was…"

"Better than those book boyfriends I hope."

The corner of her mouth lifted. "So much better."

He nipped her bottom lip before kissing her again,

shorter this time so they didn't get carried away. She needed sleep, and he needed to slow the hell down. "Goodnight, sweetness."

Chapter Twenty-Four

Hailee woke in EJ's room to bright light spilling over the bed from the uncovered windows. Peaceful silence. Tingles erupted over her bottom lip at the memory of kissing EJ. Sweet, hot, and wet kisses that were perfect in every way. Ones that made her ache in all the right places and long for more moments like those.

He asked if their kiss was better than any book boyfriends she pictured in her head. The answer caused sudden tightness in her chest. His kiss was so much better than she ever imagined. So good, she may never kiss someone with such emotion and longing again.

Yesterday, when she pulled him into the dream while he was at the club, she sensed he wasn't a one-woman kinda guy. But last night, his words and the hint of possession in his tone told the opposite. He said he didn't like the thought of others kissing her, and she believed it. He may wear the rock star vibe on the outside, but she suspected he didn't want the groupie lifestyle.

Rolling her head to one side, she peered at EJ's pillow and swallowed the disappointment that he wasn't there. Last night, he'd lain beside her until she fell asleep. She'd had the most peaceful rest in forever.

It amazed her how comfortable she seemed in EJ's room. How easy and familiar she felt inside this house.

Almost like, the moment she arrived, she turned a corner in her life. And she had EJ to thank for that.

Jittery energy soared in her blood at the thought of seeing him again. Would he kiss her like he did last night? Would he do more than kiss her?

Climbing out of bed, she padded to the bath and found her toiletries unpacked and beside the basin. After taking advantage of the extravagant shower, she returned to the bedroom feeling like a new person. Today was the day she got answers. Today was the day they figured out how to rescue Ebony. She'd tackle anyone who stood in her way.

****

At the bottom of the staircase, Raine waved her over. "Follow me."

Without further explanation, Raine led her down a narrow staircase to a basement. The air cooled thanks to the damp stone walls, making goosebumps pop along her arms. At the bottom, in front of a large metal door fit for a military facility, Raine punched numbers into a pad and the lock disengaged with a loud clunk.

Raine ushered her inside and closed the door.

"He told me not to tell you, but that's bullshit," Raine muttered, striding to a long stone bench.

"Who? Tell me what?"

She hesitated by the door, taking in the room. Three oversized benches evenly spaced in the center with various hammers and tools on each. Two furnaces on the far side, the flames from the right one warming the space. On the opposite side of the room, filled with what looked like water, stood a waist-high rectangular basin. The shimmering colors on the surface lured her closer.

Raine touched her arm. “Here.”

She stilled, glancing at the silver ring in Raine’s hand. “What’s that?”

“A dagger ring made from Purah.”

At her frown, Raine sighed, in a frustrated way that said Hailee should’ve known the answer. “Purah. Water from the Eternal Fountain in the Heavens.” She pointed at the basin. “It’s the only thing that can kill a Fallen and send its soul back to Hell until it regenerates.”

Flames from the furnace caught on the miniature blade, reflecting the same shimmering rainbow as the water in the basin.

“I don’t need that.”

Raine’s lips formed a grim line. “You will.”

“Why?”

“I knew a light Dumahel once. Thousands of years ago.”

An imaginary rope tightened around her chest. “What happened?”

“He lived for less than a year into his immortality.”

Her breath caught. “You don’t mess around with the truth, do you?”

“Why would I?”

She took the ring, turned it this way and that, inspecting it. Two pewter lines curved together on top in a teardrop shape. A thin point extended from the band like a dagger. Coolness tingled between her fingers from the Purah as though made from ice.

“EJ said I’m safe here,” she murmured, trailing her finger along the point.

“He can’t protect you in your dreams.”

A knot formed in her middle. Could a Fallen harm her in her dreams? Could Ebony hurt her? “This can protect me in my dreams?"

Raine nodded. "I forge each weapon for its intended owner. The Purah seals a connection between the weapon and owner until the two are in sync. That's why the boys never change weapons. And why EJ is so pathetic at shooting River's arrows."

"You made this for me?"

Raine gave another curt nod. "Wear it outside your dream and it will carry into your dream with you."

When Hailee slid the ring on her middle finger, the band warmed slightly and molded to fit her size. Her eyes widened, a little stunned and lost for words.

Raine clasped her hand and swiped down in a sweeping motion.

"One scrape will injure a Fallen."

She curled Hailee's fist, so the point of the ring extended past her knuckle like a mini dagger.

"A jab in the chest will send their soul to the Infernal Pits."

Holy crap. In a matter of days, she progressed from working double shifts at the restaurant to what? Dreaming of a sexy guy, finding out that guy was real, and wearing a ring that could kill Fallen—the dangerous immortals that hunted her.

This was all too much. She wasn't a fighter, and she didn't fit in this world like EJ and Raine. She trusted them to help her find Ebony, not so they turned her into a badass warrior.

She fiddled with the band. "Killing someone, even a Fallen, doesn't sit right with me."

Her stomach churned at the thought of fighting her dad, even after he killed her mother. Hailee was the survivor, the one who took care of her family. Maybe surviving and fighting were one and the same. She fought for the safety and security of her family, for some resemblance of a good and decent life. All her life she fought for a happily ever after.

Now she needed to fight the creatures who threatened to unravel all that.

Raine released her hand and strode back to the workbench, ending the lesson in miniature weaponry.

"If it's your life or theirs, you don't have a choice."

Chapter Twenty-Five

EJ opened a can of soda and drank it in one go. Gas bubbles burned the back of his nostrils, but he didn't give a shit. Today, he needed every drop of caffeine. Running on little sleep was his standard MO, but last night he didn't get a single wink. At sunrise, he slipped out of bed and let Hailee sleep longer. All morning, he occupied himself, hitting the gym and training. While the endorphins flowed, his mind stayed on track and not on their mind-blowing kisses.

Afterward, he grabbed a clean set of clothes from the laundry rather than returning to his room. If he did that, seeing her in his bed might tempt him to wake her with another kiss. That guaranteed disaster.

"Are you joining us anytime soon?" Raven grumbled from the table.

Whoops. He forgot he stood in the war room with the others, figuring out a plan to rescue Hailee's sister before she became a Fallen.

He tossed the empty can in the trash, grabbed another, then sat at the table. "Ready."

Raven straightened in his chair. "Right. This is how it's going to play out."

While Raven outlined their plan, EJ sipped the soda at a more placid pace and sifted through every tiny detail in his head to make sure there weren't any loopholes. He gave his word to Hailee they'd find her sister. He wouldn't screw this up.

So far, the plan seemed legit. He, Raven, and Aric would go to Blaine's creepy mansion to find out anything and everything.

The door to the war room swung open and Cole waltzed in with a half-eaten cupcake in his hand. "Did Ellen make these? If so, I'm moving in, so I can eat them every day for the rest of eternity."

Aric shoved his chair backward, about to pounce on Cole from across the table. "What the hell? Who iced the cupcakes? And why didn't I know?"

Cole sat in a vacant chair and stuffed more cupcake in his mouth. "Don't know, brother, but they are delish."

"Maybe you losers should leave some for Hailee given she made them," EJ snapped.

"The Dumahel made these?"

EJ threw his hands in the air. "Hailee. Her frickin' name is Hailee."

Cole narrowed his gray eyes at him while a slow smirk lifted on his mouth.

"Oh, nice one, Fate. Hailee's your—"

"Don't you dare, Reaper. You can shove that thought in your mouth with that damn cupcake."

Aric barked a laugh and slapped the table. "Told you, Raven."

Just great. Clearly, he and Hailee were the latest topic in Guardian Gossip magazine. Screw that. There were more important things to discuss. And besides, he didn't even know what their relationship meant.

What the hell? He just labeled their thing a relationship. They didn't have a relationship. One kiss didn't mean they were suddenly soulmates. He wasn't soulmate material. He'd told her that, hadn't he?

Could immortals have too much caffeine? 'Cause his brain wasn't functioning with the constant buzz.

"Cole." Raven diverted the conversation back on topic. "If the twin is in Aralim, how do we get her out?"

Cole held up his index finger while he chewed the remainder of the cupcake. When he finished, he took his sweet time wiping his mouth with a napkin.

"I haven't been to Aralim. From what I know, it's a relatively new realm in Hell. It wasn't there when Fate imprisoned Zath, which means either Zath created it, or someone else did who is equally powerful."

Raven leaned back in his chair and crossed his arms. "As an Azrael, can you enter?"

"Theoretically, but I have to find the entrance. It's not a matter of misting there and back. Gateways interconnect the many realms of Hell, and I have to find the right one to enter Aralim and then find another to get out."

"Wouldn't you use the same gateway?" River asked.

"Gateways only work one way. If you entered a realm through a gateway, turned around, and left through the same one, it would take you somewhere else. Not where you originally came from."

River popped a candy snake in his mouth. "That's very confusing."

EJ finished the soda and threw it behind Raven's chair in the trash. "Let me get this straight. Not only do we need to find the gateway into Aralim, but we have to find a different one to get out?"

Cole nodded. "Me, brother. Not we."

Not if EJ had something to do with it.

Cole continued, “Aralim is a realm in Hell. If any of you come with me, you’ll become a Fallen.”

Insert twist from Fate. Again. She was damn good at throwing doozies at them. For once, he’d love an easy, clean-cut mission without all the complications. And minus the potential soulmates.

He sensed Hailee’s presence long before she paused at the other side of the closed door. The hint of warmth on his nape, the stir in his blood, the slight hitch in his heart rate. He straightened in the chair as the door swung open. Raine entered, followed closely behind by Hailee.

Air left the room in one giant rush the moment her gaze landed on his. He couldn’t move. Not even when Raine smacked his head as she strode behind him.

Hailee hesitated just inside the room.

Raven pushed away from the table. “We’ll head out to see Blaine at dusk.”

“Wait.” Hailee stepped forward. “I want to come. She’s my sister.”

Raven narrowed his eyes at EJ, and the look communicated more than words. That was a big, fat no. Message received loud and clear.

“Can you give us a minute?” he spoke aloud to Raven.

Raven nodded, and everyone but EJ and Hailee exited the room. After the last Guardian left, Hailee stepped aside so he could close the door.

She crossed her arms over her chest. “I want to help.”

He focused on her eyes, so he didn’t look at her lips and get all sidetracked. “I know. But it’s safer to stay here.”

"I won't be pushed around like a helpless woman. She's my sister, and I came here because you agreed to help find her. Help me. Not shove me aside."

"I'm not shoving you aside. This is dangerous, and you're not prepared for it."

"Don't give me that 'leave it to the professionals' crap. This may all be new to me, but that doesn't mean I'm useless."

His shoulders slumped with a heavy exhale. "No one thinks you're useless. Especially me. Outside these walls, you have a massive red target on your soul." He curled a finger around hers. "How about I get Rave to let you join the debriefs so you know what's happening?"

A long moment passed before she spoke again. "Okay. Starting now. Where are you going?"

He pulled out seats for them both and talked her through the plan. Which wasn't much at this stage.

"Why can't I come with you to speak to Blaine?"

Using the arm rests, he rolled her chair closer until her legs were between his. "Blaine is the Fallen who wants your power. He won't hurt us…at least, I don't think he will. But he definitely won't hesitate to hurt you." He placed his hands on her knees. "I won't let that happen."

She held his gaze while he held his breath. He didn't want to be an ass about it, but he wouldn't fail this mission. He couldn't. Not this one.

The second her eyes dipped to his lips, nothing else mattered. He even forgot what they were talking about. "Tell me what you're thinking, sweetness."

"Right this second?"

"Yep."

She drew in her bottom lip. "I was thinking of…"

"Me kissing you?"

"Yeah."

A thrill burst in his veins, blazing a red-hot path through his body. "Would you like me to kiss you again?"

"Yes," she whispered.

He cupped her face between his hands, tilted her head slightly, and drew her mouth to his. If he thought it couldn't get better than last night, he was sure as hell wrong.

This time Hailee was full of confidence and he let her lead. He gave up control and sat in the passenger seat, enjoying the spectacular ride.

The kiss was sweet and soft, delicate and frickin' mind-blowing. Her tongue glided over his causing a weird, low growl to rumble deep in his throat. If he didn't pull back, he risked gripping her hips and lifting her onto his lap.

Slowing down, he eased back and gently nipped her bottom lip. "How was that?"

"Good. But I might need more practice."

"That sounds like an afternoon activity I'd be delighted to partake in."

She chuckled, making his chest expand until he thought it would burst.

"Will you promise to keep me informed?"

He nodded. "I promise."

Chapter Twenty-Six

Another cold, dreary, snowy night. Tiny snowflakes fluttered in the air while he, Raven, and Aric flew to Blaine's mansion on the outskirts of Summit Creek. Usually, the cold didn't bother him but that didn't mean the icy wind didn't suck. He should've worn a jacket. Was it possible to acclimatize from dreams? Because after having so many dreams of sunshine and warmth, he now craved it.

He took full advantage of the sun's healing rays when outside, but the dreams with Hailee were different. The sun seemed warmer, brighter, more powerful. Afterward, he woke as though he basked under the rays for a whole week. The high was addictive.

Curving his wings tighter behind his back, he descended from the cloudbank, just behind Raven and Aric. Blaine's mansion came into view.

Angling his wings, he lowered onto the roof beside Aric. "How will Blaine know we're here? Wouldn't it be more practical to use the door?"

Aric folded his midnight black wings behind his back but kept them unfurled, they all did. In case things got crazy. "He'll know we're here. Trust me."

"If he's here. For all we know, he's in Aralim."

After scoping out the rooftop, Raven strode toward them. "If he's after Hailee, he'll be in the mortal realm.

He won't leave it to Slater or the father to find her."

On cue, a whoosh behind them announced Blaine's arrival as he landed on the roof.

"Well, well, if it isn't my three favorite Boy Scouts." He nodded to Aric. "I see your wing healed nicely."

Aric glared at Blaine, his fists curled tight by his side, but he didn't take the bait. Blaine had a death wish if he picked another fight with Aric. The last time they fought, Blaine threw Hellfire at Aric's wing. He doubted Aric would let it happen a second time.

Raven stepped forward, gaining Blaine's attention. "Whatever you're up to, Blaine, it needs to stop."

Blaine cocked his head. "And where's the fun in that?"

"This isn't you." Raven motioned to their surroundings. "All this doom and gloom evil Fallen shit. It's not the real you."

"You have no idea who the real me is anymore. I was meant for this path all along."

"I'm your brother. Of course, I know, and this isn't it."

Raven's voice sounded weary, like he just wanted this over.

They all did. They'd hung out in the Snowy Mountains for over a century now and the vay-cay was getting a little old. Time to move on.

"You call yourself my brother? Where were you when I Fell?"

Raven charged at Blaine, but Aric snagged his arm, holding him back. "Are you fucking serious? I lost everything to save you. Everything. We all did. And you prance around in the mortal realm as though it's a fucking joke."

"You don't seem too sad now that you've found Tayla. You're welcome by the way. You know, for convincing her to go back to you and save your soul."

A low and feral growl came from Raven. Shit was about to get real.

"Don't you dare bring Tayla into this."

Blaine lifted one shoulder. "I'm just saying, I could have let you Fall. I could have taken her soul."

Raven was about two seconds away from shrugging out of Aric's hold to beat the shit out of Blaine. EJ needed to get this conversation back on track. "Just tell us what you want."

Done with Raven, Blaine turned to EJ. "I want the other twin."

"So, it's true, you have Ebony?"

"I have the dark Dumahel if that's who you're referring to. But Slater clearly struggles with following orders because I sent him to retrieve both. Not one. Considering you're on my rooftop, I presume the other has aligned with Team Goody Two-shoes."

Blaine peered at the Heavens for a moment and then back at him.

"How about a good old-fashioned hostage exchange?"

Something strange heated his blood, overtaking all rational thoughts. "Hailee isn't a hostage," he snapped.

Blaine straightened, all smug-like. "On a first name basis, are you? I didn't realize things had gotten so friendly."

Raven, now out of Aric's hold, paced in a tight circle. "You're taking this too far. It's one thing to harvest the souls of mortals in Fate's battle with Zath.

But taking the souls of immortals makes this personal."

"It is personal," Blaine said with a sneer.

"How? Is this about your plot for revenge against Fate?" Raven paused, shoving his hands in his jean pockets. "God, Blaine, it's been over three hundred years, just let it go."

"You wouldn't say that if she cast you out."

EJ threw his hands in the air. If this conversation went around in circles anymore, he'd get dizzy. "She did! She banished all three of us here to save your ass. Then she sent River and Raine, too, because clearly we were taking too long."

Aric spoke in a more reasonable tone. "You chose to Fall. Fate didn't cast you out. I remember the day clearly."

The corner of Blaine's mouth twitched making the hairs on the back of EJ's neck stand to attention.

"Oh, is that the tale Fate spun you?"

Raven recoiled. They all did.

"What are you talking about? Fate can't lie."

"She can do whatever the bloody hell she wants, brother. She's the queen of destiny. That amount of power is lethal in anyone's hands." Blaine's gaze slid to EJ. "I will have both Dumahel, you have my word."

"Just like you wanted Willow?" Aric growled.

Blaine's irises flared with tiny crimson flames. "This time I won't lose."

Chapter Twenty-Seven

EJ filled her afternoon with a tour of the mansion and the grounds, followed by an intimate lesson of how perfectly his lips fit with hers. Too soon, he left with the others to find Blaine. And he still hadn't returned.

After dinner, Ellen requested Hailee's cupcake recipe and suggested they make some together. But even baking didn't calm the restlessness stirring under her skin. In the end, she excused herself and found a quiet spot in the living room to hide away beside a crackling fireplace. Just her and her book boyfriend.

Leaving the unfinished mug of hot cocoa on a nearby table, she curled up on a window seat and peered into the darkness. Tayla said it snowed earlier, but without a light on outside, she only saw her reflection. She'd never seen snow. Growing up, they'd never lived anywhere cold enough. Part of her yearned to race outside right this instant to feel the snowflakes fall on her open palm. Maybe catch one on her tongue like they did in her books. Would it sting? Or would it melt before her tongue registered the touch?

Soft light from the chandelier reflected off the Purah ring on her finger. How could a small piece of jewelry wield enough power to kill a Fallen? It seemed far-fetched. All of this did. EJ and the others were Guardians, the Fallen hunted Ebony and her for their dreamwalking powers, and she and her sister were half angel. Her whole life came undone the moment she turned twenty-five.

She fiddled with the ring, turning it this way and that. Did Ebony know their dad was a Fallen? What if she thought Fallen were good?

Her stomach twisted. EJ left hours ago. What took him so long?

Sitting on the sidelines wasn't her thing, especially with Ebony in danger. She should at least warn her.

Straightening her back, she inhaled a deep breath, awakening the power flowing through her veins. It increased in intensity with each day, building and strengthening until it became an extension of herself, buzzing in the background with everything she did. Her dreams were more vivid and lifelike, and connecting with EJ was quicker and easier than each time before.

Connecting with Ebony should be a piece of cake. Closing her eyes, she summoned an image of her twin. Since they were kids, they sensed each other in different ways. She knew whenever Ebony hurt herself or was worried or nervous. When Ebony experimented with substances at rave parties, Hailee experienced some of the effects. Over the years, their connection grew stronger and now she knew why. Approaching immortality, their powers developed, linking them on an entirely different level.

When stale air filled her nostrils, she knew she'd made the connection. She opened her eyes.

A few seconds later, Ebony appeared in the living room, her eyes wide. "How did you pull me into a dream?"

Hailee drew back. "The same way you always pull me into yours."

"I have a new bracelet which should block you."

Her gaze slid to the metal on Ebony's wrist. It looked the same as hers, only black. Instead of a dreamcatcher charm, a single crimson feather hung from a loop. "What is that? Why would you block me?"

Ebony's lip curled. "Because you're with them."

"Who?"

"The Guardians," Ebony snapped. "They're trying to kill me and you're buddying up with them."

"What? No, they're not. They're helping me rescue you."

"I don't need saving, nor do I want it."

She reached for Ebony, but her sister retreated. "Who told you they're trying to kill you?"

"It doesn't matter who. What matters is I can't trust you."

She recoiled as though Ebony just slapped her in the face. "Are you serious?" They argued in the past, all sisters did, but they never had an issue with trust. "They're lying to you, Ebony. It's all lies."

"Really? You're not with the Guardians?"

She couldn't answer. If she said yes, Ebony wouldn't trust her again. If she said no, then she lied to her sister. Neither option saved her sister from those monsters.

Ebony pointed at her. "Exactly. I bet you think they're the good side. They might not be able to lie, but I doubt they told you the whole truth."

This wasn't going as planned. The last time she saw Ebony, she still sensed her sister in front of her, even after their dad appeared in the dream, too. But now, it seemed like Ebony swallowed all their lies to join their cause. Time was running out. She needed to save her sister before it was too late.

“About what?” She stepped closer, summoning an extra dose of power to anchor the dream. She needed to find out as much information as possible.

Ebony’s mood lightened as she kneeled beside the fireplace and added another log.

“The part where Fate left us in the mortal realm with our mother instead of letting Dad take care of us. Dad said she controls the universe like her personal game of chess.” Ebony glanced over her shoulder. “She took twenty-five years from us, Hailee. Twenty-five years.”

What the heck? This situation was worse than she expected. Ebony put their father on a pedestal, but she didn’t know the truth. “The Fallen you call Dad killed our mom.”

Speaking the words brought fresh tears to her eyes. The dream wavered, and she instinctively dug her toes into the carpet to stabilize her power.

Ebony stood facing her. “It was necessary. Dad needed to find us, and she wouldn’t tell him where we were.”

Hailee sucked in a sharp breath. “I was there.” Bubbles of heat rose in her chest as the memories came crashing back. “I hid under the kitchen table while he killed her as though she were nothing. Shadows in his hands sucked the life from her in a matter of seconds.”

How could Ebony justify their dad’s actions? How could she side with him?

Her hands curled into tight fists. “Mom was so freaked out. She said she promised to hide us. All this time she hid us from our dad.” Her voice rose. “You know why? Because Fallen are dangerous. They’re the ones who will kill you, Eb. Not the Guardians."

Ebony tilted her head slightly, lifting her brows. "We're dangerous too, sis."

"You're not listening," she shouted. "Every minute you spend with them puts you in more danger."

"This is who we were meant to be if Fate and our mother didn't intervene. Dad has taught me how to harness my powers, showed me how to control the dreams. He organized this protection bracelet so you couldn't help the Guardians capture me. Dad's promised me eternity. What have the Guardians offered you, sis? I bet they haven't even shown you the full extent of your powers."

She thought for a moment. EJ vowed to protect her, and the Guardians took her in, gave her a home, and agreed to find Ebony. They asked for nothing in return. Since arriving, she'd seen no evidence they planned to use her powers. She witnessed nothing but strong bonds of loyalty and love.

Ebony placed her hand on Hailee's arm. The contact made her skin burn through the fabric of her shirt.

"Come join Dad and me. We're your family. Together, you and I can pull Fallen and angels into the one dream. Think of how powerful and indispensable that makes us."

Hailee recoiled, breaking contact with her sister. Ebony made bad decisions in her life but nothing like this. Nothing that divided their family and put a loved one in danger. Siding with the Fallen did exactly that. Hailee would run from them forever, fearing for her life. She'd always try to save Ebony.

"I'll never chose evil over good, Eb. That's not

who I am and not who I want to be."

Ebony's gaze narrowed. "That's too bad. I'd rather you come willingly."

"Is that a threat?"

Her sister shrugged.

Enough was enough. This time Ebony took it too far. This time, she went beyond the point of no return.

"You know what? I'm done. If you want to hang out in Hell with our psycho father, then go ahead and do it. Leave me out of it." Tears filled her eyes, but she refused to let them fall. "I'm sick of fixing your mistakes and bailing you out of the trouble. I've done it my entire life."

"You're turning your back on your own family?"

Those tears burst free. "You've left me with no choice."

Chapter Twenty-Eight

EJ smoothed his thumb over the tear tracks down Hailee's cheeks. "Wake up, sweetness."

Her eyes fluttered open to reveal puffy, red lids. His heart clenched. Why was she crying?

"What's wrong? What were you dreaming about…while sitting?" His pulse kicked up a gear. "You were in a trance, weren't you? Who did you pull into your dream?"

"Ebony." Moving her feet to the side, she made room for him to sit facing her. "Please don't be angry."

"I'm not angry, just…concerned." He didn't know how the dreams worked or whether someone could hurt her. What if her father was there? What if Ebony became a Fallen? "Are you okay?"

"No." Her eyes filled with fresh tears and they slid down her cheeks.

He got back to wiping them. "Don't cry, sweetness. I've no practice with sad tears." He smoothed his palms over her cheeks to clear the path. "Tears of pleasure and utter satisfaction, yes, but not sad ones."

That made her chuckle. Goal achieved.

"Have you been here all night?"

"I made some cupcakes with Ellen, then grabbed my book and ended up dozing on and off in the chair." She angled to face him better. "How did it go with

Blaine? You were gone for ages."

He took her hand in his and stared at their intertwined fingers for a moment, noticing her new piece of jewelry. "Not great. He confirmed he has Ebony, and he also made it clear he intends to get you. I wish I knew why he needs both of you."

"I do," she whispered.

"Did your sister say something?"

"Ebony's convinced Fate left us in the mortal realm and hid us from our father on purpose. She kept going on and on about how wrong that was. She also said that we're more powerful together. That we could pull any angel and any Fallen into the same dream."

"Fuck." He exhaled a ragged breath, trying to calm the twitchy sensations overtaking his body. "Blaine wants to use you both to pull angels into a dream with him. That would make it easier for him to recruit them."

"Exactly how bad is that?"

"Epically bad. Like the baddest of all bad."

He needed to tell Raven so they could get on the front foot. This wasn't a game. How far would Blaine go to get to Hailee? How many angels were in danger?

He fiddled with the ring on her finger. "Did Raine give you this?"

She nodded. "She said it would keep me safe in the dreams."

"Good." He had no idea how a tiny Purah ring protected Hailee in her dreams, but he trusted Raine and her kick-ass weapons. As long as Raine didn't freak out Hailee about the fate of the last Dumahel she knew. Hailee didn't need more bad news. Nor did he want her constantly looking over her shoulder.

Hailee fell silent while he circled his thumb over

the back of her hand. "What are you thinking?"

She peered out the window. "There are so many things I've never seen or experienced." Her finger trailed along the windowpane. "Tayla said it snowed and you know what?" She angled to face him. "I've never seen snow. We didn't live anywhere cold, and it wasn't like we went on family vacations. I haven't even been to a nightclub, let alone a rave party. How pathetic is that? Ebony went to one every weekend while I worked double shifts to pay bills and put food on the table."

How the hell did he respond? As an immortal, he lived a privileged life, never worrying about where his next meal came from or how he'd afford the bills. When he had the ability to mist, he traveled the realms in a heartbeat wherever and whenever he wanted to go. More recently, he'd wasted his time in the mortal realm.

Pressure squeezed the air from his lungs. Thinking of why he frequently visited SubZero left a bitter tang in his mouth. The solitude he craved was right in front of him.

She wiped her eyes with the back of her hands. "I sacrificed everything to keep our family together."

"Come here." He drew her in, wrapping his arms around her.

Her cheek rested against his chest making his heart beat a little faster. A bit stronger. Sunshine and warmth filled his nostrils with each inhale. He could sit there all night, breathing in her scent, but it was almost dawn.

An idea sparked in his mind. He kissed the top of her head. "You know what's more awesome than seeing it snow?"

She leaned back to look at him. "What?"

"C'mon. I'll show you."

He swiped the blanket from beside her, then took her hand and led her out of the living room. At the closet by the front door, he grabbed Tayla's jacket and slipped it on Hailee, then he pulled a random scarf from a hanger and wrapped it around her neck.

"Any more layers and I won't be able to walk." She chuckled.

"Then I'll carry you."

Taking her hand again, he led her up three flights of stairs to the attic. He pushed open an extended window and climbed out, turning to help her onto the roof.

"Where are you taking me?"

"You'll see."

When he was sure she wouldn't slip and fall off the edge, he flipped out the blanket and sat, pulling Hailee down between his legs. With her back against his front, he wrapped his arms around her. That clenching thing happened in his chest again and this time, he didn't ignore it. Having her within his arms made his senses careen into overdrive, his whole body hyperaware of every inch where they touched.

To steady his heart rate, he concentrated on the pine trees in the distance. He narrowed his gaze on the spindly branches rather than thinking of her warm body cocooned in his. This was why he didn't do attachments, they came with too many weird feelings.

"What exactly are we looking at?" She whispered the words like they were being sneaky.

"Give it a few more minutes." Jesus. Was that even his voice?

They sat there in silence for the longest moment. Not an uncomfortable or foreign feeling. The others thought he needed constant buzzing twenty-four seven. They didn't know he crept up here on the roof each morning to watch the sunrise. It put everything into perspective. The sunrise on a new day meant he had another chance to prevent Fate's vision from coming true.

That he hadn't failed. Yet.

The first trickle of dawn crept over the horizon, streaming thin beams of light through the trees. A golden ball of heavenly fire chased away the last remaining darkness, splashing the sky with a deep orange glow.

Hailee sucked in a breath. "It's…beautiful."

The weight on his shoulders lifted with a heavy exhale. He'd made it another day. "Yeah. It is."

Within a few minutes, the morning sun bathed the estate. Wispy tendrils of fog swirled between the wide tree trunks. Fresh, white snow dusted branches, a thin layer on the garden beds and patches on the grass. The sun would melt it before long, which made this time of the day more special. Like he and Hailee witnessed something spectacular and rare no one else had.

She pivoted in his embrace, so he could see her face. "Thank you."

His chest squeezed so tight it might shatter his damn ribs. "Don't spill my secret spot, the others might steal it."

"My lips are sealed…" A mischievous grin curled at the corner of her mouth. "Edison Jones."

He almost told her. So close. But if he told her, then her guessing game ended. "Wrong again. How many names are left on your list?"

She exhaled an exaggerated sigh. "I'm just making them up now. Soon, I'll start listing town names."

He couldn't respond because once again, her sapphire blue eyes stole his words. With a darker rim around the outside and framed in delicate dark blonde lashes, her eyes mesmerized him. Heartbeats echoed in his ears until he no longer distinguished between his and hers. It didn't matter.

She lifted her chin toward his, and it seemed like the most natural thing in the world to meet her halfway. The moment their lips touched, a sweet thrill shot through his veins causing an ache low in his belly. Flashes of heat pulsed along his arms. He cupped the back of her neck, tangling his fingers through her hair. Without rushing, he kissed her slow, long, and deep, until every cell in his body hummed with need for her.

If this were any other girl, he'd have her naked by now. But with Hailee, everything was different. Attraction wasn't an issue, far from it. Her touch lit his body like a fireball careening to Earth, and the thought of her naked underneath him scrambled his brain. But being close, holding her in his arms, kissing her, gave him the biggest thrill, the highest high he ever experienced. At this rate, getting naked with her would blow his mind, not just scramble it.

Hailee moaned, slipping her hands over his waist and around to his back. Feeling her touch him felt frickin' amazing. He wanted her hands on him for the rest of eternity, and that scared the hell out of him. How easily she made him feel a swarm of foreign emotions. How she made him feel a tiny bit…worthy.

Slowing down, he eased back from the kiss but

lingered for a few heartbeats with his forehead pressed against hers. Hailee snuggled closer to rest her cheek on his shoulder. He held her a little tighter. He sat there in silence, content with her heart beating in time with his, until the sun lifted above the trees and the magical dawn became day.

Peace. He hadn't felt that for so long.

Chapter Twenty-Nine

"Let me get this straight. You and all other Ariel can make trees sprout from the ground using magic?" In the mirror, she gaped at Willow, who stood behind her holding a section of Hailee's hair.

Willow pulled the hair through a curler then twisted it around her finger. "It's no big deal."

Tayla exited the closet carrying more outfits. "It is a big deal. It's the most amazing thing to watch." She held up two dresses dangling from hangers. "What about these? I think the burgundy goes with your skin tone."

She eyed the choices. They were both stunning and probably cost more than her yearly wage at the restaurant. A job she no longer had. "I just…"

Tayla frowned. "You don't like them?"

"I do. They're beautiful. I'm just not a dress kind of girl."

Willow sighed, grabbing another section of hair to pull through the curler. "I don't understand how you don't like dresses."

Tayla laughed. "Cheers to that, sister. I'm a jeans and sweater girl."

"Me too!"

The bedroom door burst open, interrupting their laughter.

"Have you decided on clothes yet?" Raine said

from the doorway, one hand on her hip.

"One second." Tayla rushed back into the closet and returned with a burgundy knit top. "How's this? You can wear it with the jeans you have on."

"Perfect."

At least she'd feel more like herself wearing her own jeans. She was nervous enough without dressing like a stranger.

Raine took one look at the top then spun and left, closing the door again.

Warmth expanded through her chest as Tayla lay the shirt on the bed ready for her to change. "I appreciate you guys letting me borrow some clothes and…for all of this."

Willow hushed her. "Don't be silly. We should thank you."

"How so?"

Done with the curler, Willow placed it aside and styled Hailee's bangs across her forehead, tucking a section away with a pin.

"I've known EJ a long time. More than a thousand years. He's always hidden himself behind a joker façade. I know the visions take their toll on him, but he never lets anyone in enough to show them the real him."

"Hang on." Her jaw flopped open. "EJ is more than a thousand years old?"

Tayla laughed. "I know, right? It takes a bit to get your head around."

How did she even respond to that? A thousand years? She kissed a thousand-year-old angel? A lump tightened in the back of her throat. Exactly how many women had EJ kissed over those thousand years? In her short twenty-five years, she'd only kissed…EJ because Tim Duncan didn't count. They didn't even touch lips before she almost puked down the front of his shirt. "Okay, I'm too nervous to comprehend that right now. You said visions?"

Tayla dusted powder over Hailee face, highlighting her cheekbones.

"Fate sends him visions of the future."

"But they're tragic visions. He can never get there in time to stop what's destined to happen," Willow added.

EJ saw visions of the future? That was so much worse than dreamwalking. His reaction when she called him a hero now made sense.

Her earlier conversation with Ebony came to mind. "Is Fate really that cruel?"

Willow placed her hands atop Hailee's shoulders and met her gaze in the mirror.

"No, she's not. Fate brought Tayla and Raven together when he needed it the most. She brought Aric back to me and prevented my soul from Falling." She paused, her shoulders lifted and fell with a deep breath. "Fate works in mysterious ways. Often, we don't see the reasons behind her actions until we're meant to."

She considered Willow's words for a moment. Could Ebony be wrong? Maybe Fate left her and Ebony with their mom for a reason, they just didn't know why yet. That explained why Mom carried a picture of the Guardian mansion and constantly searched for the place every time they moved.

Willow spritzed hairspray over Hailee's hair and threaded her fingers through the curls. "Done! How do you like it?"

She studied herself in the mirror. Makeup wasn't usually her thing because it made her face all greasy in the kitchen. But Tayla applied it so lightly and flawlessly it looked natural. Bouncy curls fell to her shoulders with a few strands pulled back over the sides. She looked pretty. She felt pretty. "I love it."

"EJ's going to flip." The excitement in Tayla's voice rang loud and clear.

A smile warmed Willow's face. "Raven and River just arrived at the club with EJ."

"How do you know that?"

"Aric just told me."

"When?" She scanned the room looking for Aric. Or a cell phone in Willow's hand. Nothing. "How did he tell you?"

"In my mind."

Tayla held out the top. "Quick, get dressed."

She slipped into the adjoining bath and changed, careful not to ruin her hair as she swapped shirts. "Telepathy is pretty cool. What else can angels do?" she called out.

"Besides fly?" Willow said. "Some can use compulsion, manipulate memories, control time. The Guardians were the most powerful before Fate exiled them here."

Again, Fate sounded cruel and didn't win any points on the popularity contest.

Controlling time would be handy, especially the ability to travel back in time. Then she could save…She couldn't finish that thought. Not tonight.

She flipped her hair out from the neckline of the shirt. "I saw Gabe disappear into thin air. Can you both do that, too?"

"Not me," Tayla said. "I'm just your average immortal with no superhero abilities."

"Besides wrapping Raven around your little finger," Willow added.

They both laughed, and the sound filled her chest with hope. Maybe Fate did have a plan and things would work out as they were destined. Only time would tell.

"I can mist," Willow replied. "All angels required to leave the Heavens can mist."

Sucking in her stomach, she tucked the top into her jeans. Perfect. If she didn't eat. At least until her jeans stretched a little. "Why were they banished?" she asked, returning to the bedroom.

Willow's gaze dipped to the floor, as though the conversation made her uncomfortable.

"I'm sorry, it's none of my business."

Willow hushed her again. "Don't be. You have every right to know. You're a part of this family now. It's just not a pleasant topic."

Tayla cleared her throat. "Fate banished the Guardians here to save Blaine. Raven's brother."

"The Fallen hunting me?" She gasped. "The one who has Ebony?"

The grim line of Tayla's lips said it all. "You're safe here. The Guardians won't let Blaine take you."

What if they couldn't stop Blaine? What if the Guardians slipped up somewhere and he found her? Why would they want to save someone so evil? "This is a bad idea. I think we should stay here. I mean, what happens if—"

"There'll be enough immortal muscle in that club tonight to hold off an entire army of Fallen. It'll be fine."

If only Mom made it to the Guardians before the Fallen killed her. What the hell was she doing? "This isn't right. I shouldn't go out and have fun while Ebony is in…Hell." Saying it aloud sounded so wrong.

"Raven's working on a plan with Gabe and Cole, but it'll take time." Tayla squeezed her shoulder. "After all you've been through, you deserve at least one night. And going to a nightclub is one experience we can easily tick off your bucket list. This might be your only chance before things get crazy."

Raine barged through the door again, holding out a pair of shiny navy pumps. "These should fit." She all but shoved them into Hailee's hands.

"Really? They're gorgeous."

Raine exhaled an exaggerated sigh. "Finally, someone else in this house that appreciates stylish heels."

Tayla rolled her eyes and turned to Hailee. "Congratulations. You just won a new BFF."

Chapter Thirty

At Subzero, the DJ played the perfect mix of tunes. Hard, fast beats where the bass vibrated low in his blood and drowned out the buzzing in his ears. His heel tapped the floor in time with the rhythm, the music working its way up his spine until it cleared his thoughts. Unless that was the vodka? Could be both.

Raven sat across the table from him in the VIP area. The scowl on his face proved he didn't have the same appreciation for the DJ's epic playlist.

"What's up, Rave?" He didn't bother shouting above the music, Raven could hear perfectly fine.

He'd convinced Raven to put him back on patrol tonight with him and River. The twitch beneath his skin wouldn't go the hell away. He either prowled the streets to fight deadbeat Fallen or he got wasted. The night was a total buzzkill. No Fallen were out and that weird feeling still lingered in the background.

Right, time to get wasted.

Raven shot back the remainder of his bourbon. "No Fallen, your shit taste in music blasting in my ears, and Gabe hasn't returned from his chat with Fate. Take your pick."

Raven the grumpy bum.

River plopped into a chair beside him. "What the hell? The DJ said no. Again." He swigged his beer. "I'm thinking of compelling her. Just once."

"God, no." EJ groaned.

"I don't know what music I find worse. Yours or his," Raven grumbled, pointing between him and River.

"Your progression to the dark side is taking a frickin' long time, Rave. I thought your taste in music would improve when you met Tayla and discovered how to open the app on your cell." He laughed, pushing his chair back from the table. "It clearly didn't."

Raven straightened. "Where are you going?"

"Grabbing another drink from Jimmy, so he'll fill it with vodka rather than this one shot at a time business."

Raven's shoulders relaxed. "Grab me another while you're at the bar."

"I'll come, too." River stood.

"I can find my own way, Sunshine. There's no need for an escort."

Before River protested, EJ exited the VIP area, merged into the crowd, and took the long way to the bar. Weaving through the sea of mortals gave him a different kind of buzz. Like a natural high. Maybe that would rid the strange humming in his blood.

He paused at the rail encasing the sunken dance floor and scanned the faces. A few familiar ones stood out in the crowd. A few he'd entertained in the private rooms in the back, some who'd entertained him. A blonde on the far side of the dance floor caught his eye with a wave of her hand. Jess? He wasn't good with names and it didn't matter. Every woman he was with knew he wasn't relationship material. They enjoyed a bit of fun, a lot of pleasure, then parted ways happy and satisfied as hell.

Rocking her hips in time with the music, she curled her finger for him to join her. She backed up, separating herself from two other women in her group.

Fallen patrol, drinks at the club, sex in the private room—back to a normal routine. No shitty visions from Fate, no mission to save humanity, no failures. An existence full of distractions.

In the time it took to slide his empty glass onto a nearby table, the blonde moved around the edge of the dance floor, gaze locked on him like a missile. About an inch of regrowth at the roots showed in her dyed, straight hair. Not naturally blonde and wavy like Hailee's.

On the approach, she pivoted. With her back to him, she raised both arms in the air to move her hands in time with the music. She wore a figure-hugging singlet top teamed with a mini skirt that showed off her long, slender legs. No curvy waist or hips he could grip in his hands, like…Hailee.

Leaning his forearm on top of the rail, he watched her ascend the handful of steps. Dancing with a female, grinding his pelvis against hers while they made out on the dance floor made his top ten list of things to do. Maybe number seven.

At the top of the steps, the blonde spun toward him. Knots twisted in his stomach. Strobe lights reflected the color of her eyes. Dark. Brown? Hazel? Not vibrant blue like…Hailee's.

What the hell was wrong with him? Why did he suddenly compare every female to Hailee?

She weaved through the mortals lined up at the bar and headed toward him. The knot twisted tighter the closer she came. His heart thumped louder and faster than the music. Halfway to him, her mouth curved in a grin. Only, he didn't find it sexy.

His stomach rolled. This wasn't what he wanted. Why the hell did he come back to the club? He should've learned his lesson last time.

Before she came any closer, he pursed his lips and shook his head. She stilled, a slight frown creased her brow.

He should explain, but even he didn't know what the hell was happening. All he knew was he didn't want meaningless sex with a random mortal. He wanted...*Holy shit.* He wanted Hailee and only her. Without a word or explanation, he turned away as fast as he could.

Back at the table, he stood rigid behind his chair, gripping the backrest. "Let's split. Jimmy won't give me the whole bottle even if I asked nicely and compelling him doesn't sit right with me."

"Did you get me a drink?" Raven asked.

"Get another one back at the mansion. Let's go."

Raven checked his cell then placed it face up on the table. "Fifteen more minutes."

He clenched the chair tighter. "What the hell?"

"Despite the DJ's reluctance to play my one and only request, I'm not ready to leave yet either." River chugged from the neck of his beer.

"I am." He turned from the table.

"Sit your ass down," Raven growled.

"For real? You're ordering me to stay at the club? A club playing music you hate?"

Raven gave a curt nod.

This was ridiculous. He looked at River, who shrugged his shoulders. No help whatsoever.

"Who are you and what have you done with Rave?"

Raven didn't answer and just as well. He might bite his head off. Clearly, he landed in that alternate universe again. Next, mutant Raine would waltz into the club wearing a pink tutu.

With a huff to verbalize his abundance of dissatisfaction, he pulled out the chair and collapsed into it. He drummed his fingers on the table, not in time with the music, but as a distraction from the muscles coiling tighter and tighter in his shoulders. "I don't know what the hell's wrong with me."

"I do."

He paused the drumming and curled his lip at Raven. "Don't give me that soulmate bullshit again. That's not what's happening. Fate will never forgive me for not telling her about Blaine, she made that loud and clear. She swore to torture me for the rest of eternity, remember?"

River slid his beer to the center of the table with the other empties. "Why don't you believe in soulmates?"

"It's not that I don't believe, it's just…" He threw his hands in the air. "Why are we even talking about this? Is this why you made me sit back down? So, you could quiz me on soulmates? Can't you do that back at the mansion?"

Warmth prickled the back of his neck, flowing down his spine before branching into his veins. His whole body smoldered with a dangerous amount of heat. He knew this sensation. It happened each time…

His back straightened, gaze darting left and right. The staff exit door opened at the rear of the club. Raine strode through first, heading toward their table. His heart pounded against his ribs, faster than ever. Tayla came through the door next, followed by Willow. He leaned forward on the chair. A million butterflies replaced the twisted knots.

Hailee walked into the club, with Aric a step behind her. His breath caught.

His gaze worshiped her as though she were the midday sun, the only cure to healing his broken soul. Her hair was down just how he liked, and she wore a pair of kick-ass heels. Sweet Jesus. Images of her wearing nothing but those heels consumed his head and diverted all vital blood to his groin.

When her gaze drifted to his, the world could've exploded around them and he wouldn't have given a shit. All that mattered was her.

Chapter Thirty-One

She couldn't breathe. Marking something off her bucket list seemed like a good idea at the time. But now, as she stood just inside the club, with the thumping music and all the flickering colorful lights, she suddenly lost her nerve. What if EJ came here for space from her? The others said this was his second home, that he spent as much time here as he did at the mansion. What if she cramped his style?

Aric halted beside her. "You good?"

She nodded, not sure her voice worked in the thick, humid air. Her feet weren't convinced, though, which meant she hovered by the door.

Aric stepped to the side, and she caught sight of EJ standing a few tables away. As though in slow motion, he strode toward her. That damn swagger and the sinful way his eyes locked with hers caused a lump to expand in her throat.

EJ and Aric exchanged words before Aric continued to the Guardians' table. Leaving her alone with EJ.

"Hey, you." He twirled a curl loosely around his finger.

"Hey. I wasn't sure if this was okay…If you minded that I came—"

He crushed his lips against hers, sliding his hand behind her neck, fingers tangling in her hair. By God, the kiss not only took the words from her mouth but also stole the breath from her lungs. She met his desperation, sweeping her tongue over his. This kiss was so different from their others. Intense and all-consuming.

She clutched his shirt at the waist as he backed her against the closed door. A low growl vibrated in his chest. Clearly, he wasn't upset she came to the club.

Once she was a panting, gooey mess, EJ slowed their kiss. His forehead pressed against hers, his breath heavy. "You wanna dance?"

When she nodded, he took her hand and led her to the dance floor. Her lips tingled and her cheeks hurt. Probably from the ginormous smile on her face. But she didn't care. One carefree night was all she wanted. What better way than to spend it with EJ?

As they passed the table where the other Guardians and their soulmates congregated, Tayla returned her smile. They all told her how excited they were EJ had found her. In fact, they even suggested Fate destined the two of them together. Maybe that was true. Maybe he was the hero in her story. Her knight in rock star jeans. But she wasn't convinced about the whole soulmate thing.

Authors filled romance novels with stories of hope and triumph, love conquering all. Characters that, no matter how rocky their path, always found their happily ever after. But real life didn't guarantee happily ever after. In her experience, it rarely existed. Her parents' relationship was the perfect example—twisted, full of lies and deceit, which ended in murder.

That plot was better suited to a suspense novel, not a romance.

Holding her hand, EJ weaved through the crowd on the dance floor until they arrived in front of the DJ booth. With a wave of his arm, the DJ nodded and changed the music mid song. EJ curled his arms around her waist and backed her into the center again.

As he pulled her closer against him, she looped her arms around his neck. The music slowed. The beat softened. Not enough to slow dance like couples did at prom. Enough that she no longer felt the urge to jump up and down waving her hands in the air in time with the music.

The crowd thinned as some made their way off the dance floor. She barely noticed. All her brain power focused on EJ's cheek against hers.

His deep, gravelly voice whispered in her ear, "I can't believe you're here."

She needed water. Her mouth was so dry her tongue stuck to the roof. "I wasn't sure. I mean, the other night when I pulled you into the dream, you were here with…"

"No one. I was here with no one." His arms tightened around her. "I thought coming here was what I needed, but it wasn't."

Her heart pounded faster than the music. "Why wasn't it?"

"Because you weren't here with me."

Air exploded from her lungs in one punch. Her legs quivered. He thought he wasn't a hero. With swoony words like that, he could win over any heroine.

"I suppose Rave and the others were in on this plan?"

"Yeah. Willow did my hair while the guys kept you here until I arrived."

He untucked her shirt and slipped his hands beneath the hem. A dress would've been cooler, more practical for the nightclub, but then his hands couldn't wander.

Swaying side to side, all the horrible things she experienced this week drifted to the back of her mind. Safely cocooned within EJ's strong arms, she imagined having the strength to tackle any obstacle, the courage to keep moving forward.

EJ drew back slightly. "You're so gorgeous."

"You're not so bad yourself."

"I knew it." His smirk set her damn panties on fire. "You do think I'm sexy."

He cut her laugh short by nipping her bottom lip. Teasing a bit before taking her mouth in a deep kiss. His tongue swept over hers, making every cell in her body spark to life. Her fingers tangled in the loose strands of hair sticking out from under his beanie. This is what she wanted. One night to experience firsts.

Music blared through the nearby speakers, and coupled with the heat building between them, her body tingled in all the right places. Surrendering to the sensations came easy. No wonder he came to the club all the time.

Everything felt right. Well, except for the fact she still didn't know his full name. Not knowing drove her insane, and the others were no help, they wouldn't tell her. Did they even know?

She tucked her thumbs into the back pockets of his jeans, tempted to squeeze his ass, but chickened out. "You feel like giving me another hint about your name?"

"Only if you kiss me again."

Done. That was the easiest bargain ever. She kissed him again, slower, savoring the hint of alcohol on his tongue and the wildness in his caress.

He moved his head and nipped at the fleshy part of her earlobe. "EJ is one name, not two."

If she weren't so drunk with lust, she would've slapped him. She did a little. Slapped his firm ass. "Are you saying I've been guessing a given and surname this entire time and I didn't need to?"

He winked. Bastard.

"I came up with all those surnames—"

He cut off her words by kissing her again. Such a good way to stop someone from talking. She quite enjoyed that method.

Still underneath her shirt, his fingers slid to her hips, thumbs circling at the corners of her belly. Wild thrills pulsed between her legs. A painful ache climbed to the apex of her thighs.

Experiencing a nightclub for the first time wasn't the only thing on her list tonight. Another one crept to number one. Guessing his first name could wait.

"EJ," she murmured between kisses. "I…want you."

Lazy hands drifted to her face, cupping her jaw. His nose touched the tip of hers. "You have me, sweetness. You totally do."

He didn't get it. She needed to spell it out for him, but the thought of saying it aloud where others might hear made her cheeks flame.

Fiddling with his hair, she waited for the lump in her throat to lessen. "Raine told me that there's…you know."

"There's what?"

His black short-sleeved shirt hugged his body in all the right ways. The color blended with his ink. She couldn't stop staring at him.

"Um, rooms where we can…"

He nipped her bottom lip. "Do more than kiss?"

God. They were having a conversation about sex in the middle of a dance floor. Thank goodness for the loud music and yay for her immortal hearing, because even with all the noise, she heard EJ just fine.

He smoothed a thumb along her mouth. "Is that what you want?"

Yes. She didn't need experience to know he wanted her too. The hardness pressed against her gave it away. She may be a virgin, but she knew how things worked. "I want this, and I want it with you. I want something good amongst all the bad."

He didn't answer. His gaze diverted to somewhere behind her. Was he looking at the private rooms Raine told her about? Was he deciding? How long did he need to think about it?

"No."

Her stomach plummeted to her feet. No, beneath her feet. Maybe to the center of the earth. "No?"

"No." He nipped her bottom lip again, a little harder this time, and it sent a bolt of lightning down her middle. "When we get naked, it'll be somewhere special. Not in a scummy sex room at a club."

When, not if. Okay, that wasn't total rejection. Was it?

Hot, wet kisses trailed along her jaw before he nibbled on her ear again. "When I take you, it'll be somewhere neither of us have had sex. I wanna experience a first with you."

"I just found out you're…" Kisses drifted down her neck to her collarbone, drawing a moan from her lips. "You're over a thousand years old. Is there anywhere you haven't had sex?"

"Mm-hm." Scorching lips returned to her jaw. "My bed."

If she hadn't lost her breath, she'd laugh. "You've never had sex in a bed?"

He kissed her hard, as though there were no one else in the club. As though the universe depended on it. "*My* bed."

She panted like an idiot. The ache between her legs swelled to a new high. "You've never had a woman in your bed?"

The sinful look in his ice-blue eyes made her insides swirl with fire. So intense. So possessive.

"You'll be the first, sweetness. And you'll be the only one."

Chapter Thirty-Two

Holding her hand, EJ led Hailee back to the table where the others sat, chatting away. Dancing became too much the moment they talked about sex. Sure, he'd thought about it, but having her say it made it real, made him want it more.

He snaked his arms around her middle, pressing her back tight against him. A two-in-one move—it hid his hard-on and ticked the being social box. His brothers went to so much trouble to get Hailee here, they should at least stay for a drink. But socializing was the last thing he wanted when all his thoughts were on the woman in his arms and getting her naked.

Half of him wanted to throw her over his shoulder fireman style and get the hell out of there. More than half. Probably closer to an eighty-twenty split. But the other twenty percent didn't want to rush. Hailee had never been with a guy and he wanted her to be sure. Hell, he wanted her to enjoy sex so much she craved it with him every day for the rest of eternity.

He rested his chin on Hailee's shoulder. Directly across the table, Raven gave him a look. One that expressed his smug satisfaction like he won a bet. He wouldn't put it past his brothers to bet on him and Hailee. Assholes.

That was enough. Socializing time had ended. He and Hailee had better things to do.

Angling his mouth to her ear, he whispered, "Wanna get outta here?"

Through the connection between them, he sensed her pulse spike. She nodded.

"Throw me the keys, Ric, we're heading home." He held out a hand, ready to catch them. "You guys right to fly your wingless warriors back?"

Tayla and Willow had no problem flying with their Guardians.

Aric lifted Willow off his lap just enough to dig the keys from his pocket and throw them across the table.

EJ caught the keys in his hand. Hang on. They were his keys. "You drove Stella?"

"She felt neglected."

He wanted to punch that stupid smirk right off Aric's face. Stella was a one guy kinda gal. She didn't appreciate others taking her for a spin. Especially losers that rode motorcycles.

The plus side? If there was one. Now was a good opportunity to introduce Hailee to the love of his life.

He pocketed the keys and squeezed Hailee's hips. "Let's go, yeah?"

"Okay. See you all later." Hailee waved bye then followed him out.

Four steps away from the table, a prickling sensation erupted on his neck. His stomach churned. He froze, arm tightening around Hailee's waist. They were here.

He spun back to the table. Raven's chair flipped backward as he stood. The others followed. Eyes darted left and right, no doubt sensing the same thing.

A Fallen was close.

Get Hailee the fuck outta here, Raven growled in

EJ's mind.

He didn't need the order, he was already hightailing to the rear exit.

Hailee didn't protest. She kept up with him as they barged through the door and into a back room.

"They're here, aren't they?" she whispered. "The Fallen."

"Yep." No point sugarcoating it. As an immortal, she probably sensed them too, just didn't realize what it meant.

When they reached the door leading into the parking lot, he spun Hailee to face him. "Listen. We're gonna fly. It's the quickest way. I won't let Blaine get you."

Her chest rose and fell in rapid breaths. "When I said I wanted to experience firsts tonight, that wasn't what I had in mind."

"You're gonna do it someday, may as well be tonight. You're safe with me. I promise."

She peered back the way they came. "What about the others?"

"Don't worry about them. It's you the Fallen want."

She nodded. "Okay. What do I do? Just…hold on?"

"Yep. I'm gonna take off as soon as we step outside. They could be in the parking lot waiting, so we can't screw around."

Even in the dimly lit room, he saw her eyes bug out, but she quickly recovered. Turning to the side, he unfurled his wings, tucking them behind his back so they fit through the doorway. Adrenaline soared through his veins and he welcomed the rush. His muscles twitched, shoulders tightened. His wings prepared for flight.

Fighting produced highs equal to sex. Getting his girl to safety was one step higher on the endorphin scale. His girl. That sounded so damn good in his head.

Hailee sucked in a sharp breath. “Your wings. They’re…beautiful.”

He tapped her nose. “Less ogling, more urgency.”

“I am not ogling.”

He cocked a brow. “You totally are.”

“I’m…admiring.”

“When we get back to the mansion, you can admire all you like.”

Her hand fluttered near her chest. “Right. Okay. Let’s do this.”

Hand on the door handle, he inhaled a deep breath. All at once, he flung open the exit, scooped Hailee into his arms, and shot into the night. At a safe height, when the prickling along his neck faded, he hovered in the air, peering back at the parking lot. No Fallen. They must’ve gone inside the club.

His brothers could handle Fallen in a mortal club without him. Even Tayla could throw a decent side kick these days thanks to Raine’s self-defense lessons.

All that remained in the parking lot were a few random cars and poor Stella, waiting for him to take her home. Now she’d spend the night out in the cold and that just pissed him off. Damn Aric for driving her to the club. Why didn’t he drive Willow’s car? Or Raven’s? Anyone else’s besides his.

He mentally sent Stella a silent apology. First thing in the morning, he’d come back for her and treat her to a wash and detail. Turning away, he flew higher into the cloudbank.

Hailee rested her cheek against his shoulder, arms clinging for dear life around his neck.

"You okay?"

"Yeah. Are they following us?"

"Nope. We're in the clear."

She wiggled a little, adjusting her position in his arms. "Good." She paused a moment. "Flying is…kind of thrilling, isn't it?"

Oh, yeah, it sure as hell was. Even more so with Hailee in his arms. Her breath tickled the side of his neck sending all kinds of thrills straight to his groin. "Maybe you'd like to try flying a second and third time?"

"I think I would."

His chest puffed with some unfamiliar feeling, and it felt damn good.

Brisk night air did nothing to temper the heat radiating between their two bodies. Like Hailee had a little furnace stashed beneath her shirt that ignited when they touched.

The mansion came into view, and he lowered out of the clouds to sail just above the pine trees. Her scent of warm sunshine mixed with the earthy pine needles made his head swim.

As soon as he landed on the balcony, he folded his wings back inside his shoulder blades. But he didn't release Hailee. He carried her into his bedroom and kicked the door shut with his foot.

He lowered her feet to the floor nice and slow, adding an extra layer to his little self-torture game. Standing, pressed against his front, she peered up at him. Her eyes hooded, breath heavy, lips slightly parted. Her look undid him in the best possible way.

He stroked his thumb along her lower lip. “We don’t have to do this. You’ve had a lot of firsts tonight, we can wait until you’re ready.”

Hailee stepped back, slipped off her heels, then lifted her shirt up and over her head, dropping it to the floor. Sweet holy mother of Jesus. That lacey bra called to him as much as those shoes did.

“I am ready. I’m so sick of pining over boyfriends who don’t exist. I’m tired of never experiencing life. Tonight proved we need to live every single moment. The Fallen won’t stop hunting me, and Ebony isn’t going to magically come home. I don’t even have a home anymore.”

He cupped her face between his hands as a wave of possession soared through him. “Yes, you do. Right here.”

She shuddered under his touch.

“What if the Fallen found me tonight? What if they were in the parking lot waiting? What if they—”

He crushed his mouth to hers, stopping the words. They couldn’t think about any of that right now, it made it all too raw. The fact she put herself in danger to join him at the club created a hot, bubbling mess of…something he had never felt before. A deep-seated yearning to claim her as his. To tell the whole world that he was off the market and never coming back. Make it clear as hell she had his protection. She had him.

The urge to spend the rest of his eternity in this bedroom with her floored him like a tsunami. Right now, Hailee wanted him, and he couldn’t deny her. He fucking wanted her too.

Chapter Thirty-Three

EJ kissed her with so much heat and intensity the ache between her legs soared to a new height. Higher and higher until it became a delicious burn with no end in sight. Despite the frantic butterflies in her stomach, she wanted this. She wanted this with him.

The back of her knees hit the bed, and she sank onto the covers, crawling backward up to the pillows. He remained standing at the edge. His eyes darkened until they resembled the deepest depths of the ocean.

By the neck, he lifted his shirt over his head. It fluttered to the floor at his feet. A tangled, delicate mess like her heart. Next, he flipped off his shoes.

Her greedy eyes took in all that ink. Utterly gorgeous. On one arm, black, thick wings curved from his elbow and around his shoulder, spreading onto his pec. The other arm was the fight scene with angels and Fallen but with his shirt off, she saw the rest. A black and gray sun shone through the clouds over his shoulder. The Heavens. Another scene stretched along one side on his torso, down his ribs, disappearing around his back. Above his heart were small crosses, so many of them in neat, tiny rows.

"Now you're ogling."

His husky voice rumbled through her middle. She swallowed the giant lump in her throat. "Guilty."

The bed dipped as he crawled onto it, prowling on

all fours toward her. Reaching her feet, he nudged open her legs, and positioned himself between them.

"Why did you leave your jeans on? I know I haven't done this before, but I'm positive they need to come off."

Though, she left her jeans on too because, well, she was too damn nervous to take them off. Secretly, she hoped he'd take care of that for her. Oh, how she wished she owned some sexy panties.

His body hovered above hers, and the heat emanating from his chest, his wild scent, the thrill of flying in his arms all crashed into one massive rush. It made her light-headed.

Bracing himself with one hand beside her head, he used the other to stroke a path along her jaw, down over her collarbone. "Sweetness, we haven't even progressed past first base yet. There's no need to rush."

Oh, man.

"Do we need the other bases? Maybe tonight we could skip them?"

Scorching, hot lips nipped at the sensitive skin at the base of her neck. "Would you skip pages in your book just to get to the sex scene?"

"Of course not, a slow burning build-up is the best."

He lifted his head, and a smoldering smirk curled on his mouth. He was a sex god who'd just chosen his favorite brand of torture to inflict on her. "Slow burn it is then."

"That's not what I—"

His mouth cut off her words again. Tingles exploded throughout her entire body, centering in her core. This was her own fault, she said slow burn, and he freaking grabbed it and ran. A tiny part of her wanted him to end the ache now. A much larger part, the half of her that truly loved the sadistic torture of slow burning romances, wanted this to last forever.

Her neck arched as his tongue trailed a path back to her mouth. "So, we're starting at second base?"

"Nope."

He kissed her again, this time slow and deep. Fingers tangled in her hair and when his tongue swept over hers, her body turned into liquid, melting into the mattress. Hardness pressed against her core. Not at the ache. But so, so close.

He drew back. "Now we can progress to second."

She was a panting puddle. How did he do this to her? How did he even speak properly after that? "What happens at second base?"

Oh, she shouldn't have asked. A spark of downright sin lit in his eyes right before he dipped his head back to her collarbone, kissing a path to her breasts. The bra strap on one side slid down her shoulder. Then the other. Cool air tickled her skin when he flipped down the cup. Before she freaked out about someone seeing her semi-naked, he kissed her breast with the same slow, deliberate motions.

When his kisses moved to the other side, the ache between her legs became unbearable. Her pelvis rocked against his. Each time she did it, he responded, pressing back harder, creeping closer to her ache. The zipper on her jeans pushed on the wrong spot, preventing the friction she craved. Damn jeans. They needed to go.

He took her nipple in his mouth, rolling his tongue, and it nearly ended her.

She fisted his hair. "The ache…make it stop…"

A growl rumbled from deep inside his chest. One hand slid underneath her back, unclipping her bra in one swift movement. The guy was a freaking god. The lacy fabric disappeared from her chest and flew across the room. Cool air kissed the wetness left on her skin, making it tingle.

EJ propped himself up, his eyes liquid fire, the pupils so large they almost swallowed all the blue. "I like you lust drunk."

"Is that what you call it? I call it torture."

That sexy smile returned. "Wanna progress to third so I can take care of that ache for you?"

"Yes," she said with a little too much enthusiasm. "Are there only four bases? Because I don't know how much more I can take."

He kissed her again. Hot, deep, and rougher than the last time. The best way ever to stop her from rambling.

"Four bases, sweetness." He sat back on his legs. Fingers skated along her ribs, down her stomach, halting at the waistband of her jeans. "I'm gonna take off your jeans now, yeah?"

"Finally."

He chuckled, popping the button and lowering the zipper. She lifted her butt off the bed as he shimmied off the jeans. They dropped to the floor. Next, his fingers tucked into the waistband of her panties. Up went her pulse.

"You wanna keep your panties on for a bit longer?"

"No."

Off they went. After tossing them on the floor with the other clothes, EJ crawled back up to her, this time beside her, his bent elbow propping up his head. She rolled onto her side facing him and he hooked her leg over his hips. This close her breasts touched the smooth skin on his chest, and her hands explored his ribs and over his shoulders.

"I'm gonna touch you now."

She nodded. Words didn't work with a lump in her throat. Angling his body over hers, he kissed her. Starting with light nips at her bottom lip, progressing to deep drawn out pulls. Her hyperalert body didn't know which sensation to focus on—the kiss or his fingers inching toward the ache between her legs. Ever so slowly, he crept closer. The moment his feather-light touch stroked the bundle of nerves, air punched from her lungs. She moaned. Unable to control thought or reaction. This was lust drunk. And it felt like heaven.

He stroked and circled, easing the ache only to build it again over and over. But she was a fast learner. The louder she moaned, the quicker he stroked, the closer she moved to that blissful peak.

Just when she thought she'd break and shatter into a million pieces, his finger inched further down. Slowly and gently, it eased inside her.

Oh. My. God. This was heaven. Way better than before.

"Is this okay? Does it hurt?"

She nodded. No. Shook her head. Gah! What did he ask?

"Tell me, sweetness. Good or bad?"

"It's good. So good."

He nipped her bottom lip harder, shooting bolts of lightning through her middle. His finger slid in and out, before being joined by one more.

A sharp sting made her flinch.

His fingers paused inside her. "You okay? Wanna stop?"

"No. I don't think so. I'm okay."

His fingers curled, hitting a glorious nerve deep inside her. The pain subsided, and the ache returned with each stroke.

"Do that again."

He did. He was a good listener.

Sliding in and out, she gradually rocked her hips, gaining more friction against his hand. Taking her mouth in his, he continued kissing her until she lost herself in the feeling of every cell zapping to life. Delicious pressure built up her spine at the same time waves of heat crashed across her body. She rocked harder. He kissed harder, more forceful and possessive, until all the sensations exploded together like fireworks in the night sky, sending her free-falling over the edge of the cliff into a pool of bliss.

If she were a panting mess before, it didn't compare to now. "There's no way the next base could be better than that. They should reorder them."

He laughed, withdrawing his fingers to circle a path between the inside of her thigh, her hip, and up to her belly button. "If you ask me, they're all hot in different ways. But nothing compares to home base."

Nothing could be better than what they just did. "To be sure…I think I need to compare them all. You know, so I have an informed opinion."

"Is that so?" His hand dipped between her legs once more.

"Yes. And I think it's time you took off your jeans."

Chapter Thirty-Four

Scorching hot fire blazed through his entire body. He had never experienced performance anxiety, never worried about his ability to pleasure a woman. Now? He freaked the hell out.

This time was completely different. More intimate. More real. He was naked with a woman on his bed, in his room, in his house. Not in some skanky room at the club, or on the hood of a car.

He was at that faint pencil line again, the one that drew an invisible line between him and Hailee. The one he shouldn't cross because he was a Guardian tasked with her protection. But she wasn't a Chosen, they were both immortals, nothing forbid him from being with her. Yet something told him if he crossed this line, he'd never go back.

Pfft. Who was he kidding? He erased that line days ago when he first kissed her. That line was so far behind him he couldn't even see it on the horizon.

"EJ?"

Shit. While Hailee lay naked beside him, he mentally wrestled with the demons taking up residency in his head.

He teased her bottom lip. A lip he wanted to full-on bite but held back. That might freak her out. Just because he liked it rough didn't mean everyone else did, and until they agreed on a level, he'd stick to little nibbles.

Rolling off the bed, he stood, undid his belt, popped the button, and slid down the zipper. The weight of her gaze burned as hot as the fire inside him. Before discarding his jeans, he grabbed a condom from the back pocket.

"You…uh, don't wear underwear?"

"Nope. You could've found that out ages ago, but you didn't want my answer."

"I'm glad you didn't tell me. Knowing that would've been a little…distracting."

He ripped open the foil packet and covered himself. "Just admit it. You find me sexy."

"You win, I think you're hot." She bit that lip of hers. "And um…impossibly large."

Cocking his brow, he crawled onto the bed between her legs. "Say it again, I didn't quite hear you."

Instead of hearing her giggle, spikes of adrenaline shot through his blood. Not from him but from her. "Hey, are you okay?" Hovering above her, he skimmed his thumb along her jaw. "We don't have to do this if you don't want to."

"I want to. I do. I'm just…"

"What? Tell me, sweetness."

"I think I'm just…nervous. It's kind of overwhelming. I mean…you're real." Her hands smoothed over his shoulders. "This is real."

This time he didn't cut off her rambling. Instead, he let her get it all out, so he knew what she thought without probing her mind. No way in hell he'd do that. If she told him how she felt, then he'd know if she truly wanted this. Because sure as shit, he wouldn't force her to do a damn thing. They would take this as slow as she needed even if the slow burn approach turned his balls purple and killed him.

"Of course, it's real." She laughed, the pitch higher than usual. "I mean, I just never imagined being with someone so…perfect."

He ignored that last part. He was far from perfect. But he wanted this moment to be perfect for her.

"This is real, sweetness. We're real. I have a feeling the connection between us is also very real." He rolled his hips, gliding his hardness along the outside of her core. "But it may hurt a little at first. If it does, we can stop. No questions asked. You're in control here."

She stared into his eyes for a long moment. "Okay."

"Are you sure?"

"Yes. I'm sure."

Balancing his weight on one arm, he gripped himself and aligned at her entrance. Her eyes squeezed shut.

"Eyes open, sweetness. Watch me as I slide inside you."

The second her eyes fluttered open, he eased in. She sucked in a sharp breath, clamping her legs either side of his hips.

"Relax, baby. Just relax." When she did, he eased in further, stretching her little by little even though the pace killed him. "Does it hurt?"

"It's tight. A little uncomfortable, but not hurting."

"Tell me if you want to stop."

As slowly as he could, he withdrew part of the way.

She gasped and dug her nails into his shoulders.

"Do that again."

"What?" He slid in and out. "This?"

"Yes, keep doing that."

Lowering his head, he kissed her slow and deep, relaxing her even further. All the things he did before no longer mattered, because being inside Hailee just hit number one on his top ten things to do.

Pressure built slow and steady, deep in his gut as he rocked inside her. Her hands wandered, exploring his torso and hips. He wouldn't last much longer. It took every ounce of control not to increase the pace. Next time, he'd position her on top so there was less risk of him being too rough.

Sweet baby Jesus. She felt better than the Heavens.

Her hands stilled. Nails dug into his arms. Her back arched off the bed a second before she fell apart, clenching him from every possible angle. He didn't slow, too far gone to stop. He rocked faster, buried his head in the crook of her neck, and kissed her skin. Release punched low in his gut sending a wild rush through his body. The coil in his belly exploded again and again while a single word slammed into his mind. *Mine*.

How he didn't collapse and crush her, he didn't know. His limbs were jelly-like and tingly. When his breathing calmed down enough to actually speak, he lifted his head.

Fuck. He bit her. "Shit. I'm sorry."

"About what?"

He touched the red, swollen mark on her shoulder. "I bit you."

"I know." A sinful grin curled on her swollen lips. "You can do that anytime you want."

Holy fuck. He was so epically done for.

****

He perched Hailee on the side of the bath while he filled the tub and disposed of the condom.

"Can I get pregnant if I'm immortal?"

Swirling his fingers through the water, he gauged the temperature. "Two immortals can't create life on their own. But an immortal and mortal can, as you know. On that theory, no, you can't get pregnant with me."

"And I presume we don't get diseases because, again, we're immortal and I've never been sick."

"Yep." He added a few drops of lavender bath oil he stole from Willow ages ago. She had so much she'd never notice. "Where are you going with this?"

"I think next time I'd like to try without a condom. It felt a little scratchy."

He scooped her into his arms and lowered her into the tub, settling in behind her. "Sweetness, we can try whatever the hell you want."

"Should we check on the others?" she asked, maneuvering herself between his legs.

"Ric sent a text while we were busy. It was only Blaine." He grabbed a washcloth and dunked it in the water. "They're all good and made it back here without an all-out war at the club."

Thank Fate Aric texted because while he and Hailee were busy, he totally forgot about the others.

She shuddered. "Lucky we left when we did."

Blaine wasn't one for public displays of immortality, but they'd underestimated him a lot lately. With Hailee's life at stake, he wouldn't take any chances.

He squeezed the water from the washcloth over her shoulders. "How do you feel? Sore?"

"A little. Nothing too bad. It was worth it." She slid backward to rest her head against his shoulder. "I can't believe I waited this long. I could've been doing this for ages."

That hot, bubbling sensation returned to his middle. "I don't like the idea of you doing that with anyone else."

She shifted, looking over her shoulder at him. "So, you only want to have sex with each other?"

He gave her a playful nip on the shoulder. "Damn straight I do."

"I like that plan."

So did he. Turning around, she relaxed against his chest as he washed her front. The lavender scent mixed with the crisp hint of sunshine made his bathroom smell like Aric's greenhouse. Like they soaked in a field of flowers, and he loved every bit of it. Guess they both experienced firsts today.

"What are the crosses for on your chest?"

His hand stilled. He caught her checking out his ink when she lay on the bed but hoped she hadn't noticed those.

"You don't need to answer. It's okay."

He remained silent for a bit longer. Waited for the sinking feeling to subside. "They're…failures."

Coaxing her into a sitting position, he washed her back so she couldn't spin and face him.

"What do you mean?"

A lump grew in his throat. "As well as her never-ending doom and gloom visions, Fate sends me visions of the future. Bad things. But she sends them as they happen so I can't prevent it. Each cross is a vision I failed to prevent."

Her breath hitched. "There are so many."

"Yep." Instead of tightening, the lump in his throat eased a fraction. He glided the washcloth up and down her arms. "Though she hasn't sent me a failure for a while."

"How long?"

He swallowed. "Since Tayla."

"What happened?"

The one vision that would haunt him for the rest of eternity. "Fate sent me a vision of her car flying off the side of the mountain." He tried to warn her, but she didn't answer his call in time.

He still pictured the devastation on Raven's face, heard the agony in his scream. Still recalled the moment Cole escorted Tayla's soul to the Heavens. Those moments were hands down the worst in his entire existence. For all of them.

"Was she hurt?"

"Yep." His throat closed. "She frickin' died that day."

"Died?"

He nodded, even though she still had her back to him. "She was human. But s'all good, 'cause she's here now."

Hailee remained silent for a moment. "Willow said Fate does things for a reason and sometimes we don't see the reason until we're meant to. But to be honest, she sounds kind of nasty."

He was the first to admit Fate's overachievement on the bitch scale, but he was also one of the few that knew why she became like that. The whole story from beginning to end. "She never used to be. Until all the shit went down with Zath and then Blaine."

Before Hailee quizzed him further on the topic, he made some room between them. "Lean back, let me wash your hair."

After they washed and towel dried, they climbed back into bed, beneath the covers this time. Settling in behind her, he slid one arm under her head and wrapped the other around her waist. With her body flush against his, that same sense of peace flowed through his veins, making it crystal clear he'd chosen exactly the right path.

Chapter Thirty-Five

This was what happiness felt like. Heat radiated through her body creating weightlessness in her limbs. Absolute bliss. Cocooned beneath the covers, she rolled onto her side and opened her lids a crack. The first tendrils of morning hinted through the uncovered windows bathing the room in golden sunlight.

Her limbs ached all over. Like last night she discovered a whole new group of muscles she'd never used before. Which was true. A freaking sex god claimed her virginity. Thinking of EJ and their hours tangled between the sheets returned the ache between her legs. The things he did to her should be illegal—because if he kept doing them, she'd surely become addicted.

He was so considerate, loving, and giving, exactly how she imagined the fictional heroes in her romance novels. How could she have thought that standard didn't exist? All this time, she assumed no man could live up to an author's imagination. But EJ did, he exceeded it in so many ways.

Rolling out of bed, she grabbed a shirt and a pair of sweatpants off the floor and slipped them on. Last night was hands down the best night of her entire life. The first time she'd felt alive, and she could thank EJ for that.

Speaking of EJ. Where was he?

Rather than waiting in bed, she ventured out of the room. Out in the hall, the house was silent, peaceful, no voices or noise to suggest the rest of the house was awake. It must be earlier than she thought.

Remembering EJ's spot on the rooftop, she headed there first. So she didn't wake the rest of the house, she walked as quietly as she could down the hall and up the stairs to the attic. At the far window, warmth tingled in her chest when she spotted EJ sitting on the other side, his back against the chimney flue, arms wrapped around his bent legs.

His head turned her way and the hint of a smile made her lower belly flop. He tipped his chin for her to join him. After grabbing the blanket they left by the window last time, she climbed onto the roof.

"Morning, sweetness."

Holding her hand, he helped her sit between his legs then wrapped his arms protectively around her. "Did you get enough sleep?"

"Yep." She draped the blanket over their legs.

Toasty warm lips nuzzled her neck sending flashes of heat dancing along her skin.

"Do you come here often?"

His chuckle vibrated through her back. "No need for pick-up lines. You already got in my pants."

She gave him a playful slap on the arm.

He was silent for a long moment while his arms squeezed her tighter. "I guess I like the idea of new beginnings."

As if on cue, the sun's golden rays breached the horizon, bursting between the trees. Just like the last time they sat on the roof, patchy snow covered the ground and the outer branches of the pine trees. A chill laced the air, but it didn't bother her. Because EJ's arms were around her or because of her immortality, she wasn't sure. The temperature never really worried her, even less over the past few months.

Snuggling in, she rested her cheek against the tight muscles of his upper arm. "I'm starting to like the idea of new beginnings, too."

He softly nipped her earlobe. "I like sunrises almost as much as I like you wearing my shirt."

A smile warmed her face. She hadn't worn his shirt on purpose. She grabbed the closest one, but she didn't tell him that. Starting now, she might just wear his shirt every night, especially if he rewarded her with his kisses.

Thin, wispy fingers of fog swirled between the tree trunks, reflecting the deep orange of the sun rising. "I think maybe that's what Mom searched for the entire time. A new beginning. But every time she tried to give us one, they found her."

EJ's chin rested on her shoulder. "You know, your mom was super brave for a mortal. For twenty-five years, she remained one step ahead of the Fallen and kept you all safe."

She fiddled with the bracelet on her wrist. "Do you think her soul went to the Heavens?"

The question plagued her almost as much as not giving her mother a proper goodbye.

"I know so. Cole escorted your mother's soul to the Heavens the night she died."

Relief burst inside her chest. Knowing Mom's soul was at peace in the Heavens gave her a little closure. "One day, when everything settles down, I'd like to do something special to give her a proper goodbye."

"Whatever you need." EJ's arms tightened around her, but he didn't speak for a long moment. "You know, regardless of how high your dad sits on the douchebag scale, I think he loved your mom."

She twisted in his embrace to see his face. "Why do you say that?"

"He's an Azrael, he could've taken your Mom's soul to Hell. Instead, he left it in her body."

"Are you defending his actions?"

"No way. He's still a Fallen and still killed her." His lips formed a grim line. "It just got me thinking, you know, that maybe some connections are eternal no matter how hard you try to fight them."

She knew all about fighting feelings. Turning back to the sunrise, she leaned her head against EJ's chest.

Now that they'd stopped talking, her mind focused on their position. Heat from his chest radiated against her back. The steady inhale and exhale of his breath whispered along her neck. Firm, muscular arms wrapped around her, holding her tight in a protective embrace. She wanted to throw off the blanket but removing it made her feel too exposed.

Sitting between his legs not only sent her pulse fluttering, but she couldn't miss how her lower back pressed firmly against his growing hardness. A part of his body she explored last night in the most sensual experience she ever had. And now she wanted that again.

As though he sensed her shift in mood, EJ lightly kissed her shoulder, waited a second then did it again. Her breath quickened, and she tilted her head to one side, giving him more access. He took the hint. Light nips turned into hot, sweet kisses, trailing up her neck.

That ache between her legs returned with a vengeance, exploding tingles along her skin.

EJ's hand slipped underneath her arm, smoothed down her stomach, and halted at the waistband of her sweatpants. "How do you feel? Sore?"

A little but not enough to stop his hand from venturing further south. "No. I'm fine."

His fingers left a scorching trail as they slid under the waistband and beneath her panties. She eased back, widening her legs.

The moment his finger brushed her core, she swore stars exploded before her eyes. He stroked and circled, building her up fast.

"Won't someone see us?" she panted.

At this point, it didn't matter anyway. If he stopped, she'd likely murder him.

"Nope," his deep, thick voice rumbled against her ear. "Lucky for us, you brought a blanket."

Without slowing, his other hand crept up her shirt. His shirt. Whatever. All that mattered was how his skillful fingers careened her toward that euphoric edge.

Pressed hard against her back, he slipped a finger inside her, downright growling as he did it. That blissful edge approached with light speed. His other hand caressed and teased her breast, squeezing and rolling her nipple, sending bursts of pain and pleasure.

The moment he caught the fleshy tip of her ear between his teeth, she flew over the edge in a hard and explosive fall. He continued stroking, milking every pulse from her body until she sagged into a liquid, panting mess.

Both his hands moved underneath her shirt, stroking her belly in feather-light circles. "You wanna slip off those pants?"

God, his voice did sinful things to her lower belly. Wait. She pivoted to gape at him over her shoulder. "You want to have sex here? On the roof?"

He chuckled. "Why not?"

"Umm. Because it might be a bit hard? Or someone might see us."

"It's meant to be hard, sweetness. That's the idea."

"I meant for my back." She pressed her hand against the roof tiles to prove her point.

"Straddle me and I'll put the blanket under your knees."

Heat flamed her cheeks. They tried a few different positions last night but straddling EJ on a rooftop seemed like a whole other level. Was this how he liked it? She already knew he preferred sex a little rough, and turned out, so did she. But having sex outside? On a rooftop? In public? The jury was out on that one.

Her expression must've given away her thoughts. Unless he mindread them.

"Not ready to venture outside?"

"Sorry."

He pinched her chin between his thumb and finger. "Don't you ever say sorry. We'll take this as slow as you want. We have an eternity to discover our favorite spots."

Drawing her closer, he took her mouth in a sweet, deep kiss, turning her inside out.

"Wanna continue in the bedroom instead?"

"Yes." She panted like an addict overdue for her next fix.

He helped her up and climbed through the window first, holding out his hand for her. At the ledge, a chill skated along her neck, so lightly maybe she imagined it. Regardless, she turned and stilled. On the far side of the estate, a shadow moved between the trees, drifting ever so slowly toward the mansion.

"Hails?"

Words choked in her throat as the shadow stopped at the tree line. A male materialized. Then a female. At her gasp, EJ rushed onto the roof, positioning her behind him so fast she barely registered what happened.

Tremors raced along her body, colliding in one giant lump in her throat. Her pulse echoed in her ears, making her dizzy.

EJ spun to face her, gripping her shoulders, bending so they were eye level. "What did you see?"

She shook her head. "Not what." She peered at the now vacant spot at the edge of the trees. "Who."

Chapter Thirty-Six

"Get inside and lock the window."

Hailee stood her ground. "No. I'm not useless."

"Now's not the time for heroics." Holding her upper arm, he nudged her toward the window. Manhandling was a scummy move, but he didn't have time to argue. "I can't go down there without knowing you're safe."

Thank Fate for the Raziel spell on the mansion, preventing a Fallen from entering. Otherwise, those dark angels could waltz in whenever they damn well pleased.

She scoffed, yanking her arm from his grasp.

"You're all the same. Big tough guys hiding the women inside while you beat your chest and fight each other for alpha hero."

"You said you wanted a hero."

Her eyes narrowed, shooting daggers in his direction.

"You said you weren't one."

"Fuck, Hails. Seriously? We're gonna argue about this now?"

"No, we're not. Go save the day, anti-hero."

She climbed through the window and slammed it shut in his face.

Anti-hero? What the hell was that? A frickin' book term?

How the hell did that moment go from rip-your-pants-off hot to icy-cold in a matter of seconds?

Slater. That was how.

At least with Hailee inside, he could sort out what that loser wanted. Hopefully, she wasn't pissed at him for long. Knowing he'd made her angry, no matter the reason, didn't sit well with him.

He couldn't worry about that now.

Code frickin' red, southeast end of the estate, he mentally sent the alert to all the Guardians simultaneously. Quicker than texts and definitely quieter than running around the mansion shouting like a lunatic.

The mental replies came just as speedily, but he didn't wait for a visual. In a split second, he bolted across the roof, unfurled his wings, then leaped into the air. At the edge of the forest, he hovered above the trees, scanning between the branches, searching for any sign of their unwelcome visitors.

Below, Aric and Raine sprinted into the forest, veering off into opposite directions. Out of the corner of his eye, he caught River swoop around the far edge of the estate heading up the road leading to the highway.

Raven hovered beside him, a short sword gripped in his hand. "Who is it?"

Shit. He didn't have a weapon. Not one single dagger. "Slater and the sister." He pointed to a spot below. "Hailee saw them both standing there."

Raven nodded. "You take left, I'll take right. Meet back in the middle."

Angling his body forward, he flew to the left, keeping a few feet above the tree canopy, surveying the property. The morning sun, now risen, warmed his bare arms, tingling along the feathers of his wings. Brisk, winter wind cooled his face. Up in the air, the wind felt like it came straight off the snowfields.

Slater was somewhere in the forest. The nauseating tingle at the back of his neck alerted him to a Fallen nearby. But Slater had the ability to mist. He could disappear and reappear all over the estate while the Guardians chased him like a giant game of cat and mouse. For all he knew, Slater planned exactly that, flaunting the fact he had the power to mist. Unlike the Guardians.

EJ swooped lower, scanning the ground, flying so close to the treetops the high branches smacked his shoes. Nothing.

A branch snapped the instant a Fallen materialized straight underneath him. Without slowing, he tucked his wings and shot between the trees. At the last second, he spun his body to slam his feet into the Fallen's back. The Fallen hit the ground face first.

All at once, mental shouts flooded his mind as more Fallen appeared all over the forest. Each of his brothers engaged in a battle with at least one. Clearly, Slater had recruited some friends.

He didn't need backup anyway, he could fight this Fallen on his own. A weapon or two would be handy. He never left the mansion without one. But inside, he'd never carried. Dumbass mistake he wouldn't repeat now that the Fallen decided to make house calls.

The Fallen leaped onto his feet and spun to face him. Wait. That Fallen wasn't male. He drew back, recognizing her. "Luce? You're a…"

"Fallen. You can say it, EJ. Fate won't strike you down." Dagger in each hand, she swiped them in a tight circle by her side, reminding him again of his weaponless status. “How long’s it been?”

“Obviously, longer than I thought.”

Jesus. He wasn’t big on fighting females, especially ones he had a fling with a few centuries ago. Even if her eyes now glowed crimson.

Luce, however, used that to her advantage and wasted no time engaging. Lightning fast, she swiped a dagger across his front. He leaped back just as the blade sliced his shirt. His damn shirt!

“How ’bout you mist back to Hell?” He motioned between them. “And we forget this ever happened.”

She laughed, swiping the dagger at him again. “And miss this reunion?”

Reunions weren’t his thing either. He hated them almost as much as fighting females, which was second to angels expecting him to save the day.

If she wouldn’t back off, then he’d end this quickly for everyone’s sake. First, he needed her daggers. Hopefully, they were decent. Otherwise, this could waste time he didn’t have.

He scanned the vicinity, searching for a weapon to disarm her. A branch, a stone, anything until he got hold of the daggers. Luce caught on. She was always a thinker. She charged forward, arm raised, prepared to strike. He snatched a broken branch by his feet. Centering his weight, he swung, aiming for her middle. She anticipated his move and raised her forearm, blocking it. The branch snapped, rendering it useless.

“The mortal realm has made you weak.”

Bullshit it had. “No need to be bitchy.” He widened his stance, focusing on her body language, her facial expressions, the way she favored one side slightly over the other.

She laughed, though her arms remained raised in front of her chest like a boxer. “Stop fighting like a little mortal girl.”

Miss Snarky prowled forward.

He held his position, balancing his weight on the balls of his feet. “Hell has made you bitchy.”

Luce still had the same raven hair braided back from her face, still wore a similar style of tight-fitting pants and singlet top. But her eyes were no longer the seductive shade of chocolate brown he remembered, and the crimson wings behind her back stood out like balls of fire against her dark tanned skin.

She wasn’t the same angel he’d gotten hot and heavy with a few times back in the Heavens. Now he only saw the face of the enemy. The soul of another angel stolen and corrupted.

Luce was a Fallen. One who attacked his home and his family. A Fallen who put Hailee’s life in danger.

That last thought sent a wave of adrenaline pumping through his veins. His pulse increased, body coiled, preparing for battle. Mental updates from the Guardians came through fast as more Fallen materialized in the forest. They needed to get this shit under control before the Fallen closed in on the mansion. Hailee, Willow, Tayla, and Ellen were inside. They weren’t Guardians, nor fighters. They were no match for an army of Fallen should they somehow break the barrier spell. Raine’s self-defense training only covered so much.

He’d vowed Hailee his protection, and he wouldn’t fail. Not this time.

In one swift maneuver, he leaped forward, twisting

his body sideways at the last second, shoulder charging Luce in the chest. She grunted, staggered backward, but remained upright. Dagger raised over her shoulder, she slashed at his face in vicious motions. When the dagger was within reach, he crouched and side kicked her knee. Luce's legs flipped out from under her. Her back hit the ground. She commando rolled and leaped onto her feet in a move that impressed him.

"You've been training."

Luce widened her stance, bouncing between the balls of her feet. "We all have." She sneered.

Bad, bad news. Willow told them Blaine recruited an army of Fallen, but they hadn't seen any evidence. Until now. If Blaine and Slater trained the new Fallen, the Guardians had their work cut out for them.

Luce took advantage of his momentary distraction and lunged forward, jabbing a dagger in his arm.

"Fuck." Using her momentum to his advantage, he did a three-sixty and landed behind her. Before Luce twisted, he locked his uninjured arm around her neck in a choke hold. She thrashed, kicking backward at his legs, but he shifted his stance. With his free hand, he clenched her wrist with all his strength and shook. The dagger fell to the ground. He used his foot to drag it within reach. Luce's nails clawed at the forearm currently cutting off her airway. He gritted through the pain and tightened his hold.

He'd make this quick for her. That was the least he could do considering they once had a thing. Nothing that compared to what he now had with Hailee, but still, he kinda felt bad for her. After her soul recovered in Hell, he'd add her to the list of Fallen to save. At this rate, they'd end up with a list a mile long.

With Luce's head still locked in his grasp, he leaned to the side and reached for the dagger. Luce jabbed her elbow backward into his cheek.

Sharp pain burst in his face. "Jesus!"

Centering the weight through his legs, he overpowered her, shoving her face down in the ground. With his knee on her back between her wings, he pinned her down and made her kiss the dirt. From this position she couldn't swipe at him. The last thing he wanted was a gash from those damn talons.

She frickin' fractured his cheek. Any sense of obligation on his part vanished.

Luce kicked her legs, but she'd run out of time. He was done fighting. Dagger palmed tight, he raised it above his shoulder and aimed for the spot between her ribs, directly behind her heart.

Just as he thrust the dagger toward her back, Luce misted. The dagger rammed into the dirt.

"Damn it," he grunted.

Where the fuck did they go? Raven's voice rang in his mind.

Guess all the Fallen misted at the same time.

I've got Slater, Raine replied.

No time for rest. He raced toward Raine, using their shared Guardian connection to guide the way. He and Raven arrived at the same time from opposite directions. Raine twirled a throwing star around her finger, in an epic stare off with Slater.

Arms crossed over his bare chest and a lazy grin, Slater portrayed a relaxed stance, but he fooled nobody. Slater could turn on them at any moment. There was no sense of leftover loyalty for the Fallen Azrael. They needed to take Slater out. Blaine might retaliate, but having one less Fallen to deal with would be worth the risk.

Aric stalked through the forest, approaching Slater from behind, halting a few feet away, daggers in both hands. River hovered directly above, arrow nocked in his bow. The Guardians surrounded Slater.

Raine scoffed, pointing the tip of a throwing star at Slater's legs. "Are you seriously wearing leather pants?"

"Denim is a fire hazard, princess."

Raine got right in Slater's face goddamn fast. She jammed the heel of her dirt-covered red shoe into his boot. "I don't give a shit whose bitch you are, don't you ever call me princess again."

Slater grinned so wide Raine might just stab him in the eye with her shoe. No such luck.

Before the party started, Raven intervened. "Back off, Raine."

Raine twisted the heel a few more times before retreating. Note to self: don't get on her bad side.

"You're on our property, surrounded. Unless you want another visit to those torture pits, I suggest you mist back to Blaine." Raven's voice was full of authority.

"Relax. Blaine sent me to negotiate a deal for the Dumahel."

Raven's voice deepened. "You brought an army of Fallen with you to negotiate a deal?"

"It got your attention, did it not?"

Heat raged through EJ's blood, his hands curling into tight fists. He stalked toward Slater. No way in hell they'd negotiate over Hailee. "You can remind Blaine that Hailee is not up for negotiation."

Slater cocked his head, that smug smirk back on his face. “He mentioned your little attachment to her.”

“Shut your mouth, asshole.”

Slater barked a laugh. “EJ, the notorious party boy, brought to his knees by a half mortal.”

A white-hot rage overtook all sense and reasoning. He charged at Slater, fist curled—

Someone snagged his shirt at the same time Raven growled a warning in his mind. He spun and shoved free of Raine’s grasp, giving her a look he hoped was as dirty as the gin martini she drank. She, of course, remained unfazed.

“You lose your balls when Fate exiled you?” Slater heckled.

If he were any closer, he’d kick that Fallen Azrael in the goddamn balls and watch him scream like a little baby. They were buddies before Fate exiled the Guardians, but that all blew up in smoke the moment Slater Fell.

Instead, he ignored the smartass remark, refusing to let Slater know just how much Hailee meant to him. *Duh. Bit late for that.*

You finished? Raven snapped.

“Yep,” he replied aloud.

To prove his point, he kicked the dirt and sent a twig flying toward Slater just for the hell of it.

The tiny stick hit Slater’s leg. He ignored it. “What’s your price, Raven?”

“Hailee is under our protection. We’re not handing her over.”

“Protection?” Slater exaggerated leaning back, glancing up, then left and right. “How are you protecting her if you’re all out here with me? I hope for your sake she doesn't wander outside that Raziel spell."

Chills ran down EJ's spine. Where the hell was Hailee's sister? In all the drama with Luce, he'd forgotten about the twin. If she was still here somewhere, she might lure Hailee outside without protection.

Frickin' hell.

Without waiting for the others to catch on, he spun and bolted to the mansion.

Chapter Thirty-Seven

Hailee slammed the door closed in EJ's room loud enough the whole town could've heard. Certainly, the household.

Get inside and lock the door. EJ's words made her blood run hot. Her sister was out there with the Fallen who helped kill her mother. Her sister was with a murderer.

She paced back and forth, doing all she could not to stamp her feet. Was this EJ's idea of protecting her? Putting himself in danger? He promised protection from the Fallen and right now he was outside risking his life. Placing not just himself but his entire family in harm's way. For her.

Another death on her hands would send her over the edge. If she hadn't pulled him into a dream…if she hadn't told him her location…if she hadn't gotten in the car with him.

But she did. No point dwelling on all the choices she could've made, it wouldn't change anything.

Was this how EJ felt every time Fate sent him a vision? How he dealt with that burden, she'd no idea. Dealing with her mother's death was bad enough, let alone if the Fallen hurt any of the Guardians or Ebony because of her.

Thinking she, or anyone, could influence the future was absurd. Laughable. But a month ago, she didn't even know the immortal world existed. Maybe she could stop this before someone else paid with their life. She needed to at least try.

Pausing beside the bed, she contemplated the situation. In her romance novels, the bad guys reappeared toward the end for an all-out battle. But the battle outside wasn't some action scene in a book where no matter how brutal the fight, the good guys always won. So far, real life proved more dangerous than she ever imagined.

In her story, EJ locked her away in a fortress like a fairytale princess while he fought the baddies. Forget that. She never sat on the sidelines and watched. And she wasn't about to start. She was the heroine of this story, a grown woman, half immortal, who didn't need approval or a hero to rescue her from the tower. She would take control and save her sister herself.

Ebony chose the wrong side of this fight and until they ended this stalemate between them, the danger would continue chasing them both.

A foreign buzz stirred in her body, like millions of fireflies beating their wings, sending vibrations through her blood, the sensation was weird but not uncomfortable. She concentrated on the flutters. They swelled and intensified until her entire body felt alight. Power. Ebony spoke of power like this.

With her sister outside, and her own powers strengthening, it wouldn't take much effort to contact Ebony through a dream. Already the thread charged under the surface, preparing for connection. She sat on the edge of the bed and took a few deep breaths to steady her heart rate.

She fiddled with the Purah ring on her finger,

twirling it around in a full circle, giving herself a boost of…what? Confidence? Stupidity? Ebony wouldn't hurt her, she knew that without a doubt. By controlling the dream, she could prevent the Fallen from magically appearing. But if something went wrong, at least she had a secret weapon.

Closing her eyes, she prepared for the dream. Mentally, the connection sparked to life and exploded into the ether, finding Ebony in less than a second. Her stomach lurched, flipping upside down as though she were on an out-of-control carousel. As quickly as the sensation came, it disappeared.

Brisk air caught in her lungs. Slowly, she opened her eyes and scanned the area. No Fallen ambushed her, so that was a plus. But something seemed different. A thin veil of fog drifted along the ground. Beams of early morning sunlight streamed between giant pines, but the light didn't chase away the eeriness. An earthy hint of fresh pine needles filled the air. This wasn't the usual place she found Ebony in her dream. No living room, no lit hearth. In fact, this forest seemed awfully similar to the forest on the Guardian property.

To her left, at the base of the nearest tree was a patch of wildflowers she watched Willow grow just yesterday. Chills danced along her skin. Because she controlled the dream, had she somehow created a replica of the forest or did she unknowingly…

A lump jammed in her throat, she turned in a one-eighty and gasped. Past the tree line, a manicured lawn led right up to the Guardian mansion.

What the hell?

"Hailee?"

She spun around and found Ebony standing by a

tree. Her usual pale skin all blotchy, eyes puffy and red from crying.

"What's wrong?" She scanned the forest one more time. "How did I get here?"

"Your powers. When you connect with an angel, you can mist to where they are." Ebony wiped her cheeks with the back of her hand. "And of course, wherever I am."

Huh. That seemed like a handy skill. "Can you do this, too?"

Ebony nodded.

"Why haven't you misted to me?"

"Your bracelet." Ebony's bottom lip quivered as though fighting back a fresh batch of tears.

"Oh, God. I'm sorry." Hailee closed the distance and drew her sister in, hugging her tight. "Tell me what's wrong."

Quiet sobs rocked Ebony as she buried her head in the crook of Hailee's neck.

"I'm so stupid."

"You're not stupid. What happened?" She leaned back and smoothed Ebony's hair away from her face.

Her sister remained silent.

"Tell me, Eb, please. Has someone hurt you?"

Ebony shook her head. "I just…I've made a huge mistake."

She started crying again and laid her head back on Hailee's shoulder.

When the sobs softened, Hailee drew Ebony down with her to huddle at the base of a tree, cradling her sister's hands in her lap. If they were on the Guardian property, and all signs pointed to exactly that, then she and Ebony needed to remain hidden. That murderous

Fallen could find them at any minute.

She wiped the tears from Ebony's cheeks. "What happened?"

Ebony inhaled a deep breath, seeming to steady her voice. "I thought being with Dad was the right thing to do. I thought he'd help me. But all he did was trick me." Her voice cracked. "I'm sorry I didn't believe you."

Her body tensed at the mention of their psycho father. "Of course, he tricked you. I told you that from the start, but you refused to listen. He murdered Mom."

"I know. I'm sorry."

She checked her anger. This wasn't the time nor the place to lash out at Ebony. "What did he do?"

"He made a deal with this other Fallen, Blaine. I have to pull him into a dream, but I don't want to…I just want to go home."

Some part of her hoped the Guardians were wrong, that Ebony wasn't with Blaine. But this proved otherwise. From what she knew, Blaine sounded like the baddest of all bad guys.

"Don't do it. Just leave. If you can mist like I can, come here. I'll take the bracelet off so you can find me. The Guardians will keep you safe."

Ebony shook her head. "I can't. He has me locked in Hell and won't let me leave until I pull him into the dream." Her lip quivered again.

God, she'd never seen Ebony this upset in her entire life. Growing up, she'd just adapted and moved on, without letting her emotions get in the way. For her to cry like this…

Ebony squeezed Hailee's hand tight. "I hoped that…maybe if you were there too, I could do it. He promised to let me go once I helped him. But I'm too scared to do it alone in case something goes wrong."

A heavy, sinking sensation swirled low in her belly. She let go of Ebony's hands and stood. "No way. I'm not helping you pull a Fallen into a dream. They're dangerous, Ebony, haven't you realized that already?"

Her sister stood. "I know that now. That's why I need your help!"

Hailee backed away, shaking her head.

"Please, Hailee. I don't want to be here anymore. I want to be with you. He won't free me until I do it."

Ebony once again expected Hailee to come to her aid. Connecting with a Fallen wasn't like sweet talking a police officer down at the local station, convincing him to take it easy on Ebony. Our mom's sick, she's just acting out, blah, blah, blah. No, this was far worse, and a thousand times more dangerous. How dare Ebony expect her to bail her out whenever she felt like it?

She wanted this to stop, for the fighting and danger to end. It ended now. Now she needed to push down her emotions and do the right thing.

"I can't, Eb. I'm sorry, but I won't do it. Sooner or later, you need to face the consequences of your actions. Now is that moment." She retreated a step, even though it shredded her heart. "I told you I wanted no part in this. You chose them and got yourself into this mess, so now you can get yourself out."

She turned to face the mansion and the bracelet on her wrist exploded with iridescent blue. A Fallen was near. Her time was up.

"Don't leave me," Ebony cried.

Before she changed her mind, Hailee mentally snapped the dream connection with Ebony. Her vision swirled, skin tingled, stomach flipped. In a split second, she was back in the mansion, sobbing on the floor at the foot of EJ's bed.

Chapter Thirty-Eight

EJ burst through the front door as though Hailee's life depended on it. Because it did. He didn't give a shit about hinges or splintered wood. All he cared about was her, and why the hell Willow and Tayla couldn't find her.

Racing up the stairs, he took two, then three at a time, bolting to the second floor. At the top, he swung left and nearly knocked Willow flat on her ass. "Where is she?"

"I don't know. Tayla is checking the garage. She's not in any of the rooms on this floor, I already checked."

He ripped off his beanie to rake his fingers through his hair. "How the hell could she disappear from inside the house?"

"We'll find her. The Raziel magic prevents a Fallen from entering, and we'd know if someone broke the protection. She's safe inside."

"Unless she went outside."

What if Ebony lured Hailee outside? While he and the others were dealing with the damn Fallen, Hailee could've gone outside to find her sister and ended up getting kidnapped.

Willow clasped his shoulder. "Use your connection with her. The one you refuse to acknowledge."

He didn't refuse to acknowledge it, he just didn't

know what the hell to do with it. Or how to deal with it. Or how it even functioned. For his brothers, it seemed like this shit came naturally. For him, not so much. But he'd use every means possible to find Hailee.

Slowing his breath, he focused on the tendrils of light entering and exiting his soul like a wireless transmitter. That same light only he saw suddenly burst from him and shot forward, straight through the door to his room. He raced past Willow, along the hall, and flung open the door. Hailee huddled on the floor by his bed, with her head in her hands.

"Sweetness," he whispered through the weight crushing his lungs.

Mentally, he sent out a message to the Guardians to cease their search. Willow needed a serious lesson in search and rescue if she couldn't find Hailee in his own damn room.

Hailee lowered her hands, her eyes puffy and red.

In an instant, he was beside her, pulling her up from the floor and into his arms. "Jesus. I thought you went outside." He squeezed her tighter, breathing in her summery warmth. "I freaked out when the girls couldn't find you. Were you hiding from Willow? She said she checked all the rooms."

Hailee curled into his embrace, wrapping her arms around his waist, her cheek against his chest.

"I'm sorry. I wanted to be alone."

He stroked his fingers through her wavy hair, twirling bits of loose strands, more to calm himself but it probably had the same effect on her.

They stood there for what seemed like hours. When his breathing steadied and that damn ache in his chest eased, he drew back slightly to look at her face. "Hey."

He smoothed a thumb over her cheek. “I’m sorry for being an ass before, shooing you away. I…don’t want you to get hurt.”

Instead of answering, she rose on her toes and kissed him. It started light, a touch of her warm lips against his, but within seconds she took control and he let her.

Minutes ago, he thought he lost her, that a Fallen had captured her. Now she was here, in his arms, kissing him in a way that made him want to strip her naked and have her right here against the wall. Her mouth on his set that light in his soul on fire.

The kiss was a distraction to avoid talking about what made her cry, he knew that. Hell, he had used that technique on her a few times. But they couldn’t rely on distractions forever. For once, he needed to be responsible and sort out the emotional shit first. Something made her cry, and that didn’t sit right with him. Not one bit.

He slowed the kiss and drew back, much to his dissatisfaction, and cupped her face in his hands. “I’m sorry. I won’t push you aside like that again.”

She didn’t answer for so long he wondered if he spoke or just thought the words. Her gaze drifted to his arm.

“You’re bleeding.”

“I’m fine.” He lifted her chin, redirecting her attention back to him. “I really am sorry, sweetness.”

As she nodded, her eyes filled with unshed tears. “I’m worried about Ebony.”

What a douchebag. Big fat douchebag. So focused on what made her cry, he totally forgot to tell her about her sister. “I didn’t see her. Only Slater and his team of losers. Ebony wasn't there."

The tears fell freely, and he scrambled to brush them away with his thumb. When he said he wanted to sort out the emotional shit first, he didn't want to make her upset again. "We'll find Ebony, she'll be okay. I promise."

"No, she won't. She's scared, and I left her there with those monsters."

He stilled. "Wait. She contacted you?"

Hailee nodded.

"What did she say?"

"She doesn't want to be there. She wanted me to help her, but I just can't. I can't do it anymore. I'm sick of being the one who carries the burden. I'm not her mother, I'm her sister."

He tucked her head back against his shoulder. Seeing those tears caused strange, wild, caveman feelings he couldn't identify or unpack right now. "Sshh. I've got you."

He'd hold her for as long as it took for her to get it all out. That's what soulmates did. His brothers spoke of a bond so strong it felt as though a second heart beat alongside their own. Right now, he felt exactly that. A bond that made him want to do anything for her—comfort her, protect her, even kill any deadbeats that dared to look at her sideways.

He couldn't deny it any longer. Hailee was his soulmate.

His. One single word had never felt so right or made him feel so whole. For some bizarre reason, Fate sent Hailee to him, and he wasn't gonna let that slip through his fingers.

****

Hailee's mind was a hazy mess from all the tears. At some point, EJ helped her undress and climbed into bed with her. For the past hour or so, she lay there wrapped in his arms while he dozed on and off. With one arm tucked under her head and the other curled around her waist, he held her tight against him. Almost like he subconsciously feared she would leave.

All she did was stare at the bare wall. The perfectly painted light gray wall.

Dread filled her belly. She couldn't sleep even if she wanted.

Did she do the wrong thing? The first time in history Ebony asked for help, not expected it, actually asked. In the forest, Ebony looked like a mess. And she'd abandoned her sister in the presence of a Fallen.

What the hell was she doing lying in bed with EJ while a Fallen imprisoned her sister in Hell? At the time, Ebony didn't know how bad the Fallen were. But she refused to listen no matter how many times Hailee warned her. If her sister made better choices, she wouldn't be in this position.

Without moving too fast so she didn't wake EJ, she grabbed her book from the nightstand and opened to the last chapter. Anything to distract herself from the back and forth.

It didn't matter where she started, she'd read the novel so many times she could recite the whole thing. The ending was her favorite. The part where the couple was in love and blissfully happy. They overcame every obstacle, defeated all the baddies, and finally realized they were stronger together. That life was better together. The last chapter of a romance gave a warm tug on her heart, proving that love always triumphed above everything else.

Just not for her.

EJ stirred and tightened his arm around her waist. He snuggled closer, molding her body against his until they were almost one. She closed the book and slid it back onto the nightstand.

"Elijah."

His sleep groggy voice murmured against her ear.

She glanced over her shoulder. "Huh?" He loosened his hold a little as she flipped onto her other side to face him. "Who is Elijah?"

He remained silent for several heartbeats before answering. "Me. My name is Elijah."

Oh, no. He finally told her, and the timing sucked. She didn't respond. She couldn't. While he opened his heart to her, she lay in his bed torn between staying and leaving to save Ebony.

He swept the hair from her face.

"I shortened it when Fate banished us to the mortal realm."

"Elijah isn't cool enough for you?" Lightening the situation masked the ache building in her chest. Kind of.

He didn't laugh, just kept touching her, trailing a feather-light path along her skin. Starting at her jaw, his hand slipped under the covers to continue along her arm, over her hip and back up again.

"Elijah comes with all this pressure to save humanity. Responsibility. Expectations I couldn't live up to anymore."

He paused, and she bit the inside of her lip so she didn't interrupt.

"When Fate banished us from the Heavens, I left

that part of me behind. Created a new me." His brows drew together. "EJ can't disappoint anyone if no one takes him seriously. No one expects great things from him if they know he's always destined to fail."

That ache swelled in her chest, squeezing her ribs. Suddenly, his reluctance to be the hero made sense. "What happened?"

He took her hand and placed it over the tiny black crosses inked above his heart.

"I failed the one Guardian who truly needed me." His gaze grew distant. "I knew Blaine planned to Fall. I knew it and I didn't tell Fate. I didn't tell anyone."

He curled his fingers between hers.

"I figured he wouldn't actually follow through. He'd threatened to Fall before. I didn't see it coming."

"You can't blame yourself for someone else's choice." The irony of that statement wasn't lost on her.

"Why not? Fate does. When I told her, she cursed me with visions of the future and said I'd never have that excuse again." He exhaled a long breath. "If I stopped Blaine, none of this would've happened."

With her free hand, she cupped his cheek. "Maybe. Maybe not. But if you weren't here, we wouldn't have found each other."

That last thought broke a massive crack through the center of her heart. If they hadn't found each other, then she wouldn't need to choose between him and Ebony. But did she really need to? She couldn't blame herself for Ebony's actions. Ebony was a grown adult and half immortal, just like her.

He released her hand to brush his thumb over her lips. "You know, all this exclusive kissing made me realize something."

“What?” she whispered, almost afraid to hear his answer.

“I like you, sweetness, a lot. In fact, I’m damn sure I love you.” He paused, the back of his hand resting on her cheek. “Having a soulmate scares the hell outta me. I don’t wanna fail you.”

Her reply jammed in her throat. His soulmate? She suspected all along, hoped even, but hearing him say it aloud made the whole situation a thousand times worse. Again, the timing was so horribly wrong.

If she were honest, she fell in love with him long ago, but what would saying it now achieve? It only made her choice harder.

Instead, she tried to lighten the mood again. “I thought you didn’t believe in soulmates?”

That sexy grin of his did wicked things to her belly.

“I’m man enough to admit when I’m wrong.”

He gave her hip a playful squeeze.

“I didn’t think a lot of things were possible, but I can’t deny what’s between us. I don’t know what Fate’s game is or why she matched you with a broken Guardian like me. All I know is if this is a soulmate connection, then I want it for the rest of eternity.”

Propping himself up on an elbow, he leaned over and kissed her nice and deep, slow and delicate. A kiss that bled right into her soul.

Before things progressed, he drew back. “Let’s go grab some food. Emotions make a guy hungry.”

He grinned, and just like that, he sucked her back into his world until staying with him seemed so right she couldn’t imagine it any other way.

Chapter Thirty-Nine

Sitting at the dining room table, Hailee pushed a slice of carrot around her plate with her fork. She couldn't eat it. Not because of the lack of seasoning or Ellen's cooking skills, the food was delicious, but because of the churning in her stomach.

She felt like a fraud. This makeshift family took her in, protected her from the Fallen, and vowed to find her sister. EJ said they were soulmates, told her he loved her. Now she sat at the table, acting as though everything was fine when it wasn't. Far from it.

The entire household gathered for an evening meal every night and the room bustled with different conversations. Tonight, EJ sat beside her chatting with Aric across from him, laughing at something Aric said. The entire time, his hand remained on her thigh. A protective and reassuring gesture that was all wrong given the turmoil happening in her gut.

After finishing his meal, EJ grabbed the back of her chair and pulled her closer so he could whisper in her ear. "When I woke earlier and found you reading that book, I got all ragey. Like I have competition in the form of a burly kilt-wearing guy. Have you forgotten I don't like sharing?"

She glanced at him, holding back a smile. "You're jealous of a book boyfriend?"

"Pfft. Let's not get carried away, sweetness. A

fictional dude can't make you scream their name like I can."

She gasped, slapping his leg. "EJ!"

He relaxed in the chair with a smirk of utter satisfaction and total smugness. "Yeah, like that, only much louder."

She shook her head. How did she even respond? He was so full of himself. And rightly so, he made her scream his name. Loud and often.

In the split second of silence between them, her smile faded, and the dread returned.

"You're not hungry?"

She moved the carrot to a different position and stared at it some more. In case it sprouted wings and flew around the room. "I guess not."

He tilted her chair toward him, balancing it on two legs. She gripped the edge of the table to avoid sliding off. "Clearly, you need to work up an appetite. I can help with that."

She forced a fake smile.

Down went her chair, back on all fours, though his arm remained along the backrest. "Hey, what's wrong?" He pinched her chin so she couldn't turn away. "Are you all right?"

Before she answered, Cole strode through the double doors. His long, heavy strides made the dread sink lower until it consumed her body. Although they hadn't really spoken, she knew who he was and his role in the immortal world. Cole was the angel in charge of finding Ebony in Hell.

When Cole's gray eyes focused on her and EJ, his expression tightened, mouth forming a grim line.

Cole halted beside Raven at the head of the table.

"Raven, I need to speak to you about the…twin."

Ice froze her veins. She couldn't move. Conversations around the table halted all at once, filling the once bustling space with eerie silence.

EJ's hand moved to her shoulder, his thumb drawing circles at the base of her neck. "What's going on, Reaper?"

Aric pulled out the vacant chair beside him. "Have a seat, man."

Cole glanced at Raven. When Raven gave a curt nod, Cole sat at the table. "I tracked the sister."

EJ lightly squeezed her shoulder.

"She is in Aralim with the Fallen Azrael, just like Hailee said." Cole's gaze landed on her. "Her soul is clouded with darkness. The Azrael blood running through her veins will allow her to travel to Hell, but it won't prevent the change. If your sister remains there much longer, she'll become a Fallen."

That dread in her belly exploded like an avalanche, taking out everything in its path. If they didn't save Ebony soon, she'd turn into a monster like their father. Like Blaine. For over three centuries, the Guardians attempted to save Blaine. What if Ebony became a Fallen, and it took that long to save her? Or longer?

She was so stupid. Ebony had begged for help. The longer Ebony denied Blaine's demand, the more her soul blackened. She turned her back on her sister and played happily ever after with EJ. She left her sister in Hell.

Guilt threatened to swallow her whole. Protecting her family, protecting Ebony, came first. Not some fantasy fairytale.

She shoved away from the table. "I can't do this."

****

EJ raced after Hailee. “Hails, wait up.”

She didn’t stop. She ran to their bedroom, throwing open the door and rushing inside. He followed. Chills danced through their connection, a clear indication she was freaking the hell out.

But when she started shoving things in her backpack, he joined her little freak out session.

He slowed his steps and leveled his voice. “Hey, sweetness. Whatcha doing?”

“Leaving.” Backpack in hand, she whooshed past him to the bath.

It took a second for the word to register in his brain, but when it did, he snapped into action. Leaving? Not on his watch. Not without him.

He stood in the doorway as she shoved her toiletries in the backpack. “Leaving, as in we’re going on a vay-cay? Because I don’t think that’s a smart idea. You know, with all the Fallen shit.”

Her hand stilled, clasping her toothbrush. “As in I’m leaving.”

He figured she meant that, but he needed to be sure. Women sometimes said things when they meant the complete opposite and he never understood it. He had hoped this was one of those moments.

Finished gathering a handful of toiletries, she tried to exit the bath, but he blocked her.

“EJ, please. Let me pack the rest of my things.”

“No.” When her beautiful, endless blue eyes locked on his, a sharp, crippling pain ripped through his chest. “Not until you tell me what’s going on. Tell me why you want to leave so suddenly.”

Jesus. He needed to get his breathing under control.

It rushed in and out so fast it made his pulse buzz in his ears.

"It's not sudden. I've been thinking of leaving for a while."

He stepped into her space, so close she tilted her head to maintain eye contact. "You're lying to me. I can feel it."

Her face blanched, but she didn't back down. "I won't sit around waiting until you and the other Guardians come up with a plan to save Ebony." Her voice rose. "Her soul is at stake. Don't you get that? She's in Hell!"

"Of course, I do. I get that more than you think." He moved to cup her jaw, but she retreated a step. "I'll come with you. You, me, and Stella. We'll go together. Just tell me where we're heading."

She shook her head. "No."

"Sweetness—"

"I don't want you to come with me."

What the hell? Hailee took advantage of his shock and pushed past him into the main bedroom. He spun and found her on the other side of the bed. "You don't mean that."

"This was fun, amazing, but that's all it was meant to be. A snippet of time, a distraction from reality. Something good in a world full of bad. But it was never going to last."

He stepped toward the bed, raising a hand, palm facing her. "Hold up. Are you saying you used me for sex?"

Her heart thundered as fast and as loud as his, in perfect unison. No doubt about it, she was his soulmate, not some one-night stand at the club. Why wouldn't she tell him the truth?

She snatched her book off the nightstand. "You said so yourself. You don't want responsibility or people expecting things from you. All you want is a carefree lifestyle. No commitment. I want the complete opposite. This would never last."

He rounded the bed in an instant. She gasped, staggering backward until her back pressed against the wall.

"I'm familiar with the concept of casual sex. In fact, it's all I've been familiar with for my entire existence."

Flattening his hands on the wall on either side of her head, he pinned her in place.

"What we have between us is more than just mind-blowing sex. It's a connection that's destined to be forever. I know you feel it. You can't walk away from that."

"You can't give me what I want. I want a knight in shining armor to spend the rest of my existence with. Someone who pulls me free from the shadows into the light. Someone to fight the demons in my nightmares. It took until this morning for you to even tell me your real name."

He flinched.

Her gaze held his, full of conviction and downright stubbornness. "I want a hero, EJ, and you passed on that role."

"Fuck, Hails."

He snatched the book from her hand and waved it in her face.

"This is fiction. Made up. Heroes like this don't really exist. You put these dudes on a fucking mile-high pedestal that an ordinary guy like me can't possibly compete with." He tossed the book onto the bed. "Is that what you want? To live your immortality with a fucking imaginary guy?"

Tears welled in her eyes. "I don't want this mess."

"Too bad. Life is messy. Real life is raw, hard, and full of shit. But that's what makes it life." He invaded her space once more, cupping her face. "This between us is as raw and real as it comes. Stop pretending you don't feel it."

She yanked the neck of his shirt and slammed her lips against his. Hard. Not the heated, slow burn kisses they usually started with, but a teeth clashing, breath punching, rough kiss that flipped his mind into a frenzy. She ripped off his belt then his shirt. Buttons from her shirt pinged across the hardwood floor as he tore it off. Bits of lacey fabric fell to the ground. He stripped off the remainder of her clothes and lifted her with ease to lock her legs around his waist, while unbuckling his jeans.

Using the wall for support, he surged inside her. Not eased. Almost like proving a point that life was raw and full of moments like these. Moments that forced emotions and fears to the surface.

Within seconds, she screamed his name, balanced at the edge of her release. He wasn't far behind. Tiny tremors pulsed through his blood while her nails dug deep into the flesh on the tops of his shoulders. He hoped they left tiny half-moons all over his skin.

She bit his lip, hard, drawing a possessive growl from deep in his chest. An urge to not only have her, but to properly claim her as his, surged through him. Here and now. None of that half-hearted shit. He ignored the connection for too damn long.

They needed moments like these. Not rough, all-consuming sex, but real, raw emotions on display. With one hand behind her head and the other gripping her thigh, he pounded deep inside her. Each thrust a reminder of what they built together in the short time she was in his existence. How she found his heart and tattooed her name on it without him even realizing.

The humid, heady scent of sex filled the room. Sweat slid down his torso, smearing between his chest and her breasts. Kissing became too much. One of them would surely crack a tooth. Instead, he put his mouth to better use sucking the crook of her neck.

Her thighs squeezed his hips a second before she fell apart, clenching him inside her over and over. Still, he didn't stop, continued to drive into her heat.

After this, he'd take her in the tub and show her how those raw and gut-wrenching moments turned into sweet, tender ones. Because life was about balance. Taking the good with the bad. He realized that now.

Digging his fingers into the top of her thigh, he thrust harder, faster, until release quaked through her again. The sensation so powerful it lit up their soulmate bond like an exploding sun, flinging him over the edge with her. He erupted inside her as a brilliant white light burst between their souls until he thought it would never end.

Their heart rates steadied and the last of the ripples faded, leaving them both a sweaty, tangled mess. He rested his forehead against hers, clutching her tighter in his arms while their hot, panting breaths collided between them.

Moments like this made life worth living. They

made him look forward to the future. Moments like these made him feel whole. Worthy.

"Sex doesn't fix everything, I know that. But whatever it is, I'll fix it. We'll fix it together." He brushed his bruised lips against hers. "I won't fail you."

Chapter Forty

Hailee lay in EJ's bed with his strong arms wrapped protectively around her waist while he slept. Only this time, she felt like an imposter. As though she were inside someone else's body or living someone else's life. In a way, she was.

Her mind refused to quiet, filled with a mental countdown of Ebony's remaining time as a Dumahel before she became a Fallen. Soon, the bomb would detonate, and she'd lose her sister for good.

EJ stirred, making her heart leap. She didn't dare move. Instead, she inhaled a ragged breath through her nose to steady her heart rate. Although the soulmate bond confused and intrigued her in equal parts, she knew enough of the basics by now. EJ sensed her emotions and she could feel his. A single invisible tether connected the two of them and she was about to tear it apart.

Even though he refused to admit it, he was her hero from the beginning. Everything she ever wanted. But now wasn't their time. Right now, she needed to put Ebony first.

The gravity of her decision caved in from all directions. EJ lay behind her while she turned her back on their new beginning. Should she write him a note? Tell him not to follow her? No, there wasn't time. If she didn't hurry and connect with Ebony, EJ would sense her decision and try to stop her. Just like he did earlier.

This time she couldn't let him. Nor would she put him or his family in any more danger. She needed to do it on her own. Tears pooled behind her closed lids, and she bit the inside of her lip to prevent them falling while her heart tore into tiny pieces.

Time was of the essence. She couldn't waste another second thinking about what could've been or what her life with EJ would've been like. Ebony was her family, and she couldn't rest until they were both safe.

After inhaling a deep breath, she unclipped her bracelet and gently lay it on the nightstand next to her book. She wouldn't need it anymore. Where she headed, the jewelry would constantly illuminate in the presence of Fallen. She left the Purah ring on her finger though. Having a hidden weapon was just plain smart.

Closing her eyes, she summoned the Dumahel power. It buzzed and swelled inside her. She stretched out her senses, searching for Ebony's soul amongst the millions of white lights. As soon as the mental connection between her and Ebony sparked to life, she latched onto it.

Waves of nausea rolled through her stomach, her body swayed this way and that. Every cell stripped down to single molecules, blew apart, scattered across the universe, then came together again like metal attracted to a magnet.

The moment her dizziness ceased, the link between her and Ebony fused together. Without opening her eyes, she knew she no longer lay in EJ's bed, in the safety of the Guardian mansion. She'd arrived in Hell.

Chapter Forty-One

"Fuck." EJ slammed open the doors to the war room. The wood splintered and something snapped. Probably the door stopper. He couldn't care less.

Raven glared at him, but he didn't give a shit about that either. They could replace the doors. Nothing could replace Hailee.

He'd called a code-frickin'-red for the second time in twenty-four hours. Not because an army of Fallen misted to the property but because his soulmate misted away.

Fuck.

He knew something was wrong. The pit of his stomach spun round and round like a carousel high on sugar. He thought he'd convinced Hailee to stay.

Guess not.

"Are you sure she misted away?" Raven asked, standing behind his chair, hands gripping the back rest. "Are you sure she's not hiding somewhere in the mansion?"

"One second she was in my arms, our connection alive and kicking, then next second poof she vanished along with the connection. She's gone."

"Why the hell did she leave?"

EJ threw his hands in the air. "Oh, I dunno, Rave, maybe because her sister's soul is at stake? The sister we've been planning to save but never acted. I should've realized when she was being all weird." He scanned the faces gathered in the room. River, Aric, Raine, Willow… "Where's Cole?"

Ripples appeared to his left a second before Cole materialized. Not a second too soon.

He forced his feet to remain stationary, so he didn't get in Cole's face like a crazed lunatic. "You'd better have a solution, Reaper, because I'm about to lose my frickin' shit here."

Cole nodded. "Hailee took off the bracelet, which means we can track her soul."

EJ clutched Hailee's bracelet in his fist. He hadn't let it go since he found it on the nightstand. "And?"

"She's in Aralim. With the twin and father." Cole paused. "And Blaine."

"Double fuck."

"Look who's swearing with the big boys." Raine snarked from her usual spot butting against the side table.

He glared at Raine. "Now's not the time to be all preachy. Sometimes big boys have to use big words to get their point across."

With a lightning fast flick of her wrist, a throwing star shot toward him. He ducked just in time as it whizzed past his head and slammed into the wall. How the hell Ellen or Raven didn't lock Raine up was anyone's guess.

"Jesus, Rae. You're more unhinged than me." Unhinged was an understatement. He straightened and rounded the table to stand beside River, out of Raine's direct throwing path. If she threw another one, it would hit her brother, not him. Serves River right for wearing those palm tree shirts. "How the hell did she mist to

Hell?"

Cole squeezed his shoulder. "She's half Azrael, remember? She can enter any realm in the Heavens or Hell. Plus, I suspect her powers have almost fully developed. Through her dream connection, she can mist to any angel, including her sister. She can also mist out of Hell…if Blaine isn't holding her captive."

"Blaine's wanted Hailee from the beginning, I think it's safe to say he'll hold her captive. I didn't even know she could frickin' mist!"

"Maybe she didn't either?"

"She took off the bracelet. She knew where she was going." He grabbed a soda from the mini fridge and drank the whole can in one go. Then crumpled it in his fist before tossing it in the trash. "Why the hell did Fate create a soulmate for me and then let her mist to Hell? The one time I would've welcomed a vision, she didn't send one."

Raven exhaled a heavy sigh. "He finally admits it."

He gave Raven the most exaggerated eye roll in the history of eye rolls. "Drop all the confetti you want when I have her back. First…help me get her back."

"We will, my man. We'll get Hailee back."

A nod was all he managed because the damn lump in his throat prevented words.

Leaning over the table, Cole grabbed a blank piece of paper and a pen and drew a rough map. Very rough. His drawing skills were terrible. "Here are the gates of Hell. This is Aralim." Cole tapped a circle in the middle of the page with the pen. "And these are the gateways in."

Aric leaned back in his chair. "Cole, that's a shitload of scribbly lines."

Pen marks went in every direction, making the sketch look like a porcupine's self-portrait. A mortal toddler could draw better than the Azrael.

Cole nodded. "There're many gateways. Most of them interconnect from other realms and back and forth from the gates of Hell. But this one here." Cole pointed to one squiggly line. "This one is the only gateway connecting Aralim with the mortal realm."

That wasn't so hard. They identified the way in and out. Easy-peasy. "Awesome. So, we use that one. Let's go."

Cole pinned EJ with a hard stare. "That's not how it works. Gateways connected directly to the mortal realm are like secret tunnels. Emergency exits. I can't enter through this, only exit."

Triple fuck. "How do we get into Aralim?"

"The most direct route is through the gates of Hell, then entering this gateway here." He pointed to another squiggly line.

At this point they all looked the same.

"Hang on." EJ straightened. "Did you say through the gates of Hell?"

Cole nodded.

If EJ went through the fiery gates, he'd become a Fallen. His soul would blacken and jump onto Team Zath. Fate and her frickin' twists.

Going through the gates was the only way to reach Hailee. Oh, well. Only his soul was at stake, he couldn't die from the transition, and if it meant saving Hailee, then so be it. After thousands of years without a soulmate, he wouldn't abandon her in Hell.

Besides, he was always up for a new adventure.

He crouched over the table to memorize the

scribbles, so he knew where they headed once they passed through the gates. "Not an ideal solution, Reaper. But we'll make do. Give me your word you'll take Hailee out that emergency exit when I get stuck in Hell. You know, literally."

Cole's gaze flickered to Raven then back to EJ. "I told you before, brother. There's no we. I do this alone. I'm the only one who can enter the gates and leave without it affecting my soul."

"By the looks of that poor excuse for a map, you'll need to get past a helluva lot of Fallen. You think they'll say hi and offer cupcakes? Nope. You'll have to fight your way to Aralim."

Cole's eyes widened, then zeroed in on EJ. "Are you doubting my fighting skills?"

Yes. "Blaine chose this realm for a reason. For all we know, Blaine created it. He's not stupid. I doubt he took the twin to a location where one Azrael could waltz in and steal her back."

Raven squeezed the chair so hard the leather squeaked under his grip. "He's right. Blaine would've chosen Aralim because it's difficult to infiltrate. You need backup, Cole."

EJ slid Hailee's bracelet in his pocket and pointed to himself. "Exactly. I'm the backup."

Willow gasped. "EJ, no. You can't do that. You'll become a Fallen."

"If it means saving Hailee, then it'll be worth it."

"Like fucking hell it will be." Aric shoved his chair out from the table and stood. "I feel you, man, I truly do. But I won't let you do this. I won't lose another brother."

"Oh, right, because you weren't prepared to do the

same thing for Red?"

"Learn from my mistakes and all that."

EJ ripped off his beanie and threw it on the table. "You're such a hypocrite, Ric."

"That's enough," Raven growled. "Both of you. Only an Azrael can enter the gates of Hell and return without becoming a Fallen. I'll summon Gabe and request more Azrael go with Cole."

Cole squeezed his shoulder again. "EJ, I'll bring her back. You have my word."

Only an Azrael can enter Hell... "Hang on." He spun to Raven. "I have an idea. Summon Gabe and tell him I have an urgent message for Fate."

A smirk curled his lips as an awesome plan formed in his mind. He would either be in more shit after this stunt or dead. Fifty-fifty chance. Those odds were totally fine.

Chapter Forty-Two

Thick smoke caught in Hailee's lungs, making her cough with each ragged inhale. A sickening stench of rotten flesh mixed with something like death layered the air. She didn't want to open her eyes. The image would no doubt fill her head with countless nightmares for the rest of her existence.

Icy shivers erupted across the back of her neck. Two hands locked around her upper arms. She screamed, eyes flying wide.

At least ten Fallen surrounded her. Maybe more. All wearing black military style clothing and boots. Some shirtless. Crimson wings unfurled behind their backs. Their eyes blazed red.

From behind, one held her in a tight grip.

She shoved at the Fallen. "Let me go."

Still clutching her arms, the Fallen pushed her forward until she'd no choice but to walk. Or he would no doubt drag her.

Complying, for now, she scanned her surroundings. As inconspicuously as she could, she twisted the Purah ring on her finger into position, with the sharp tip pointing down. The perfect angle to strike. When the opportunity arose, she'd stab the monster holding her.

She didn't expect Hell to look like this. Yellow light from a low full moon swirled through the bare, ghostly branches lining the dirt path, providing enough light to not trip in any holes. Further ahead, the air cooled, became fresher with a hint of winter in the stillness. At least here she could breathe without choking on smoke.

Where were the fire and screaming souls?

She jerked against the Fallen again, trying to gain the upper hand. “Where are you taking me?”

The Fallen shoved her forward again. “To Blaine.”

Mixed feelings collided together in one giant ball through her middle. Relief, dread, anticipation, and fear. Even though she knew Blaine capturing her before she found Ebony was a high possibility, it didn’t make the situation any less terrifying.

The Fallen halted at the tree line. Directly across from a clearing stood a creepy stone gothic style mansion. A handful of Fallen guarded the perimeter. Crimson wings at ease behind their backs.

Out of nowhere, a dangerous-looking guy appeared a few feet away. She tried to retreat but slammed into the rock-hard chest of the Fallen behind her.

“Hello there, love.”

The guy took a determined step closer, acting not the least bit surprised to find her there.

“I’ve waited an awfully long time to meet you.”

Dressed all in black, with matching jet-black hair and equally dark eyes, his bad guy vibe was off the charts. Even without a set of crimson wings and glowing red eyes, everything about him screamed Fallen. But the confidence in his step and the cocky tilt of his head radiated authority. No, superiority. This wasn’t any Fallen. This guy was the baddest of all.

“You’re him.”

“Blaine.” He extended his arm in a low, regal bow.

"I'm a tad disappointed the Guardians didn't tell you my name. That's plain rude."

"They did. But not what you looked like."

He smirked. "Raven will never get over the fact I got all the charming looks."

Add self-obsessed and plain arrogant to his description. She shoved against the Fallen holding her.

Blaine tipped his chin, and the Fallen released her.

She stumbled forward, rubbing her upper arms. "Where's Ebony?"

"Relax. Your sister is perfectly well, inside. I presume you're here to help her?"

She nodded, swallowing the lump in her throat.

He offered the crook of his arm. "Shall we?"

"Wait." This might be her only opportunity to negotiate Ebony's freedom. "I want to make a deal."

The corner of his mouth twitched as he lowered his arm. "You're in no position to make a deal. But I'll listen."

She straightened her shoulders, but kept her fists curled by her side in case she needed to use the weapon on her finger. "Once Ebony and I do what you need, I want you to guarantee our freedom."

He tapped his chin with his finger for a moment then clapped his hands together. "Deal. You help me out with a teeny, weeny little dream and I'll let you and your sister leave Hell whenever you want."

Was that what she said?

Freedom. No more bad guys chasing her and Ebony. She could finally stop, build that little house with the white picket fence. Live without fear or the pressure to rebuild every couple of years. Get her life back on track.

"How do I know you'll really let us go?"

He was a Fallen after all. From what she'd seen, they couldn't trust them.

"I give you my word." He offered the crook of his arm again. "Now, shall we head inside?"

With only his word, she needed to trust that he'd let them go. Now all she needed to do was pull him into a dream. She could do it.

Not bothering to link her arm in his, she strode past Blaine toward the mansion. He chuckled and caught up with her. This situation was bad enough without having him charm her. A few feet from the entrance, the door swung open and two figures stepped onto the porch. Ebony with their dad standing directly behind her.

Ebony dashed down the steps, arms outstretched, and embraced Hailee in a tight bearhug. "I knew you'd come."

Blaine strolled onto the porch to stand beside her dad, who completely ignored her before he walked back inside. Not a single hello or even a wave. Why expect anything else when the guy abandoned them and killed their mom?

She loosened her arms to step back to see Ebony's face. "Are you okay? Are you hurt?" Her palms touched Ebony's warm cheeks, swept a strand of violet hair back from her sister's face. Anything to make sure this moment was real.

Ebony clasped Hailee's hands and lowered them from her face. "I'm fine."

"But when we last spoke, you were upset and scared, begging me to get you out of here."

Adrenaline spiked in her blood, that fight-or-flight reflex kicking into gear. Something felt wrong. Why was Ebony so calm? Why was she standing out here?

"Chop-chop, ladies. As much as I love reunions, I'm on a tight deadline," Blaine called out.

Ebony slung her arm around Hailee's shoulder, ushering her toward the front door. As they reached Blaine, Ebony chuckled. "I told you that would work."

Chapter Forty-Three

Clearly, Fate had her listening ears on because as soon as the words were out of EJ's mouth, the room flipped upside down with everyone in it. More accurately, his stomach flipped, but it felt like the whole room.

One minute they stood in the war room at the Guardian mansion, the next they were in an identical room in the Heavens. How did he know they were in the Heavens? Because a burst of heavenly light shot through his veins and crashed into his soul so hard, he stumbled backward from the impact.

Tingles erupted along every inch of his skin, repairing even the tiniest of scratches he didn't realize he had. Oh, wait, they were marks from Hailee's nails. He'd rather keep them but didn't have a choice.

By the wide-eyed expressions around the room, the others had the same experience.

"What the fuck did you do?" Aric snapped, positioning Willow slightly behind him.

Like that would help. They should thank him. They hadn't experienced this much concentrated heavenly light in one shot since before Fate exiled them. Talk about a high.

Before he replied, Gabe and Fate strolled through the shimmering wall and into the room. Together those two oozed so much power and authority a lesser angel would've run for cover. Not the Guardians. Fate didn't create a brotherhood of warriors so they cowered in fear every time she entered the room.

"You're dead," River muttered under his breath.

Raven stepped forward and gave a brotherly handshake to the Archangel. "Gabe." He inclined his head. "Fate. I'd say it's great to see you, but I'm not really sure why we're here."

"Thanks for the boost of light though," Aric added.

Fate, looking as radiant as ever, inclined her head to Raven and then swept her gaze over the others in the room. "Guardians. Cole. It has been a while."

Understatement of the millennium.

EJ stepped forward, braving an up close and personal with Fate. "Yeah, three hundred and seventy-three years, four months, and twelve days, give or take."

If the time shocked Fate, she didn't show it. "Elijah."

He cringed at the use of his name in front of the others.

Raine snorted. "Your name is Elijah?"

He glared at the crazy woman with a death wish. "It's a noble name. At least I'm not named after the weather."

Raine's lips set in a hard line, no doubt she mentally stabbed him with a thousand daggers.

Turning back to Fate, he inclined his head. "Your Grace."

Fate's eyes narrowed. "Since when do you abide by proper greeting etiquette?"

"Since I…we, need your help to rescue my soulmate from Hell."

"I see. And what plan have you devised?"

Fate asked the question even though he guessed she already knew the answer. She knew everything.

He clapped Cole on the shoulder. "Link me with Cole."

"What the hell?" Cole barked. The Azrael recoiled from his touch.

EJ continued as though Cole didn't just react like he'd sold the Reaper's soul to Zath. "Link me with Cole, so his Azrael powers can protect my soul and allow me to enter Hell without Falling."

Ha! And everyone thought Aric was the badass strategist. He just showed them.

In a split second, his insides flipped again as Fate misted him and Cole to another location, leaving the other Guardians with Gabe. Sweet cherry blossoms assaulted his senses, the first sign she misted them to her Pool of Reflection. Ugh. The last time he came here was the day she exiled him and the other Guardians.

Fate strolled to the circular pool and perched on the raised stone edge. He held back, a knot tightening in the pit of his stomach. Cole glared at him, clearly not a fan of surprises.

He thought the gamble would work. But the odds were probably more like seventy/thirty, and not in his favor.

Leaning over the edge, Fate swirled her finger through the crystal-clear water. An image appeared on the surface as though it were a mirror into another realm. Which it was. The mortal realm.

"The last time you came here, Elijah, you told me you knew Blaine planned to Fall. You told me after he Fell."

Yep. Then she cursed his ass for the rest of eternity. "Maybe it's best not to dwell on the past. I think you proved your point with the whole curse thing."

"Every choice happens for a reason."

He inched closer to the side of the pool before sitting on the edge. Below, an ordinary city bustled with traffic while mortals carried on with their lives oblivious to two angels spying on them.

"Why do you make me fail all the time? A handful of times, maybe a decade or two, sure. But for over a century?"

"I do it to remind you of what's at stake, so the Guardians don't abandon their mission in the mortal realm."

Fate straightened, her sapphire blue eyes narrowed at him.

"I do it to remind you of the consequences of ignoring your path."

"Okay, let's get this all out in the open. Blaine told me his plan to Fall and I'm sorry I didn't tell you. I really am. Maybe if I did, we could've prevented his Fall, maybe not. But as far as I know, you didn't stop him."

Her eyes swirled with silvery clouds, brimming with power he hoped she didn't unleash on him. "That is true."

Cole joined the poolside gathering. "Why didn't you stop him?"

Fate peered into the pond and swirled her finger through the water again. "Blaine must fulfill his destiny."

She talked in more riddles than Gabe. "If Blaine's

destiny was to become a Fallen, why did you send us on this wild quest to save him?"

"He isn't just any Fallen." As Fate spoke, the image in the pool swirled and morphed into something much more sinister.

Roaring flames and ominous shadows consumed the dark water. He peeked over the edge. *Holy shit.* That wasn't a mirror into the mortal world. Fate created his repeating end-of-the-world vision. Like he needed to see more of that.

From the side of the pool, he watched himself standing on the rooftop of a building, peering down at a city in flames. The acidic stench of death and sulfur burned his lungs even though he was only a spectator. Beside him, Cole muttered something under his breath, but he couldn't decipher the words.

Thick, black, smoky clouds blanketed the sky in darkness. Endless fires burned the streets. Explosions erupted throughout the city, though he heard nothing but silence. Thank Fate. Because if he heard those mortals scream one more time, he'd fall to his knees and beg Fate to stop.

Knowing how it ended, he turned away from the carnage.

"Watch," Fate commanded.

He did. Bile rose in his throat. When the sedan exploded directly outside the building, he braced for the next part. Counted the seconds in his head. This part made his stomach lurch every time. Like clockwork, a Fallen swooped down, soaring low over the demolished road, its target in sight. Just as the Fallen snatched the mortal off the street, Fate paused the vision with a flick of her wrist.

Then he saw it. Holy frickin' hell.

Two blocks over, Blaine perched on the peaked roof of a church, his crimson gaze locked on vision-EJ standing on the rooftop. A Fallen stood beside Blaine. With violet and black hair, and fiery red eyes, the Fallen looked nothing like Hailee but the resemblance in her features was identical.

"Is that…?" Cole whispered.

EJ shot to his feet and staggered back from the pool. He'd experienced that vision for over three centuries. He never once noticed Blaine. All this time he'd focused on the Fallen snatching the mortal off the street. Lately, he turned away as it happened, knowing he couldn't stop it. Never did he look on the church roof.

Blaine was there the entire time, with Hailee's twin beside him.

The water in the pond swirled, sucking the vision to the bottom in a violent whirlpool.

Fate stood and straightened her dress. "I will grant your request on one condition."

He nodded, not able to speak.

"The other Dumahel must remain in Hell."

His eyes widened so far they could've fallen out of the sockets. "You can't be serious. Hailee misted to Hell to save her sister." He pointed to the pool. "Look what will become of her."

"The choice is yours. Leave one twin in Hell or leave them both."

Cole swore and turned away.

"Jesus, Fate. You don't like doing things the easy way, do you?"

He raked his fingers through his hair. The choice

was easy. From the moment he first met Hailee in her dream, he knew there was something different about her. Something different about this mission. He didn't just need to protect a mortal Chosen, Hailee was his soulmate. He wouldn't fail her.

"I choose Hailee. I'll always choose her."

Fate nodded before addressing Cole. "Cole, do you agree?"

As Cole's gaze hardened, EJ had a mini freak out that he might say no. If that were the case, he'd need to find another Azrael he trusted with his life. That list was short considering it only contained Cole.

Cole jutted his chin. "I agree. But the next time you reincarnate my soulmate, I want it to be the last time. I want her repeated torture to end."

"For real?" EJ snapped. "Reaper, now's not the time for your own demands. Wait your turn."

Fate didn't act surprised by Cole's bargain. She inclined her head. "The end is near."

What the hell? Did they both just get what they wanted? Who was this angel and what did she do with Fate? Was he stuck in an alternate universe again?

Fate plucked a pale pink cherry blossom from her crown and tossed it in the air toward EJ. Midway, it morphed into a miniature tornado of dark clouds swirling over his body. Starting at his shoes, the clouds curled around his legs, up his torso before surrounding his head. He turned his hands this way and that, inspecting the gray tinge on his skin. A thin thread formed inside his soul, sparking and bursting with light until it locked onto its target: Cole.

The Reaper pressed the heel of his palm against his chest, his brows drawn tight. "Don't do anything reckless, brother."

"Who? Me? Never."

Cole rolled his eyes.

Once EJ became one with the shadows, Fate lowered her hand by her side. "Use your shadow abilities wisely, Elijah. They will remain linked with you for three mortal days."

He nodded. How the hell would he convince Hailee to leave Hell without her twin? And how the hell would he do it in three mortal days?

He turned to Cole. "Three mortal days. How much time does that give us in Hell?"

"Hours."

"Nice one, Fate," he said with a sneer, not bothering to hold back the sarcasm.

Fate smirked. For the first time ever, he saw humor in her expression. "You're welcome, Elijah."

Chapter Forty-Four

"You tricked me?" Hailee shrieked.

Ebony halted in the doorway. "Would you have come otherwise?"

"No! No, I wouldn't have. You tricked me into misting to Hell, Ebony. Hell! You lied to me. I thought you needed me."

"I do." Typical Ebony remained unfazed. "I'm sorry. But you were being so stubborn."

Too stunned, Hailee couldn't reply.

Ebony took her hand and ushered her into the house. The place reminded her of a boarding house. Along the hall, they passed a handful of Fallen all dressed in the same gear as those guarding the front. Conversation bustled from a room to the left, but as they approached, the door closed, silencing the words.

When her sister led her to the living room, Hailee pulled up short. The room was the exact one from her dream with Ebony. The house was real.

The living room reminded her of a sitting room in the olden days where wealthy men drank whiskey and played cards. Smoked a few cigars. It had that vibe, but instead of a handful of gentlemen, there was only Blaine and her dad.

Ebony gestured to the Fallen. "Hailee, meet our dad, Asher."

The guy who called himself their dad stepped

forward. "I've waited twenty-five years to meet you."

She couldn't deny the resemblance. Although shorter, his hair was the same wavy golden blond as her own, but slightly darker. He had the same pointed tip of his nose and pouty bottom lip as her. God, she even got her widow's peak from him. His jaw was squarer and dusted in dark golden stubble. About the only thing she got from Mom was her lack of height. Asher stood a good two feet taller than her and Ebony.

Eyes, a dull shade of crimson, locked with hers. Not blazing like the other Fallen she saw around Blaine's place. Not flaming like the night he killed Mom.

Before she knew it, a hot, wild mess of rage exploded inside her.

"You bastard," she screamed, charging at the Fallen.

A Fallen. He wasn't her dad, he wasn't the Azrael who loved her mother. He was a murderous Fallen.

Her fist crashed into his hard chest. "You killed my mother!"

Asher didn't move or defend himself. Simply planted his feet and took every blow she delivered. Each punch to his chest a symbol of all the things she blamed him for—leaving her mom, abandoning her and Ebony. She resented him for their years of running, for the torment he put Mom through, the doctors who insinuated she was crazy. Her fists pounded into him for the double shifts Hailee worked to put food on the table, to pay the bills.

Tears burned in her eyes. She blamed that sorry excuse for a father for taking Ebony to Hell. Her throat tightened. She hated him for turning Ebony against her.

That monster made her leave EJ.

Flood gates opened, and hot tears streamed down her cheeks. But she kept hitting, though her fists lost their power and were more like slaps.

Asher gripped her wrists, stilling them. "Sweetheart, are you done?"

"You're crazy." She gulped in a breath and jerked her hands free. "You're all crazy."

Ebony gently squeezed Hailee's shoulder and offered her a tissue. A tissue! They were in Hell and her sister offered a tissue.

She retreated, her brain threatening to explode from the emotional overload and sheer ridiculous scenario unfolding before her.

Ebony turned to Blaine. "We should postpone until Hailee's had a chance to…adjust."

"No can do, love. Your sister is a Guardian's soulmate. And if there's one thing I know about soulmates, he'll stop at nothing to get back at her."

"You mean get back to her." Asher shrugged out of his jacket and sat on the couch.

"That's what I said."

Asher leaned forward with his forearms on his thighs. "Blaine's right, girls. You need to do this now."

Ebony curled her arm around Hailee's back, turning her around. "Okay, give me a second with her."

They talked about her as though she weren't in the room. Pain stabbed her temples, and she pressed her hands against them to ease it. Now was not the time to lose her mind.

Ebony moved in front of her, hands on her shoulders. "Hailee, get yourself together. Once we do this for Blaine, we'll be free to catch up." She chuckled.

"You can even hit Dad some more if it makes you feel better."

"You think this is a joke?" She lowered her voice. "Do you know what he wants us to do?"

"Of course, I do. I wouldn't agree to do anything I didn't want to." Ebony squeezed her shoulders. "One dream. That's all."

She freed herself from Ebony's grasp to address Blaine. "Then we can leave?"

Blaine relaxed into the couch with a lazy arrogance. "You keep asking the same question. My answer hasn't changed. After you pull the angel and me into the dream, you are free to leave. If you wish."

"Or you can stay," Asher added.

She glared at her father. "And play murderous family with you? No thanks."

Asher smirked. "You have your mother's sass."

"Don't you dare speak about my mother."

He raised his palms in surrender. If he thought they'd suddenly become a happy family just because she was in Hell with him, he'd be disappointed.

Arm around her, Ebony led her to a couch, sitting beside her. Blaine threw back the remainder of his drink and slid the empty glass to the center of the table.

"I don't know how to do this," Hailee mumbled, wiping her clammy palms along her pants.

Ebony pivoted to face her. "It's easy. Close your eyes and concentrate on the angel and you'll pull them into your dream. I'll do the same with Blaine. Once Blaine and I are linked, I'll connect with you."

Her heart thudded so fast it bounced up her throat. "Where will we set the dream?"

Blaine crossed his leg, resting an ankle on his knee

and motioned around the living room. “Set it here.”

She stared hard at Asher. “What’s your role in this?”

From inside his boot, he removed a dagger and lay it beside him on the couch. “I make sure no one gets killed while you’re all in a trance.”

She swallowed the lump in her throat. Killed? Stupid. Of course, there was a chance someone could kill them. They were in Hell.

Ebony clasped Hailee’s hand between both of hers and squeezed. “Ready?”

“Nope. But I don’t think I’ll ever be.” She glanced at Blaine. “Who’s the angel you want me to pull into the dream?”

Blaine’s eyes lit with fire as a grin curled on his lips. “Fate.”

Chapter Forty-Five

"You know, for the entrance to Hell it's a little pretentious." EJ waved his hand at the two huge black wrought-iron gates in front of him and Cole. Flames licked the air along the top of the gates making them resemble something out of a bad horror movie. "I mean, look at those flames. It's a bit over the top."

Cole snorted. "Well, Fate created Hell. She has a thing for flaunting her power."

"Don't let her hear you say that."

They both laughed, though the mission they were about to embark on was anything but funny. Crazy. Reckless. Downright stupid. Mortals joked about doing anything for the one they loved. He took that advice and frickin' leveled up. Not only would he do anything for Hailee, but right now he prepared to bust through the gates of Hell to save her. This hero business wasn't so bad after all.

"Show me again." Cole nodded to EJ's hands.

EJ held his palms facing up and awakened the shadows swirling inside his body. Dark clouds emerged from the center. Little tornadoes of blackness twisted and turned, growing in intensity the more he concentrated. This was the coolest power ever.

After their mission in Hell, he'd petition to keep the shadows a little longer. They would come in handy in the mortal realm.

"Good." Cole exhaled a long breath. "Let's hope you can summon them quicker if we run into any trouble."

"Can do, Reaper. I'm good." *I hope.*

Because they would run into trouble, without a doubt. Blaine wouldn't make it easy for them, nor would any of his Fallen minions. And if they ran into Zath…

An icy shudder ran down his spine.

Instead of relying solely on the epic shadow ability, he also strapped himself with weapons. A Glock tucked into the rear waistband of his tactical pants, daggers sheathed on his chest on full display. He even stole some throwing stars from Raine's stash at the mansion before Cole misted them here. Raine could kick his ass when he got back. He also changed into combat boots because according to Cole, canvas shoes were a fire hazard in Hell. That explained the Reaper's questionable wardrobe.

Palming a dagger, he hid the blade against the inside of his wrist and turned to Cole. "Let's do this."

Cole nodded, and they strode forward.

A few feet away, the gates magically swung inward, inviting them to Hell. Hysteria set in as he imagined greetings like the signs on the outskirts of mortal towns. Welcome to Hell, population six hundred and sixty-six billion dead souls. With some slogan from that hotel in California song scribbled underneath and a Fallen smiling, his arm outstretched, welcoming them to their doom.

Once inside, the gates closed. Instead of a polite, friendly welcome, a town burned to ruins and a crumbled road covered in a thin layer of soot greeted them. Buildings flanked the sides, blackened bricks, windows smashed or missing entirely. A blaring sun consumed the red sky, beaming down making the asphalt sticky beneath his boots. Dirty gray ash fluttered in the air, dancing in the stillness.

Burning sand had nothing on this heat.

He paused for a minute and concentrated inward. No evil darkness swirled inside his soul, no Fallen poison traveled through his veins. Not a single change in his body or wings. Linking himself to Cole worked.

Thank Fate.

EJ caught up with Cole. As their quick steps tore up the road, he couldn't shake the sense he'd been here before. The buildings, little spot fires along the sidewalk, they all seemed familiar. Which was impossible. He hadn't misted to Hell, and Fate created this realm long before streets like this existed in the mortal realm.

Soulless Devoid milled along the sidewalk, wearing clothing that spanned centuries—tattered cloth, nineteenth century dinner suits, faded, baggy denim jeans, and modern tight-fitting outfits that showed more flesh than it covered. Apparently, their clothing was fire retardant. Slater probably just had a thing for leather.

Hundreds of mortal souls corrupted by Fallen before they died now went about their business as though they weren't living in the underworld. Only, they didn't walk like ordinary people. Their motions were slow and corpse-like, with a zombie vibe.

Cole interrupted his train of thought.

"The shop front we need is this way on the left-hand side of the road. Ignore the Devoid but stay sharp. Fallen frequent this street like it's a New Year's Eve party every night. If one of them recognizes you…"

That added another layer of danger to their already crazy mission. And they didn't have time to waste.

"Got it."

As they darted past different establishments, EJ peered through the open doorways. After all, this was his first and, hopefully, last visit to Hell.

Through door number one was a torture room of the worst kind. From his cursory glance, he spied Fallen torturing several Devoid. Some strapped to wooden tables, some pinned against a wall. The stench of blood and ooze spilled out onto the street. He fought every fiber in his body not to bust in there and rescue the poor souls. But then what would he do? They already signed their soul to Zath and his evil buddies. Nothing could save them.

They were souls added to his never-ending list of failures. One day, when they won this war, all those souls would enter the Heavens and finally know peace. Then, and only then, was his job done.

The churning in his stomach made him turn away and pick up the pace. He crossed to the other side of the road and kept up with Cole.

The road seemed to never end.

"Can't we just run?" he asked the Reaper.

The giant sun made his shirt stick to his skin. Sweat dripped down his back, making him irritable. Changes in temperature didn't bother him in the mortal realm, but clearly Hell didn't get that memo.

"We'll draw more attention to ourselves if we run. We need to blend in."

Right. They were Azraels. They were in no hurry. Only, secretly, they were. Every stride, no matter the pace, was too slow. They only had a few hours to find Hailee.

Passing another open doorway, he peered inside. His feet faltered. A Hell sex club. Both Fallen and Devoid flesh on open display, thumping music muting the cries. Pleasure or pain, he wasn't sure. Writhing bodies tangled together in every available space. Twosomes, threesomes, groups. The whole scene made him bolt in the opposite direction. After all these centuries, he never would've guessed he'd reach the point where he craved only one female for the rest of his existence. But here he was, craving exactly that.

After they covered two blocks, Cole pointed ahead. "The gateway is inside an abandoned shop on the next block."

He nodded and quickened his pace. The ticking clock on his link to Cole had an expiration date.

Five Fallen rounded a building at the opposite end of the street, chatting like it were an ordinary Friday night out on the town. Before they spotted them, Cole shoved EJ off the sidewalk and through the closest doorway.

His stomach lurched, a prickly sensation exploding onto this skin.

"Jesus," EJ growled. "Why did you mist us here? This isn't the shop we need."

The Reaper shook his head. "I didn't mist us, we went through a gateway. We needed to get off the street before the Fallen saw you."

Sounds registered. Clangs, grunts, shouts of pain. Definitely not pleasure.

Cole's eyes widened as he stared at something over EJ's shoulder. Pivoting, he followed the direction of

Cole's gaze. Holy shit. They were in a Fallen training center.

Two boxing rings in the center, punching bags attached to stands off to one side, gym equipment that made him exhausted just looking at it. A lot of Fallen. From first glance, he guessed close to twenty. Some made use of the enormous ceiling height to fight in the air, others engaged in battles on two feet without using wings.

Cole gripped his shoulder. "Let's get out of here before one of them realizes we gate crashed."

EJ turned to the door but paused when a familiar face caught his attention. The Fallen pinned a dude on a wrestling mat beneath her, a knife held against the guy's throat.

"Holy shit. That's Luce."

At the mention of her name, her eyes snapped in his direction. Double shit. Her gaze narrowed, fire lit her pupils.

He didn't wait to say hi. "Run, Reaper. Now!" He shoved Cole through the door. Disorientation washed over him, and he did a three-sixty. "What the hell?"

They were in a different part of the city.

Cole peered up and down the street. "The entry and exit gateways lead to different locations, remember?"

"Why does this have to be so frickin' hard?"

Cole's deadpan expression met his stare. "You're in Hell."

That wasn't the point, but they didn't have time to bitch about it.

"This way." Cole pointed right, and they bolted down the street, racing toward an unknown destination.

He glanced over his shoulder just as Luce and three

other Fallen burst from the gateway and chased after them.

"Was that Luce…as in your ex-Luce?" Cole shouted, his feet pounding along the pavement.

"Yep."

Though he wouldn't class Luce as an ex, they weren't officially an item. Again, that was beside the point.

Just as Cole spun, EJ grabbed the sleeve of his shirt and jerked him forward. "Don't stop, idiot. She's a frickin' Fallen now." Across the road, he spotted a side street and dashed down it. Cole followed. "And she's hella good with a knife."

He didn't know where they headed, only that they needed to get away from Luce. So much for a sneaky in and out rescue.

Pounding boots rounded the corner after them. Luce and her three evil buddies.

He and Cole skidded to a halt at the end of the alley, faced with a brick wall. The only thing in this flaming city that remained intact. Too high to scale without the use of his wings. Just their luck.

They spun and faced their chasers. He'd fight Luce again even if the idea made him a little queasy.

Revealing his Guardian wings without cloud cover made them more of a target. He wouldn't risk jeopardizing his mission to save Hailee.

Luce and the other Fallen halted midway down the alley. Their crimson wings unfurled, ready for flight.

Switching the dagger to his less dominant hand, he snatched the Glock from his back and aimed it at the Fallen beside Luce. Without hesitating, he fired the first shot. It hit the Fallen in the chest. A split second later, the Purah bullet entered the Fallen's heart, exploding heavenly light through his veins. By the time the others realized what happened, the Fallen burst into mist and fluttered away with the dry, hot breeze.

Luce, seeming unfazed by the disappearance of her buddy, edged closer. "Twice in as many days. This time I won't go easy."

He held his ground, gun aimed at the Fallen on her other side. "You misted away without so much as a goodbye."

Luce narrowed her eyes. "Bye."

Before the word finished, she threw a dagger at him. It shot through the air with lightning speed. He kissed the ground a second before the blade flew past and ricocheted off the brick wall.

He bounced back to his feet, resumed aiming the gun at the Fallen, but addressed Luce. "I live with a constant knife thrower. You'll need to do better than that."

Cole snorted.

Luce wasn't impressed. The other two Fallen didn't wait. They flew forward, short swords raised, charging at him and Cole. Luce held back with a stupid smirk.

Cole raised his hands, palms out. In an instant, shadows surrounded them. The shadows swirled a few feet above their head and out to the sides, shrouding their end of the alley in complete darkness.

The Fallen hovered in the air, brows drawn tight, gazes darting left and right. They couldn't see through the shadows, but he and Cole could.

"So cool," EJ whispered.

Cole jerked his chin at the Fallen and EJ got the

hint. He aimed the gun and fired two shots in quick succession. The shadows didn't impede trajectory or speed. Those bullets buried straight into the chest of both Fallen. The dark angels burst into mist.

Now to Luce. As he pointed the gun at her, she flew down the alley in the opposite direction and swooped around the corner.

"Shit, shit, shit." Still palming the Glock, he bolted after her. "Let's go, Reaper. She'll lead us to Blaine and we're running out of time."

Chapter Forty-Six

Hailee shot to her feet. "Fate?" she squawked. "You can't be serious."

Blaine appeared unfazed by her outburst.

"Oh, I am, love. Deadly serious." He pointed to the couch. "Now sit back down so we can begin."

She shook her head, glanced at Ebony who was no help whatsoever, then back at Blaine. "I can't do that. How do you expect me to pull Fate into my dream? I've only connected with two people, and not at the same time. I haven't even met Fate." She sidestepped toward the exit. "I can't do it."

Faster than she could track, Blaine vaulted off his chair and grabbed Ebony's arm, jerking her to her feet. With his free hand, he ignited a tiny crimson flame and held it against Ebony's head. Ebony flinched, struggling against Blaine's hold.

"You either sit down and connect me with that Ice Queen or I send your sister to the Infernal Pits for a few centuries. The choice is yours."

The Infernal Pits didn't sound fun. If Blaine used the flame in his hand to transport Ebony there, it was likely a horrific way to travel.

Blaine lied to her. Fate wasn't an ordinary angel she could connect with.

"You said you wanted me to pull an angel into a dream. Not the creator of the universe."

He didn't reply.

"Please," Ebony pleaded.

The last of Hailee's restraint faded away. How was she so stupid? Both Ebony and Blaine tricked her, and still they exploited her one weakness. Family.

Blaine wiggled his fingers, increasing the size of the flame. "I'm losing my patience."

Once this was over, she didn't want anything to do with them. Ebony could hang out in Hell with these monsters while Hailee headed back to the Guardians. If EJ still wanted her.

"Fine. But then I'm leaving."

Blaine nodded.

Once Hailee sat back down, Blaine released Ebony and returned to his armchair as though nothing ever happened. "Shall we try again?"

She stared at the Fallen sitting across from her. The Fallen that called himself her father, yet, when Blaine threatened Ebony's life, Asher did nothing to stop him. Not even a twitch.

Jerk.

Inhaling a deep breath, she calmed her nerves. At least to the point where she thought more clearly. "I'm ready."

Ebony took her hand and squeezed it gently. Closing her eyes, Hailee pictured what she imagined Fate looked like—a beautiful, mesmerizing queen, wearing a golden ballgown and matching crown. The image was the best she could think of given the situation. In her head, she chanted Fate's name, hoping the words summoned her and were enough to connect them both in the dream.

Lightness flooded inside her body, pooling deep in

the center of her chest. A different light than when she pulled EJ into the dream. This light felt purer. Brighter. Heavenly.

A soft, balmy breeze brushed her cheeks, and she angled her head toward the sun. It felt like forever since she dreamed of the beach. If Blaine wanted her to pull the most powerful angel into her dream, then she'd do it on her terms. In a familiar setting. One that required less effort and concentration to maintain control. A dream she could control and anchor herself to prevent Blaine throwing her out.

When the sweet smell of spring replaced all scents of Hell, she opened her eyes. She gasped. This wasn't where she imagined. Instead of the beach, she stood in a garden.

Mature cherry blossom trees in full bloom towered over her head creating a floral shelter. A rickety timber bench to her left, a manicured lawn to her right. No sand or ocean.

Crap. She screwed up and now she was stuck somewhere. Just as she was about to break the connection, a rustle from behind made her spin around.

An angel approached, and her sheer beauty took her breath away. Wavy, light blonde hair cascaded over her shoulders. Pure porcelain skin shimmered in patches of sunlight streaming between the branches. Her eyes were crystal blue with flecks of silver. The most glorious, breathtaking iridescent white wings unfurled behind her back.

"Fate," she whispered.

Fate halted at the bench and inclined her head. "Hailee."

God, even her voice was pure.

"Where are we?"

As her wings folded into her shoulder blades, Fate sat on the bench. "Neither here nor there." She patted the spot beside her for Hailee to sit.

"Blaine," she blurted, urgency filling her veins. "He has Ebony. He's making me link you in a dream with him."

Fate remained silent and stared at the manicured lawn for quiet moments. When she turned to face Hailee, silver darkened the rim of her eyes. "I've been expecting this day."

"What does he want? What will he do?" What if he hurt Fate or Ebony?

"Make the connection. Bring him to me."

Connecting a third, or even fourth angel in her dream was so far above her abilities. Not to mention Blaine wasn't an angel. But she had to at least try for her sister's sake. Inhaling another breath, she concentrated on her link with Ebony, envisaging Ebony and Blaine in the garden with them. Ripples formed in the air, pulsing in heavy beats, but they didn't appear.

She turned to Fate. "I can't do it. I'm not strong enough."

"You're half Azrael. Heavenly light fills your soul. Harness the power within you."

Closing her eyes, Hailee concentrated on the light flowing through her veins, the bundle of energy centered in her chest. Warmth streamed down her arms to the tips of her fingers. Ripples in the air reappeared, this time stronger, like large waves crashing against the shore. Fuzzy versions of Blaine and Ebony materialized before them. She concentrated harder until they solidified.

Ebony gaped, peering at their surroundings.

Blaine smirked as though he wasn't at all surprised to find himself in a cherry blossom garden instead of his living room. He cocked a brow at Hailee.

"Someone's come into their full powers."

Was he talking about her? Before she replied, Blaine turned to Fate.

"Hello, love. You're looking rather angelic."

Fate stood and smoothed invisible creases in her dress. "Hell suits you, Blaine."

"You betcha it does." Blaine offered the crook of his arm to Fate. "Shall we?"

Did Hailee hit her head in the living room? Did Blaine want a dream with Fate so he could stroll through the garden? This whole situation was beyond weird.

The moment Fate looped her arm through Blaine's, she waved a free hand in Hailee's direction. In one swift motion, the dream collapsed.

Hailee fell to her knees on the floor in Blaine's living room in Hell, gasping for breath. A second later, Ebony did the same.

Black boots appeared in front of her eyes. She lifted her head.

Asher glared at her, dagger gripped tight in his hand.

"Where's Blaine?"

She turned to the vacant armchair where Blaine sat earlier. "I don't know what happened."

Ebony scrambled to her feet. "She tricked us. The dream was somewhere else. She misted us there and left Blaine with Fate."

By the collar of her shirt, Asher jerked Hailee from

the floor. The fabric cut into her neck, choking her. His eyes flamed with crimson.

“Where did you send him?” he growled.

Fierce determination and strength soared through her. She came to Hell to save Ebony. Nothing worked out how she anticipated. Everyone betrayed her. Ebony continually sided with their father, who showed no affection for Hailee. Even Blaine tricked her. That wasn’t just any angel. He forced her to connect him with Fate. Somehow, beyond her understanding, he knew she’d pull him and Fate into that unknown place, yet, he never said it.

Her hands curled into tight fists. “Get your hands off me.”

Asher narrowed his blood-red eyes and tightened his grip. Instead of coming to her aid or helping, Ebony backed away.

Hailee’s heart sank. Ebony made her choice. She chose her side.

That same ball of light she sensed in the presence of Fate grew and grew, until it consumed her entire body. It didn’t stop. Muscles in her back clenched and trembled as the light expanded, swelling in intensity until it stretched open two slits in her shoulder blades. Blinding white light burst from the openings, exploding into the room the moment heavy wings unfurled behind her back.

Ebony staggered back, her eyes wide. Asher’s lip curled in a wicked snarl.

She stared over her shoulder at the silvery-gray wings. Stunned, she didn’t notice the dagger until it lodged deep in her side. Searing pain ripped through her middle.

Asher tore the dagger free and struck again. This time she anticipated the blow and swiped her fist across his chest. The Purah ring burned through his skin. She didn't stop. Consumed with fury, she slashed again and again.

"No!" Ebony shouted, leaping in front of their father. The ring stabbed Ebony's shoulder a second before Ebony and her father misted away.

Hailee's legs wobbled, her vision blurred. A burning sensation spread from her side, through her middle, wrapping around her torso like a web of poison. Heavenly light internally fought against the darkness seeping into her veins, until she couldn't fight it any longer. She collapsed on her side.

Heavy boots, pounding down the hall, grew nearer. The Fallen were coming for her, and she didn't have the strength to fight back.

Chapter Forty-Seven

EJ raced around the corner of a building with Cole close behind him. He watched Luce fly between the buildings like a fighter pilot in an arcade game. Angling her wings left and right, she squeezed through the narrowest openings.

His legs did an amazing job keeping pace. But the burning in his chest may halt that, and if so, unfurling his wings was the only remaining option. Flying was quicker than running but also alerted nearby Fallen a Guardian had arrived in Hell. Zath would love that information, considering the last time Zath saw them, Aric tore off his wings.

Across the deserted road on the next block, Luce disappeared between two smaller buildings. He ran faster. In this part of the city, Devoid were few and far between.

Reaching the building, he bolted around the corner but skidded to a halt. A giant ball of heavenly light burst from his chest. If the other Fallen hadn't discovered their presence, they would now.

Cole stopped beside him. "Uh, you're glowing, brother. Time to get off the street."

The ball of light dulled in brightness but not intensity. It stretched and lengthened, forming a single line outward from the center of his chest. Like a rocket, the light shot forward down the road and curved left between two buildings.

"Do you see that?" He pointed at the glowing line.

"All I see is your body lit up like the northern lights."

The light tugged him. Urged him forward. This wasn't just any ball of light, this was his soulmate connection to Hailee. It guided him to her. "I know where Hailee is."

Forgetting about Luce, he took off down the street, following the line joining him with Hailee. It led them between two brick buildings, around the rear to a closed door. As they approached, he and Cole slowed their steps.

Half the building lay in a crumpled heap, leaving a gaping hole in the wall. Climbing over the fallen bricks, he peeked behind the closed door. Nothing. No Fallen waiting to ambush them but no line of light either. The light ended at the door and vanished.

"The coast is clear, Reaper," he called out before leaping to the ground and jogging back to Cole's side.

Cole kicked open the damn door like a ninja. No more quiet sneaking. Glock raised, they both entered the building.

His stomach flipped. What the hell? Complete darkness greeted them, except for a thin veil of light running parallel along the floor near his foot. He kicked his boot and a door creaked open. It took a second for the scene to make sense. They busted through another gateway, this time disguised as a wardrobe. He had heard of that happening before, though at least on this side there wasn't a foot full of snow and an evil queen waiting to kill them. Yet.

They exited the wardrobe into a study. An antique

desk sat to one side. Two-seater leather couch on the other side of the room, coffee table and even an old-fashioned lamp with dangly tassels. The single half-full glass on the side table was the only sign at least one Fallen used this room.

His soulmate connection with Hailee projected from his chest, streaming out a door and around the corner. Either they had the right place, or this was some elaborate job to capture a Guardian and his Azrael sidekick. They'd find out in a second.

"This way," he whispered to Cole, pointing at the open doorway.

Cole nodded. EJ slipped the Glock into the back of his pants and palmed a dagger. If a Fallen owned this hideout, then he and Cole needed to be in stealth mode. The last thing they wanted was to alert Hailee's captor and risk them misting her to another location. Whether that was her soon-to-be-evil sister, her deadbeat father, or Blaine.

With Cole close behind, he slipped out the door and followed the glowing line to the left. Rolling his feet with long strides kept them undetected until the end of the hall. They spotted the first Fallen, standing at the top of the stairs guarding the upper level.

Clearly, something important was on this level. The Fallen was completely unaware they sneaked up behind him. Dumbass. At the last second, the Fallen spun but not quick enough. EJ stabbed a dagger straight into the Fallen's heart and he exploded into mist.

Where did a Fallen's soul go when a Guardian stabbed him in Hell? A question for Cole once they found Hailee.

The glowing line led them down the stairs.

At the next level, noise and commotion drifted up from the ground floor. Heavy foot falls, shouts of orders, slamming doors. Shit went down on the ground below and it didn't sound fun. When someone said Dumahel, his body stiffened, on full alert.

"She's downstairs," he growled to Cole.

"Let's do this."

Right there, in that moment, his respect for the Reaper burst into best-friends-forever territory. He owed that guy with his life. Certainly, Hailee's. And he would never forget it.

Cole summoned shadows, concealing their presence in darkness as they crept down the stairs. At the bottom, their adventure in Hell turned to shit. Fallen. Everywhere. Some rushed in from outside, others burst from a hall closet. Another gateway?

The handful of Fallen in the living area stole his attention. His ray of light streamed right through the center, curving around Fallen until it ended in a ball of brightness on Hailee's limp body. Her golden hair glowed as bright as her…holy fuck. Silver wings glittered like an exploded star from behind her back. His brain registered the rest of the scene. A soon-to-be-dead Fallen slung Hailee over his shoulder in a fireman hold.

Red spots clouded his vision. Code frickin' red. No, this was more than code red. This was burn-this-fucking-place-to-the-ground-and-save-his-soulmate.

He and Cole didn't waste time, they used their surprise attack to their advantage. EJ raised the gun and fired. Seven Fallen in the hallway exploded into mist, but that also alerted the whole room to their arrival. He tossed the Glock and held a dagger in each hand. Fallen attacked from every direction, but thanks to Cole's epic shadows, the Fallen fought blind.

Gaze locked on his target in the living room, EJ pushed forward, arms slashing left and right at anything that dared step in his path. Vaguely, he registered Cole, grunting and fighting behind him.

In his haste, he stepped free of Cole's shadows. The bastard who had Hailee spun and locked his crimson gaze on him. EJ staggered back. The resemblance punched him in the stomach. Hailee's dad held her like a prized bounty with her sister standing by his side. He needed to stop them. If they misted with Hailee, he might never find her again.

Throwing a dagger at the father was too risky with Hailee over his shoulder. What if he hit her?

Instinct made him drop the knives. He summoned shadows from his hands. Black clouds swirled in the air, gathering into a ball in front of his chest. Hailee's father narrowed his eyes, his body fading molecule by molecule as he started to mist.

Like hell. Hot rage coiled inside him. He raised his hands and shoved them forward in the air at the father. Shadows slammed into the Fallen, sending him flying backward. Hailee fell, smacking the floor. Still, he kept the shadows locked on the dad. The Fallen struggled to move, pinned against the wall.

How dare that piece of shit use his own daughter as a pawn in this war. EJ shoved the shadows into the Fallen's chest.

No one treated his soulmate like that. She deserved nothing short of worship. If that bastard lay another finger on her…

He clenched his jaw, spreading the shadows

through the Fallen's body. Twisting his wrist, he grasped the father's black and corrupted soul. The Fallen thrashed against the shadows. EJ tugged harder, disconnecting the soul from his body.

Everything happened all at once. The Fallen summoned his own set of lethal shadows and launched them at EJ. His chest jerked forward as darkness gripped his soul.

Ebony threw a dagger aimed at Hailee's chest.

In a split second, he chose between finishing the Fallen or saving his soulmate. He dove for Hailee. Shielding her body, he braced for the dagger's impact. It didn't. Silence filled the room. A sudden quietness so out of place.

Peeking over his shoulder he found the dagger suspended in the air just millimeters from his back, held there by long shadowy fingers connected to Cole's outstretched arm. He glanced at the Reaper who nodded, then with a flick of his wrist, tossed the dagger to the floor.

EJ exhaled a ragged breath. That was frickin' close.

Scanning the room, he wasn't surprised to find Ebony and the father had misted away. It didn't matter. He came here for Hailee, not them. Other Fallen inside the house were either toast or they'd misted away, too.

Folding Hailee's wings as best as he could, he curled her into his arms and rolled her over, supporting her head. A bright red patch stained the side of her shirt, her breathing labored, pulse fluttering in and out. Under her shirt, a spiderweb of faint black lines spread beneath the surface of her skin. Fallen venom. In Hell, her body wouldn't heal. She needed the sun.

With Hailee cradled in his arms, he stood and turned to the true hero of this nightmare. “Cole, get us to that emergency exit.”

Chapter Forty-Eight

Sunshine washed over Hailee's body. No, not over, through. As though the sunlight penetrated each layer of flesh and bone directly into every cell. The sensation spread from the tips of her toes, along her spine, extended out her arms, and washed back down again. A niggling pain in her side tugged as though the surrounding skin stretched and stitched back together.

Rest now, my angel, a familiar female voice whispered in her mind, but Hailee lacked the energy to identify its owner.

Gradually, gentle waves rolling onto shore registered in the depths of her mind. A light balmy breeze tickled her cheeks. The sun's rays warmed her exposed legs, arms, and face without burning. The sensation was divine. Better than any sunbathing she ever did.

A light touch swept over her forehead and she instinctively leaned into it. Another scent more intoxicating than the salty air drifted through her nostrils, awakening something deep inside her soul.

"She'll be fine," the same female said aloud.

"Thank you," a male replied. "For everything."

That thick, rough voice stirred in her heart, pulled imaginary threads, urging her from the darkness.

"Hailee chose the Heavens. All is as it should be." There was a pause. "Use this blossom to mist back."

"Would you consider reinstating that ability?"

"The Guardians' mission is not complete, Elijah. You must remain in the mortal realm."

He huffed. "It was worth a try."

Sweet floral notes filled her senses. Spring. She must be dreaming again.

Hope swelled in her chest. If she dreamed, then maybe her gallant rock star knight would join her. She sucked in a sharp breath as the memories resurfaced. Leaving EJ. Blaine and Ebony tricked her. Fate—

Her eyes shot open. "Gah." She flopped an arm over them to block the brightness.

Fingers glided along her jaw. "Welcome back, sweetness."

Slowly, she lifted her arm as her eyes adjusted to the sun's glare. Kind of. "Was I…" She swallowed, moistening her dry throat. "Was I asleep?"

"Yeah, I guess you could say that. How are you feeling? Any pain?"

EJ lay down beside her, propped up on his elbow.

She peeled herself into a sitting position. "Pain? Besides my eyes from that glare, no."

He chuckled, removing his reflective shades and offering them to her.

"It's okay, I'll be fine once they adjust. Provided it doesn't blind me first."

As though she hadn't spoken, he sat up and slid the shades on her face. Instant relief.

"Where are we? I don't remember coming here."

EJ wrapped an arm around her lower back and scooted closer. "We're in the Heavens."

"What? How?"

"You needed to heal." He tucked a loose strand of

hair behind her ear. "The sun has a higher concentration of power in the Heavens."

A niggling hazy thought made her lift the hem of her shirt, where she spotted a faint white scar about an inch long. She'd rather forget her father stabbed her.

"You saved me?"

"Always."

Tears burned in her eyes. If EJ didn't come after her… "Hang on. How did you find me? And how did you enter Hell without becoming a Fallen?"

His eyes lit with a mischievous glint. "Cool shadows, a dodgy map, and a kick-ass Azrael sidekick."

That brought a smile to her face. "An ordinary day in the life of EJ."

"You got it."

For several quiet moments, she stared at the waves rolling in and out. Despite leaving EJ, deserting him when he begged her to stay, he still rescued her. She trailed a finger through the sand. "I guess that means you still like me?"

Butterflies fluttered in her stomach while she waited for his response. She even held her breath.

He took her hand, raising it to his lips to place a gentle kiss. "I don't like you, sweetness. I love you."

Those butterflies exploded from their cage in one giant rush. "That's a relief. Because…I love you, too."

Craving physical contact, she laid her head on his shoulder as tears slipped down her cheeks. His strong arms held her tight, while he rested his cheek on her head. All this time she pined over fictional heroes when a real-life version was out there waiting for her. How did she get this lucky?

Sobs of happiness and relief quaked her body.

They may not have all the answers yet, and the battle with the Fallen, including her father, wasn't over, but at least they had each other. Everything else they could figure out together.

"I'm sorry for leaving. Ebony tricked me into thinking she needed me. She said Blaine wouldn't release her until she helped him pull Fate into a—" She jolted upright. "Fate. She's with Blaine."

EJ drew back, his brows drawn tight. "No, she was just here with us. As soon as we made it out of Hell, Fate misted us here so you could heal."

She thought for a moment. "I don't understand. Ebony and I pulled her and Blaine into a dream and then it just ended. Like Fate broke the connection."

EJ coaxed her back to the crook of his arm. "Don't worry, sweetness. Fate is fine. Everything she does happens for a reason. If she and Blaine were in a dream together, then that's what Fate planned."

Her Purah ring glistened in the sun, catching her attention. "What happened to Ebony?"

The last thing she remembered was her sister misting away with their father after Hailee stabbed him several times with the ring. Ebony chose Asher over her, and that cut deeper than any knife.

EJ kissed the top of her head. "Fate has a plan for Ebony. She needs to stay with Blaine for a while."

"Ebony is a Fallen, isn't she?"

He remained silent for the longest time. "If she isn't one yet, she will be soon."

"I couldn't save her."

EJ squeezed her tighter. "Sweetness, you did everything in your power to save Ebony. Sometimes, Fate paves a different path and we need to let that play out. Trust in Fate." He pinched her chin and turned her head to face him. "Ebony won't be in Hell forever. We'll save her, I promise you. We'll save her and Blaine."

No mention of her father, but she wasn't sure how she felt about that yet. Asher killed her mom, tried to kill her, and corrupted Ebony. He could stay in Hell for a bit longer until he showed qualities worthy of redemption.

She sensed Ebony had turned into a Fallen when she saw her in Hell. At least she was with Blaine. Was that good? No. But Ebony wasn't on her own and some psycho Fallen wasn't torturing her. In fact, inside the mansion, the other Fallen regarded Ebony in a way that made her think they respected her.

For now, she swallowed all those fears and peered back at the ocean. She'd tackle each day as it came. With EJ by her side, she sensed everything would be okay. "This beach looks identical to the one in my dreams."

"It is the beach in your dreams. I think your soul misted here while your physical body remained in the mortal realm." He shaded his eyes and peered up at the sun. "That's why I felt so fantastic each time I woke. I mean, I felt awesome because I saw you, but also because the sun's healing power in the Heavens is like being injected by a supernova."

"Ha. That sounds kind of cool and hot."

He pivoted to face her with a cheeky grin. "You bet it is. You know what's even hotter?"

"What?"

His voice lowered to a husky growl. "Your wings."

"My what?"

"Wings. You have the sexiest wings." He brushed a finger along her jaw. "Unfurl them, sweetness. Show me again."

"How do I unfurl—" Before the words were out, a rush of heat and energy burst from her back. She gasped. Over her shoulder, silvery-gray wings extended out to her sides, the sunlight refracted in the feathers making them sparkle.

She stretched them wider, longer, then pulled them in, tucking them behind her back. "That's so cool."

EJ pulled her in, kissing her. "And so frickin' hot."

Epilogue

One week later

EJ glided his hands over the taut leather steering wheel, tracing his thumb along the groove, reacquainting himself with Stella. Relaxing in the seat, his body temperature warmed the leather against his back and thighs. He inhaled a deep breath of rich birch and musk, the scents taking the edge off his nerves.

This was a big moment. The biggest in his entire existence. Never had he gone this far or become this seriously involved with a woman to even consider taking this step.

"She's a cool chick, Stella," he murmured, moving his hand to the gear shaft. "She'll respect our relationship. She won't make me choose between you and her. I know it."

Though the weird fluttering in his stomach made him doubt his decision. No, he was being stupid. Even though he'd only known Hailee for a short time, she was his soulmate. She wouldn't make him choose. Would she?

"You'll like her, Stella," he continued the reassurance, for himself or Stella's benefit, he wasn't sure. "In fact, I'm positive you'll love her as much as I do."

The garage door swung open and Hailee strode

through, heading in his direction. Those flutters turned into death-defying somersaults. He hoped to Fate he made the right decision here. If Hailee made him choose between his first love and his soulmate…

Nope. That wasn't an option.

Hailee opened the passenger door and slid into the seat. "Hey."

"Hey, yourself." He leaned over the console and kissed her, lingering for a moment to breathe in her scent. Mixed with the freshly conditioned leather from Stella, Hailee's salty sunshine made for the perfect combination inside his car. Like they were destined to blend together.

"Where are we heading? And why did we need to leave so early? It's five o'clock in the morning." The grin on her face turned sexy as her eyes heated. "And why couldn't we fly? I like us flying together."

So did he. A lot. Flying with his soulmate was a pleasure he wanted to experience for the rest of his existence. Nothing compared to the thrill shooting through their connection into his blood. The fact each flying outing landed them in bed naked made the experience that much more enjoyable. But now wasn't the time to get sidetracked.

Diverting his attention back to her questions, he swiveled in the seat to face her and took her hand in his. "I wanted to introduce you to someone who's special to me."

Her brows furrowed as she peered into the backseat. He guessed looking for the "someone."

"Okay…"

Those acrobats flipped up to his throat, building a ginormous lump there. "Hailee…meet Stella." He smoothed his free hand along the dash. “Stella, meet Hailee.”

“You’re introducing me to your car?”

He nodded.

Please don’t make me choose…

Hailee peered around the inside of the car, up to the roof, then settled her hand on the dash. A smirk lifted at the corner of her lips. “It’s lovely to meet you, Stella. From what I hear, you and EJ have a special bond, and I’m honored you’re including me. I wouldn’t want to steal him away from you.”

Relief burst through him like an explosion of confetti. Hailee understood.

“Stella’s an important part of my life, sweetness. I dunno, I just want you to know that.”

With one hand still on the dash, she slipped her other from his and held it against his cheek.

“I get it. It’s a little strange, but I get it.” She chuckled. “Just so we’re clear, Stella is the only woman I’ll agree to share you with.”

“Deal.”

Closing the distance, he took her mouth with his and kissed her with all the love in his soul. Hailee was perfect in every goddamn way. How the hell did he score such an awesome soulmate?

Before they progressed any further, he slowed their kiss and rested his forehead against hers. “I love you.”

“I love you, too.” Hailee drew back. “Now, is Stella taking us somewhere or did you wake me at five a.m. for a meet and greet?”

Hailee calling Stella by name made his chest swell. Best soulmate ever. “We’re going for a drive. I have something to show you.”

On that, he turned the ignition and Stella roared to life. Out on the highway, heading up the mountain, Hailee flipped off her shoes and threw her feet up on the dash. He all but careened off the road.

"Sweetness, have some respect." He shooed her feet off the dash. "This isn't Raven's car. And I just gave Stella a detail. She's all nice and shiny and doesn't want smelly feet on her dash."

Hailee dropped her feet and burst out laughing. "One, I'm sorry Stella, I won't do it again. And two, my feet are not smelly."

"True. But still…"

Hailee chuckled again, folding her legs up on the seat.

"That's better."

Without any further incidents, they drove the rest of the way, singing along to a playlist he created just for her. When they reached the lookout, he veered off the highway and pulled Stella into a small parking lot.

"We're here." While getting out, he took the small box from inside the door and stuffed it in his back pocket, then reached into the backseat and grabbed a blanket.

Hailee hopped out, and he rounded the hood to meet her in the middle. He flipped out the blanket on the grass in front of Stella and pulled Hailee down beside him, careful not to sit on the box in his pocket. This was the first time the three of them were together and he wanted everything to be perfect. Better than perfect. He just hoped he pulled it off.

"Do you think Stella likes me?"

He grazed his knuckles along her jaw, calming his nerves. "I know so."

Her smile flooded his soul with so much peace he wondered how the hell he'd gone without it for so long. Ever since they returned to the mortal realm, Hailee joined him each sunrise on the rooftop. In a matter of days, the ritual went from his thing to their thing. Fine by him. Because he progressed from fearing he'd fail her to embracing a new beginning with her every single day. He'd probably screw up along the way, but he'd spend the rest of his existence making damn sure he was worthy of her love.

With his hand in hers, he kissed her again. Number four on his top ten things to do with Hailee. Slow and soft, he glided his tongue over hers, loving every second the light seeped between their souls.

"I thought we could watch the sunrise here today, rather than on the rooftop."

Holy shit, he was so nervous his voice shook.

"This is nice."

Her fingers slid around his neck then under the back of his beanie.

"Being here with you, and Stella, is perfect."

Exactly. For a grand gesture as big as this, he pulled out all the stops.

As a deep orange glow spilled over the mountain in the horizon, he straightened, taking both her hands in his, and inhaled a deep breath. "We're soulmates and I know we have the rest of eternity together, but I wanted to show you that I'm not going anywhere. I want your home to be with me. Forever."

Releasing one of her hands, he pulled the small velvet box from his back pocket and held it open between them. "You're a warm bundle of sunshine that lights up my soul like a supernova. I want you, and only you, for the rest of my existence."

"Are you asking me to marry you?"

"I'm asking you to be mine. This Guardian has been off the market since the minute I walked into your dream. Now, I want the whole damn universe to know it."

Her eyes watered, but when her gaze dipped to the box, she burst out laughing. "A key?"

Not quite the reaction he hoped for. "It's a key to Stella."

Understanding dawned on her face and she fought back the smirk. "Of course, I'm sorry, I didn't mean to laugh." She cupped his jaw between her palms and gave him a light kiss. "I accept. I'd be honored to have a key to Stella."

"I got our names inscribed on the key. I figured you'd prefer that rather than inking my name on your skin."

"I wouldn't mind both."

The thought of her tattooing his name on her set his heart on fire.

He closed the lid, and she accepted the small box, placing it on the blanket beside her.

"Does this mean I can drive Stella whenever I want?"

He cocked his brow. "Sweetness, let's not get carried away."

Hailee chuckled again. Every damn time she did, it made him feel like the luckiest Guardian in the universe.

Hands cupping her cheeks, he kissed her again. Little did she know, he wasn't the hero in her story. She was the heroine in his, who saved him from the brink of madness. She pulled him from the shadows of destruction and gave him light.

"I love you, Hailee. More than I thought this broken heart of mine was ever capable of."

Her smile was worth all the nerves and doubts over the past few days.

"I love you, too. The key, Stella, and you. I love all of it."

"More than those book boyfriends?"

She chuckled and playfully patted his cheek. "Let's not get carried away."

A word about the author…

…an award-winning Paranormal Romance Author.

Growing up in a military family, Cassie had a childhood filled with countless crazy adventures. Eventually, sunny Queensland stole her heart, and she now calls it home with her husband and their two BMX-crazy boys.

Borderline obsessed with the paranormal world, Cassie loves nothing more than crafting stories involving strong, otherworldly characters in need of redemption. She's a self-confessed book-a-holic and a sucker for a gut wrenching happily ever after.

When she isn't narrating imaginary characters, Cassie loves binging on TV shows, spending time at the beach, and curling up listening to the rain.

If you love exclusive previews and giveaways, join Cassie's newsletter (https://www.cassielaelyn.com) or her Facebook reader group, Cassie's Log Cabin (https://bit.ly/FBLogCabin).

You can also stalk @cassielaelyn on Facebook, Instagram, Twitter, BookBub and Goodreads.

Thank you for purchasing
this publication of The Wild Rose Press, Inc.

For questions or more information
contact us at
info@thewildrosepress.com.

The Wild Rose Press, Inc.
www.thewildrosepress.com

www.ingramcontent.com/pod-product-compliance
Lightning Source LLC
Chambersburg PA
CBHW051133030726
47504CB00004B/856
* 9 7 8 1 5 0 9 2 3 3 3 1 1 *